Praise for

ON WHAT GROUNDS

"A great beginning to a new series . . . Clare and Matteo make a great team . . . *On What Grounds* will convert even the most fervent tea drinker into a coffee lover in the time it takes to draw an espresso." —*The Mystery Reader*

"The first book in Coyle's new series is a definite winner! The mystery is first rate, and the characters leap from the page and are compelling, vivid, and endearing. The aroma of this story made this non–coffee drinker want to visit the nearest coffee bar." —*Romantic Times*

"A fun, light mystery. Recommended." —*Kliatt*

"[A] clever, witty, and lighthearted cozy. Cleo Coyle is a bright new light in the mystery horizon." —*The Best Reviews*

Praise for

ⱦHⱤOUGH ⱦHE GⱤINDEⱤ

"Coffee lovers and mystery buffs will savor the latest addition to this mystery series . . . and for those who like both, it's a guaranteed 'Red Eye.' Fast-paced action, coffee lore, and incredible culinary recipes, brewed together with some dark robust mystery, establish beyond a doubt that this one certainly isn't decaf. All hail the goddess Caffina!"

—*The Best Reviews*

"*Through the Grinder* is full of action and murder with a little romance thrown in on the side. The ending is exceptional and completely unexpected."

—*The Romance Reader's Connection*

"A fascinating mystery . . . a brave, quirky heroine."

—*Books 'n' Bytes*

"There were ample red herrings in *Through the Grinder*'s story to lead the reader astray. I did not guess the outcome until I had finished the book. This is a great mystery in the Coffeehouse Mystery series."

—*Roundtable Reviews*

LATTE TROUBLE

CLEO COYLE

BERKLEY PRIME CRIME, NEW YORK

THE BERKLEY PUBLISHING GROUP
Published by the Penguin Group
Penguin Group (USA) Inc.
375 Hudson Street, New York, New York 10014, USA
Penguin Group (Canada), 90 Eglinton Avenue East, Suite 700, Toronto, Ontario M4P 2Y3, Canada
(a division of Pearson Penguin Canada Inc.)
Penguin Books Ltd., 80 Strand, London WC2R 0RL, England
Penguin Group Ireland, 25 St. Stephen's Green, Dublin 2, Ireland (a division of Penguin Books Ltd.)
Penguin Group (Australia), 250 Camberwell Road, Camberwell, Victoria 3124, Australia
(a division of Pearson Australia Group Pty. Ltd.)
Penguin Books India Pvt. Ltd., 11 Community Centre, Panchsheel Park, New Delhi—110 017, India
Penguin Group (NZ), Cnr. Airborne and Rosedale Roads, Albany, Auckland 1310, New Zealand
(a division of Pearson New Zealand Ltd.)
Penguin Books (South Africa) (Pty.) Ltd., 24 Sturdee Avenue, Rosebank, Johannesburg 2196,
South Africa

Penguin Books Ltd., Registered Offices: 80 Strand, London WC2R 0RL, England

This is a work of fiction. Names, characters, places, and incidents either are the product of the author's imagination or are used fictitiously, and any resemblance to actual persons, living or dead, business establishments, events, or locales is entirely coincidental. The publisher does not have any control over and does not assume any responsibility for author or third-party websites or their content.

LATTE TROUBLE

A Berkley Prime Crime Book / published by arrangement with the author

PRINTING HISTORY
Berkley Prime Crime mass-market edition / August 2005

Copyright © 2005 by The Berkley Publishing Group.
Cover design by Rita Frangie.
Cover art by Cathy Gendron.
Interior text design by Kristin del Rosario.

ISBN: 0-425-20445-6

BERKLEY® PRIME CRIME
Berkley Prime Crime Books are published by The Berkley Publishing Group,
a division of Penguin Group (USA) Inc.,
375 Hudson Street, New York, New York 10014.
The name BERKLEY PRIME CRIME and the BERKLEY PRIME CRIME design
are trademarks belonging to Penguin Group (USA) Inc.

PRINTED IN THE UNITED STATES OF AMERICA

10 9 8 7 6 5 4 3 2 1

This book is dedicated to
Julie and Kerry Milliron
cherished friends
steadfast supporters
gracious, generous, giving
Village people
original thinkers
what E.B. White had in mind
New Yorkers

ACKNOWLEDGMENTS

Special thanks to Martha Bushko, an editor of buoyant brilliance, and John Talbot, a literary agent of the highest caliber, for their valued support.

Behind every successful woman . . .
is a substantial amount of coffee.

—Stephanie Piro, Comic Artist

PROLOGUE

"*How do you like your poison?*" whispered the voice in the dark. "*Light or black?*"

Hearing the voice, the body in bed twisted back and forth, choking pillows, strangling bedcovers, sleeping, dreaming, considering . . . *Light or black?* . . .

"*Tomorrow you'll make it happen,*" continued the voice. "*So many egos will be there, watching themselves walk, hearing themselves talk, none will notice that bit of venom in the cup . . .*"

A splash of cream . . . a dash of sugar . . .

"*Then it will be over. And, after the deed is done, only one person in the room will know the reason.*"

Me. Only me. Only I will know.

"*It won't even be murder. It will simply be—*"

Justice . . .

One

〜〜〜〜〜〜〜〜〜〜〜〜〜〜〜

"Men are pigs. They should die!"

Tucker Burton's words were audible over the steam wand's hiss, the buzz of conversation, even the throbbing electronic dance music pulsing out of the Village Blend's speakers. To punctuate his declaration, my best barista butted the bottom of the stainless steel pitcher against the steam wand's spout. The result was a tooth-grinding clang of metal on metal. Then Tucker, who should have known better, pulled the pitcher away too quickly. A geyser of milk froth flowed over the brim, scalding his hand. He cursed, dumped the excess into the sink, and doused his reddening fingers in a rush of cold tap water.

It wasn't that I disagreed with Tucker about men. When they acted like pigs, I wanted blood too—so to speak. But Tucker's lethal tone, like the pounding Euro synth-pop, which was temporarily replacing our typical mix of new age, jazz, and classical, was disquietingly out of place. Not five minutes before, my buoyant barista was pulling espressos and chatting amicably to anyone within earshot. Obviously someone or something had thrown the nasty switch on the lanky, floppy-haired actor-playwright, who was now slamming around behind the coffeehouse counter like a jealous yenta.

And, believe me, it takes one to know one.

Twenty years ago, I'd been a naïve bride destined to discover that my handsome husband's extramarital romps were as commonplace as his rock climbing, mountain biking, and cliff diving expeditions during his buying trips to third-world coffee plantations. Matteo's defense—that his sex-capades were no more meaningful than any other extreme sport—was supposed to have assured me of his emotional fidelity. I'd responded by pouring a latte over his head. At least, I think it had been a latte. It may have been a cappuccino. In any event, I vividly remember white foam dripping down his bewildered features, so froth most definitely had been involved.

Behind the low-slung silver espresso machine (out of which a properly trained barista can pull 240 aromatic shots of ebony an hour) Tucker's platonic gal pal Moira McNeely paused to reassure him with a friendly touch to his shoulder. A young Bostonian now studying at the Parsons School of Design, she'd taken an interest in the art of coffee preparation (and, I suspected, my thespian-cum-barista) and had volunteered her services for this Fall Fashion Week "after dinner coffee and dessert soiree", now well underway. And I was thankful because, at the moment, the Blend was severely understaffed.

So what, might you ask, is Fall Fashion Week? Well, for concrete-loving, highly caffeinated New Yorkers, who seldom take their cues from nature, the magical appearance of the white canvas runway tents amid the tall London plane trees of midtown's Bryant Park is the quintessential sign of autumn's arrival.

Every September, the peaceful, green, eight-acre rectangle behind the imposing granite edifice of the New York Public Library is transformed into a fashion mecca. Inside the hastily erected tents, the "Seventh on Sixth" organization (whose name defines the temporary moving of the fashion industry's usual Seventh Avenue address to Bryant Park's Sixth) stages an international fair where top designers drape their spring lines on reed-thin models for all the trade, and, via the intense media coverage, the world to see.

During this week, countless parties are held in top restaurants and locations as diverse as the Museum of Modern Art and Grand Central Station. The Village Blend had never before hosted a Fashion Week party—and now that it had started, the space was admittedly tight. At the moment, even with most of the coffeehouse's marble-topped tables crammed next to our roaster and storage areas in the basement, there were so many hyperdressed bodies jostling for elbow room, not one inch of the polished, wood plank floor was visible. However, designer Lottie Harmon had insisted her party be held in this century-old, Greenwich Village coffeehouse. For one thing, she said, *she* was practically an historical landmark herself.

Two and a half decades ago, Lottie's name had been almost as recognizable as Halston's. Then, suddenly, Lottie had dropped out of the business—only to return last year to take the fashionistas by storm with an accessory line as successful as any she'd ever created, which is the second reason she'd wanted her Fashion Week party held at the Blend. Her new collection of "Java Jewelry" had been inspired by the many coffee drinks she'd consumed here.

As I moved to get behind the coffee bar and check on Tucker, I spied Lottie herself. The designer was chatting with Christina Ha, fashion critic from the Metro New York Full Frontal Fashion television network. Lottie wore her auburn hair long and dyed a bold scarlet. She'd been thin to begin with, but tonight she appeared to have dropped even more weight. She'd also shed the simple flowered skirts she'd favored since Madame (the eighty-year-old owner of this landmark coffeehouse) had introduced me to her over eighteen months ago, when Lottie had first moved back to Greenwich Village from her former residence in London. Now, clad in a chocolate Fen suit accented with striking pieces from her line—a caramel latte swirl brooch and sheer espresso scarf sprinkled with "coffee-bean" beads—she appeared at least ten years younger than her fifty-something years.

Luminaries of the fashion world surrounded her—designers, critics, models, magazine editors, along with a sprinkling of pop singers, HBO stars, and supporting actor film types. Her two young business partners were here as well. Tad Benedict and Rena Garcia had risked everything, along with Lottie, to see this spring collection succeed. Her fall line (launched last February) was already selling out in Saks and Herrods, Neiman Marcus, Bergdorfs, and Fen's international boutiques. Now it was imperative that Lottie prove herself with her spring line to be more than a one-season wonder, a fashion fluke.

So, of course, the last thing I needed right now was for Tucker to lose it in the middle of this production. For the past two hours, I myself had been the one making the coffee drinks, but I needed a break and had assumed Tucker could handle it for at least the next thirty minutes. If he couldn't, I'd have to get back in the saddle—pronto.

I moved behind the counter to speak with him, but Moira was already hovering protectively and blocking my path. "Is he all right?" I asked.

Moira frowned, brushed aside a lock of auburn hair with the back of her long, narrow hand. "I don't know, Clare. I'll take care of him and find out what's wrong."

I waited for Moira to step aside, but the girl gestured toward the crowd. "Seems like Esther needs help at the door."

She wasn't kidding. The Village Blend's front entrance looked like the mouth of the Lincoln Tunnel on a Jets game day, so I hurried over. On my way, I tried not to worry about Tucker's uncharacteristic freak out and prayed it was not some kind of omen for the deterioration of what had been, up to this point, a fairly smooth running affair.

Shoot me, but I believe in omens. My Italian grandmother who primarily raised me while my father ran a bookie operation in the back of her Pennsylvania grocery had given me the "411"—as my twenty-year-old daughter Joy would put it—on the *malocchio*, the evil eye, the curse. And although I liked to think I'd shoved this vaguely primitive philosophy behind me, I still could not dislodge an increasingly uneasy feeling that something bitter was brewing.

I arrived at the door to find the line of new arrivals fronted by a young man with short, blond-streaked brown hair. He wore a charcoal gray suit over an electric blue Egyptian cotton shirt with a lime green handkerchief blooming out of the suit's breast pocket. On his arm were two women.

The first was a typical, barely twenty-year-old model with streaked blond hair uptwisted and a tangerine leather outfit. The other, however, was memorably striking, even in this air-brushed crowd. She was well over six feet in her spike-heeled boots, had beautiful Asian features—straight black hair, worn all the way down to her hips, and almond-shaped eyes of an unusual deep blue-violet, which she'd emphasized with violet eye shadow and a matching violet minidress that glittered with metallic threads.

The trio was obviously impatient to make their entrance, but they had been stopped for a guest list check by the Blend's resident iconoclast, New York University comparative literature student Esther Best (shortened from Bestovasky by her grandfather), who chose to make a consciously *un*fashionable statement with faded khakis, an oversized green sweatshirt, her long dark hair done up in four tight anti-fashion braids, and "so five minutes ago" glasses with thick black frames.

I understood where Esther was coming from. Trendy, flamboyant dressing wasn't my style, either—mainly because I could never pull it off. On the other hand, at forty, I thought protesting "the frivolous pointlessness of high fashion" (as Esther put it) by deliberately dressing down was pretty much a pointless gesture in itself. So, I'd at least attempted to dress appropriately for the evening in the boring, prototypical New York outfit—black dress, black stockings, black boots—with my chestnut brown hair pulled into a high ponytail for barista work with that oh-so-elite fashion accessory, a discount store velvet scrunchie.

As I approached the crowded doorway, I heard Lime Green Kerchief man coo to Violet Eyes. "You should have seen it. The model's wardrobe was deconstructing on the runway. It was Milan, of course, but my god. How postmodern can you get? Use a stitch or two for chrissakes."

Violet Eyes smiled and nodded.

"And what about the Timmy Thom show?" offered Tangerine Leather Girl. "It was so . . . you know . . ." She bit her lower lip and searched the ceiling for the right word. Possibly any word. "You know, *done* before."

"Yes, it was *derivative*, darling," replied Lime Green Kerchief man. "Everybody's talking about how Timmy's just out of ideas. A barely disguised re-tread of the '02 line. And did you see the mandals he put on that hairy-legged boy toy?"

I pulled Esther aside. "Where's Matteo?" I asked.

Esther pointed across the room, but there were too many men wearing black Armani to make out which was my ex-husband. *He* was supposed to be checking invitations against the guest list at the door—not Esther. She'd volunteered to wipe spills, and gather the empty glass latte mugs and lipstick-smeared napkins.

"Boss," she whined, "these people are ridiculous."

"Only one more hour, Esther," I whispered. "And, remember, Lottie's paying you very well."

"Not well enough to be repeatedly told I'm a fashion victim and should immediately call 911. I'll call 911, all right—after I strangle one of these half-wits!"

I sighed. As diverse a town as New York City was, cliques and enclaves tended to reinforce the idea that everyone around you thought the way you did—and should dress, speak, and think like you, too, for that matter. The fashion industry was really no more unique in that regard than a cadre of New York University undergrads—and I should know, having listened to every butcher, baker, and candlestick maker prattle on from behind my espresso machine.

Theater people, stock brokers, publishing professionals—everyone had their forged attitudes, jargon, and fakery, their what's hot and what's not lists, their correct opinions, perceived winners, losers, and arbitrary size-'em-up yardsticks. Institutions meant institutional thinking, after all, but the dirty little secret after you've lived in New York long enough was that the "arts" were no more immune to this than the advertising industry, and, in fact, even "rebellion" was an organized racket—with its own line of coffee mugs and T-shirts.

I pulled away from Esther to check Lime Green Kerchief man's gold embossed invitation. "Lloyd Newhaven, Stylist, and Party," I read, then checked the name against the guest list, greeted him with a smile, and gestured for them to join the flowing mass of hyper-dressed beautiful people.

"By the way, what are mandals?" I innocently asked Lloyd the Stylist before he and his party walked away.

"Male sandals, sweetie," he answered with a brisk snap of his fingers. "And in my opinion the only man who ever looked good in sandals was Jesus Christ."

"Really?" I said. "What about Russell Crowe? In *Gladiator*?"

Violet Eyes actually laughed. "Oh, yes," she agreed, her words tinged with a slight exotic accent. "I did like that movie."

I turned back to Esther and asked her to handle the door a little longer. Then I went looking for my wayward ex-husband—something I'd done far too many times in my life to count.

As I crossed the room, I nervously dodged willowy young women dressed in Fen's new fall line—brown suede skirts, matching silk and suede blouses and mid-calf boots. All night, they'd been precariously balancing trays of lattes, biscotti, and a dozen specialty pastries while simultaneously modeling preview pieces of Lottie's spring line—from faux roasted coffee-bean Y necklaces and frothy cappuccino scarves to caramel loop bracelets and raw sugar earrings and brooches.

Unfortunately, Lottie had hired the models for their beauty and not their ability to handle full trays of hot liquids. Thank goodness Tucker had volunteered to give them all a crash course on serving customers—including a bonus lesson on the bunny dip, made famous by a once upscale but now defunct men's club.

Dressing them in Fen was calculated, too, of course. An internationally known clothing designer, Fen had worked with Lottie during her heyday over twenty years before, and he was now the key to her current success. He'd not only given Lottie a substantial financial investment to mass-produce her line, he'd also provided a spectacular launch pad by agreeing to pair her jewelry with his fall collection on runways around the world. Her new spring line would be showcased on Fen's models once again—at the end of this week.

I had hoped to see what the legendary Fen thought of one of the Village Blend's lattes, but he hadn't attended. "Too busy finalizing the upcoming show," Lottie had informed me.

I finished crossing the length of the packed room, squeezed around the wrought-iron spiral staircase and finally spotted my ex-husband next to the roaring fireplace, one hand casually braced against the exposed brick wall, which was adorned with coffee antiques gathered over the last century: a French lacquered urn, a cast-iron, two-wheeled grinding mill (used in the late 1800s, when the Blend was primarily a wholesale shop), copper English coffee pots, Turkish side-handled *ibriks*, and an array of 1920s tin signs advertising coffee brands.

Matt's attention, however, was not on the aforementioned décor, but on (no surprise) an attractive woman.

TWO

Just a few days ago, Matteo had returned from Ethiopia looking like something my cat Java had dragged in from the Blend's back alley. But tonight, even I had to admit he'd cleaned up well. In fact, he looked better than a French-pressed pot of Jamaica Blue Mountain. His muscular shoulders were draped in fine Italian fabric, his chiseled jaw, usually brushed in black stubble, was closely shaved, his Caesar haircut in masculine trim.

Matteo wasn't just my ex-husband. He was also the Blend's coffee buyer, an astute coffee broker, and the owner's son. Thanks to his French-born mother, Madame Blanche Dreyfus Allegro Dubois, Matt and I had not only remained partners in the raising of our daughter, we were now partners in the running of the Blend. Madame had offered me co-ownership of the Blend's business and the multimillion dollar Federal-style Greenwich Village townhouse to entice me back into managing the family business, only to reveal later that her pirate of a son was slated to be the *other* co-owner.

After a decade of divorce and my self-imposed exile to

raise my daughter in New Jersey, I knew that a reconcilia-
tion with my ex-husband was, in the words of *The Godfa-
ther*'s Michael Corleone, "an impossibility that would
never happen," so I subsequently convinced myself that the
Blend was worth the aggravation. I bit the bullet and
agreed to put up with Matteo's intermittent stays in the duplex between coffee buying expeditions.

Admittedly, it wasn't always an aggravation. Our
daughter Joy loved her father, and saw more of him now
(since she'd moved to Manhattan to attend culinary school)
than she ever had growing up in New Jersey. And in rare
moments of truth I had to admit—to myself and myself
only—that Matt had changed for the better lately. Not that
he wasn't still exasperating. But he'd been helpful and sup-
portive in ways that actually astounded me.

I approached my ex-husband and the elegant, fortyish
woman with whom he was now deep in conversation. She
was a sleek New York sophisticate type, tall and Waspish
with salon-highlighted blond hair smoothed into a perfect
french twist and a sexy suit with a plunging neckline and
fabric the color of a mochaccino (not surprising since Fen
had made brown the new black this season). Earlier in the
evening, Matt had cornered a young pixie-haired bubble-
head in a spandex minidress. I hadn't felt a thing when I
saw him speaking with that type—it was just Matteo being
Matteo. But, for some reason, seeing him with this woman
closer to my own age sent an annoying and totally unwanted twinge of jealousy through me.

I, of course, instantly repressed it.

"Excuse me," I said through a smile of gritted teeth.

"Clare!" said Matteo, snaking an arm around my waist.
He flashed an easy smile at the elegant woman. "This is my
business partner in the Blend," he informed her, then turned
his big, brown innocent eyes back on me. "What's up?"

"Well, *partner*, you're supposed to be stationed at the
door."

"I asked Esther to cover for me."

"Ah, but you see," I told him, "that's problematic."

"Problematic?"

"You appointed an openly hostile anti-fashion activist to meet and greet a crowd of people who mainline designer labels."

Matt laughed nervously and shot a glance at Miss Elegant, who sipped her latte and looked away as if bored. Then he leaned close to me.

"I'll be there shortly," he whispered into my ear, "and if Esther turns out to be a problem, then *you* can always look after the door until then."

With that, I felt his muscular arm spin me at my waist. Then his hand dropped to my lower back and pressed me back toward the front door in a gentle but infuriating send-off. Capping more steam than a two-boiler espresso machine, I marched away—but *not* to the front door. Instead, I returned to the coffee bar for a much-needed shot to calm my nerves. In the words of Moe Howard, "*I wanted to brain him.*"

Back at the bar, I found Tucker pulling espressos and chatting with Lottie's two business partners, Tad Benedict and Rena Garcia.

"How's Tuck doing?" I whispered to Moira.

The girl shrugged. "He won't talk about it. Just said, 'Men are pigs, and they should die' again and left it at that."

Well, whatever happened, Tucker seems over it now, I thought with relief.

Just then, Esther Best appeared at the bar. I blinked in surprise. "Shouldn't you be at the door?" I said.

Esther shrugged. "The frou-frou train has slowed considerably. I left one of those walking brown string beans to guard the entrance since it sure looks like Matt is too busy hitting on Breanne Summour to relieve me anytime soon."

"What's her name again?" I asked, since Matt hadn't bothered to mention Miss Elegant's name.

Rena Garcia, Lottie's business partner, overheard me

and replied, "Breanne Summour is the editor-in-chief of *Trend* magazine. And *Trend* is very influential with the upscale crowd. *Vogue* and *Women's Wear Daily* are Seventh Avenue staples, but *Trend* covers more than fashion . . . it follows whatever is on the cutting edge for a wide range of . . . well . . . trends."

I thanked Rena, then turned back to Esther. "For someone who doesn't care about fashion, you certainly seem to know your *fashionistas*."

"New York One's running their annual *Fall Fashion Week Is Here Again*! story," Esther replied with a shrug. "They interviewed her in the piece and ran it every hour over the weekend. It was hard not to recognize her when she walked in tonight."

My disturbed state must have been more than a little obvious because Lottie's other business partner, Tad Benedict, sidled up to me. "So how are you holding up, Clare?" he asked, genuine concern in his voice.

"Fine. I just desperately need an espresso," I said.

"Coming up," said Moira, overhearing.

"Well, you're doing a great job," said Tad. "The drinks are delicious—and so are the pastries. Lottie's very pleased. She said she only wished she could have gotten another of those little white diamonds before they all disappeared!" He smiled and patted his chubby stomach. "What were those anyway?"

I smiled. "Ricciarelli. They've been a popular celebration cookie for a long time—a really long time, actually. Documents from the Renaissance describe the cookie as being served in Italy and France during lavish, important banquets—"

Tad's eyebrows rose and I realized I was lapsing into "too much information" again. But for years, while I was raising my daughter in New Jersey, I'd written a cooking column for a local paper, and ever since obscure details about food and drink had looped themselves into my everyday conversations. So sue me.

"Well, everything's just delicious," Tad replied.

I was grateful for the positive word. Tad was a good guy. A thirty-something, self-employed investment banker who lived in the neighborhood, his receding hairline and paunchy physique presented a stark contrast to the chiseled male models packed into the coffeehouse, but the leprechaun-like sparkle in his eyes, along with his gregarious nature, made him instantly likeable.

At his side, Rena Garcia—clad in a Fen caramel silk blouse with cream collar and cuffs and a long, brown leather skirt—smiled and sipped a latte. A pretty, vivacious Latina with a savvy head for marketing and publicity, she'd become Lottie's other business partner after losing her job at Satay and Satay, an advertising and marketing firm just a few blocks away.

"So, you must be excited with what Matt's up to," said Tad, gesturing to the private conversation I'd interrupted by the fireplace.

"Excuse me?" I could think of a lot of words to describe what I felt about Matt's behavior and "excited" was not one of them.

"Matt's just being smart," he said with a reassuring look.

"Smart?"

"Chatting up his kiosk idea with some key players."

Before I could ask Tad what the hell he was talking about a familiar voice interrupted.

"Pardon me, but can I get a latte with soy milk?"

It was Lloyd Newhaven, the stylist, sans his two beautiful companions. He was suddenly hovering near Moira, who was lining up more tall glass mugs for Tucker.

"Of course," said Moira. "But we've really backed up so it will take a few minutes."

"I'll wait," he said with a sigh.

Soy milk was a fairly common request, and the Blend had an ample supply. As Moira went back to her work, Lloyd glanced our way. "I'm just dying for one, but, you know, I'm lactose intolerant."

Tad, Rena, and I nodded. That's when I noticed Tucker hoisting a tray of drinks and scanning the crowded room to find one of the model waitresses to deliver it. I was about to grab the tray from him to help out when a model swept in and whisked the tray off. But she hadn't gone four feet before a crowd swarmed her and snagged every last latte.

"Is my soy latte coming?" Lloyd Newhaven prompted, impatient after barely a minute. Moira glanced up with annoyance on her face. Before she could say a word, I decided my short break was over.

"I've got it," I declared, then moved around the coffee bar to search the fridge beneath the counter. "Figures," I muttered when I realized we were out of soy milk up front. I ducked downstairs to retrieve a fresh container from one of our two large storage refrigerators in the basement.

"Hey, Tucker . . . I can do that," I heard Moira insisting as I returned to the coffee bar. A tray with a single glass latte mug was sitting on the blue marble counter.

"Nonsense, dear," Tucker told Moira. "You volunteered to help me behind the coffee bar, not hustle drinks to this monstrously catty cartel, and you're doing great."

With that, Tucker swept up the tray and headed across the crowded room.

At some point after I'd gone downstairs, Esther had stepped away from the counter to gather used mugs. She passed Tucker on her way back. "Uh-oh," said Esther when she saw where Tucker was headed. "Watch out for fireworks."

"Excuse me?" I said, preparing Lloyd Newhaven's soy milk latte. "Where's Tucker going with that drink?"

"After you went downstairs, Tucker made Lottie a latte. That's where Tucker's headed, to give it to her—only *Ricky Flatt's* in his way."

"Who?" I asked.

"He's the fashion writer for *Metropolitan* magazine," Rena informed me.

Esther pointed. "He's standing in the group next to Lottie's. And before you ask how I know, it's because Tucker used to date him. He's stopped in the Blend a few times."

"He has?" I murmured, handing the finished soy milk latte to Lloyd Newhaven. I followed Esther's pointing finger, but I didn't recognize anyone.

"John Waters-esque mustache," said Esther by way of description.

I nodded, spying the tall, lean, thirtyish man with a pencil-thin moustache and long black hair that fell down his back in oiled ringlets. He wore a brown silk jacket and a canary yellow shirt opened practically to his navel. At his side stood a blond young man in tight jeans and a V-neck cream sweater, his teeth bone white behind a Miami Beach tan on a hard-muscled frame.

"I've never seen him in the Blend before," I said.

"You were probably off roasting beans or dealing with a delivery or something whenever he passed through. Ricky burned Tucker about two weeks ago—romantically, I mean. They had some kind of quarrel and Ricky totally dumped him. And not in a nice way. Now the jerk's obviously here flaunting his newest boy toy. If you're Tucker, that's gotta hurt."

As Tucker approached Lottie, Ricky Flatt stepped out to block his path. Esther crossed her arms and cocked her head, as if she'd just taken her seat at a WWF event. "Check it out, boss, this is going to be interesting. Five dollars says that latte Tucker's carrying ends up in Ricky's face."

But it didn't. Before Tucker could stop him, Ricky snatched the latte off Tucker's tray as if the drink was meant for him. Then he gestured to the hard-muscled young man seated next to him as if he were ordering Tucker to bring him another for his date. Tucker snapped something at Ricky—and Ricky snapped his fingers in Tucker's face. Of course, I couldn't hear either man's conversation over the loud music, but it was easy to see Ricky was baiting poor Tucker.

Finally, Tucker turned his back on the two men and returned to the coffee bar. I'd never seen him so upset. "Someone . . . someone took the latte I made for Lottie," he managed. "I need another."

For a long moment, we all just stared at Tucker.

"Clare," Tuck said loudly. "I need another latte for Lottie!"

I turned quickly, loaded the espresso machine and pulled another shot, then prepared the latte and set it directly on the tray in Tucker's hands.

"Thanks," said Tucker. He lifted the tray and made a wide detour to avoid Ricky Flatt's spot. After he handed Lottie her drink, Tuck crossed the center of the room, strolling past Ricky's group. The fashion writer lifted his latte, saluted Tucker. After swallowing a huge gulp, he passed the glass mug to his partner, who drained it dry.

Tucker shook his head in obvious disgust, then returned to the coffee bar. Just then, a commotion broke out among the audience. A woman cried out, "Are you all right?" Then a man shouted, "Someone help!"

I looked up, saw Ricky Flatt grimace as he clutched his throat. His mouth opened and closed like a fish on a dry dock.

"Oh god, I think he's choking," cried Esther.

My pulse racing, I pushed through the crowd toward Ricky. When I reached him, however, I saw Ricky Flat's face wasn't turning blue from lack of air, but a bright shade of pink! Then he slumped over his table and slid to the wood plank floor.

"Ricky! Ricky!" keened a hysterical voice. Ricky Flatt's muscular date knelt at the man's side and shook him.

"Get away from him," a short, older man in a Truman-Capote-wannabe white fedora said. "Give him some air."

Suddenly, Ricky's boyfriend also turned a bright shade of pink and clutched his stomach.

Standing over the pair, I felt someone at my shoulder— Tucker. The kneeling boyfriend looked up, his eyes wide. He raised his hand and pointed an accusing finger at my barista.

"That . . . that bastard poisoned me and Ricky!" he cried, then collapsed across the inert form of Ricky Flatt.

THREE

∾∾∾∾∾∾∾∾∾∾∾∾∾∾∾∾∾∾∾∾∾∾∾∾∾

To say a hush fell over the crowd would be a cliché. What really happened was this.

First every human noise fell silent—no more uproarious laughter, catty banter, or jostling for position around a B-list celebrity. Every fashionable body in the room was suddenly doing an impersonation of a dummy in a Bloomingdale's window. The only sound remaining was the relentlessly throbbing electronic dance music, which seemed to swell until it filled every corner of the place. Behind trendy glasses and black liner, wide eyes stared at the two young men sprawled, one atop the other, on the polished hardwood planks.

Ricky Flatt, the unfortunate victim on the bottom of the two-person pile, remained motionless. The unconscious boyfriend was still gasping for air, his labored rattle barely audible against the pounding, insistent rhythm of the synth-pop beat.

Someone bumped past my shoulder, suddenly shaking me from my paralyzed stupor. It was Esther, the house emergency First Aid kit clutched in her hands. But she was beaten to the stricken men by a tall figure in black Armani—my ex-husband.

Matt rolled the gasping man off his still partner, opened his gaping jaw even wider to peer inside, then carefully probed the victim's mouth with two fingers.

"No obstructions," he announced.

Esther was still holding the First Aid kit, unsure what to do next. It was Tucker who snatched the kit and dropped to his knees beside Ricky, checked his ex-boyfriend's mouth and throat, tilted his head back to open the airway, then unwrapped a plastic CPR mask, placed it over Ricky's bright pink face, and began the first stages of cardiopulmonary resuscitation.

So what was I doing during all this? You would think after everything I'd been through—enduring a harrowing attack on a Greenwich Village rooftop, braving the business end of a loaded gun in this very coffeehouse, raising a teenaged daughter at the dawn of the twenty-first century—that I would instantly spring into some sort of competent action.

But you'd be wrong.

Like an idiot, I stood there, silently gawking, along with everyone else in the room. That is, until I heard someone urge—

"Clare? Clare? Shouldn't you do something?"

It was Esther, and she was addressing me as Clare. Not "boss" in that urbane, near-sarcastic tone she typically used. She called me "Clare"—a word that only came out of Esther's mouth when things were bad.

"Call 911," I heard myself say.

Esther pointed to the crowd around us. "I think that ship's already sailed." Dozens of beautiful people were whipping out color-coordinated cell phones from designer bags or secret hidden pockets in their skin-tight rags. A few standing close to us were definitely talking to 911 operators—others, unfortunately, were calling their limo drivers and car services to arrange hasty retreats.

Within minutes, the front door opened and two NYPD officers came through, dark blue uniforms, nickel-plated

badges, squawking radios. I recognized the pair at once—
Officers Demetrios and Langley from the nearby Sixth
Precinct. The Village Blend wasn't just part of their regular
beat, they were also regular customers (Turkish coffee and
House Blend drinkers, respectively.)

Tucker was still giving CPR to Ricky. Matteo looked up
at the two policemen. "We have a medical emergency
here," he informed them.

"Help's coming," said Langley, raising his radio.

And it arrived soon after. An ambulance pulled up to the
curb, siren's blaring, red lights rippling through our tall
front windows. Two paramedics hurried into the coffeehouse, both laden with medical equipment.

Officer Demetrios touched my arm. I jumped, startled
out of my entranced disbelief that something like this
could have happened tonight of all nights. "Choking victim, Ms. Cosi?" asked the young, raven-haired Greek cop.

I stammered an unintelligible reply.

Esther quickly translated. "Choking seems really unlikely. The odds against two people choking at the same
table are phenomenal—and I'd say the odds are just as
high against double heart attacks . . . unless of course they
were both smoking crack cocaine and simultaneously
OD'd or something like that."

Demetrios frowned. He turned from Esther to face me.
"I'm sorry, Ms. Cosi, but if this was the result of a crime,
or criminal activity was involved, we're going to have to
secure the area."

"What do you mean exactly by 'secure the area'?" I
asked. "Does everyone have to clear out?"

"No. The reverse. They can't leave. They're all suspects."

I closed my eyes, not entirely surprised but sick to my
stomach nonetheless. "My god, this is a private party . . . all
these people are here by invitation. What will they think?"

Demetrios glanced around. "They'll probably think
they'll have another story to tell at their next party." The
Greek officer turned, waved to his tall Irish partner, gestured with his chin toward the front entrance. Already

some of the partygoers were attempting to slip out the door. Langley jumped to the exit before a pair of young women could flee the scene.

"Just hang out awhile, ladies," Langley told them. "Once we get names, addresses, and statements, everyone can go home."

"Statements? Why in the world do you need statements?" whined the short, white fedora-wearing, Truman Capote wannabe, standing near me. "Those young men were poisoned. Surely you can see that for yourself."

"Just take it easy," Demetrios replied. "It's not our job to rush to judgement. The docs will rule on that."

I frantically scanned the room for Lottie, finally catching sight of her on the edge of the crowd. The sponsor of the party seemed worried, but not overly distraught. Thank goodness, I thought, because I felt horrible. Seeing these two men collapse made me feel bad enough—but poor Lottie had chosen the Village Blend as the perfect location for her preview party. Now the entire event was ruined. I could only pray the negative publicity (which, with this catty crowd, was as sure a thing as the rising sun) would not ultimately ruin her runway debut with Fen at the end of the week. And, of course, I was worried about the Blend's reputation.

While I pondered a possible rocky future, most everyone else watched with varying levels of interest as the two paramedics checked vital signs on the two stricken men. For Ricky Flatt, things looked bad. The medical technician hovering over him lifted a stethoscope from Ricky's stiffened chest and shook his head. I felt sick to my stomach as I watched both paramedics abandon Ricky as gone, then move to the man who was still breathing. They checked his pulse, blood pressure, and the dilation of his eyes, and they snapped on an oxygen mask.

Finally the paramedic with the stethoscope looked up—addressing the crowd in general. "What happened here? This isn't a heart attack, and it's not a choking incident either."

"That man said he was poisoned!" cried a young

woman in a metallic gold minidress and matching stiletto
ankle boots. She pointed to the gasping victim. "His face
turned so pink, he looked like an ad for Juicy Couture!"

"Juicy Couture?" I whispered to Rena, who was standing behind me.

She shrugged. "West coast designers. A few seasons ago
they made pink the new black."

As the two paramedics continued to work on Ricky's
date, I noticed Matteo standing by, watching. Behind his
eyes, I saw that something was upsetting him—that is, beyond the level of distress anyone would feel over two
strangers possibly dropping dead right in front of you. I
simply knew Matt too well not to recognize when he was
personally disturbed, but I also knew now was not the time
to ask him what was wrong.

At Matt's side stood Tucker, face flushed, hands trem-
bling as he stared in disbelief at Ricky's corpse. The paramedics primed a needle and shoved it into a vein on the
other man's arm, then attached it to a bottle of intravenous
fluid of some kind.

At the front doors, officer Langley stepped aside to admit a third paramedic who entered rolling a stretcher in
front of him. He joined the other two and the trio quickly
laid Ricky's still-alive boyfriend on the gurney. Then they
pushed through the crowd, out the door, and across the
sidewalk. While the boyfriend was loaded into the ambulance, a second ambulance rolled up. Its siren cut out and
the brakes squealed as it bounced onto the sidewalk and
stopped just outside the Blend's front entrance.

After a short conversation with the first group of paramedics, the second pair opened the rear doors of their vehicle and wrestled a gurney to the sidewalk. As the first
vehicle pulled away, the two paramedics from the second
ambulance hustled inside. The pair, a young Hispanic man
and a middle-aged Asian woman, wore patches on their
shoulders that indicated they worked for St. Vincent's, a
hospital not far from the Blend (whose sleepless interns
also happened to be excellent triple espresso customers).

But when this pair tried to move Ricky, Officer Demetrios prevented them from touching the man.

"This is a possible crime scene," he said. "The victim isn't going to be moved until the detectives clear it. I don't want the area contaminated."

The young paramedic exploded. "What?! Who do you think you are, man? The freaking coroner? This guy ain't officially dead yet, which means we're taking him to St. Vincent's."

Demetrios stared at the paramedic. "He looks dead to me."

The female paramedic sighed. She examined the body. "He looks dead to me, too."

The obviously overwrought male paramedic shot daggers at Officer Demetrios but finally stepped away from the body.

Another commotion erupted at the front door. I rushed over to find a fashionista riot brewing. Members of the crowd were voicing their determination to get to the other Fashion Week parties being thrown by designers tonight—a bellini bash at Cipriani, a sushi soiree at Nobu, and a Proseco party at Otto. The only thing keeping them from their appointed rounds was Officer Langley, who stood like an unmovable Irish seawall against the swelling tide.

"Everyone stay calm!" I cried, downright relieved to have something constructive to do at last. "I'm sure everything will be fine."

"*Fine?!*" a woman exclaimed. "For all I know I've been poisoned, just like that poor man dead on the floor."

"Nobody's been poisoned," Matteo loudly barked.

I shot my ex a grateful glance, and noticed Breanne Summour sashaying up to stand beside him. He turned and she whispered something into his ear. He nodded. I frowned. Ms. Summour's high cheekbones and gazelle-like neck were annoying me. Not to mention her forehead, which had to be at least as broad as one of those widescreen TVs at the Twenty-third Street Best Buy.

"Please, everyone calm down and return to your seats,"

Officer Demetrios cried over the increasing din of complaints. The crowd ignored his command and more people pressed for the door, forcing Langley's body inches from the beveled glass. Unfortunately, Demetrios could do no more than yell orders, since he was left to guard the area immediately around Ricky Flatt's corpse from "contamination."

Good lord, I thought, Demetrios and Langley certainly had come a long way. When I'd first met them, they'd been so green they'd let me traipse all over a crime scene—that is, before Detective Quinn had shown up and chewed them out.

The thought of Mike Quinn striding through my front door again made me feel a little better, until I heard Esther say, "Maybe everyone would like some coffee?"

"NO!"

Suddenly the front door opened from outside, the frame smacking Officer Langley in the back of his head. He stepped to the side as the portal yawned. The mob began to surge forward, sensing a chance for escape. Then, strangely, they all took a step backwards again and parted with biblical soberness.

A tall, imposing woman in navy blue slacks, a white blouse, and an open gray trenchcoat swept through their ranks. She strode in on three-inch platform heels, an NYPD detective shield dangling from a black strap around her neck. She looked to be in her mid-thirties, her expression hard and sharp as a razor, her blue eyes cold and challenging. She wore no makeup, and her long straw-blond hair was pulled back into a ponytail so tight it seemed to stretch the flesh of her face.

Coming through the door behind the woman was a far less impressive figure. Well into middle age, the wrinkled Asian man seemed nearly as wide as he was tall. Under a flapping beige overcoat, he wore a dark suit, white shirt with a fraying collar, and a wide striped tie that had been out of fashion since Jimmy Carter was president. His expression was bland, neither tired nor bored—more like he was suffering from a mild but chronic case of irritation.

Officer Demetrios let out a soft, unhappy moan at the sight of the pair, but he quickly shook off the momentary distress, straightened his uniform, and corrected his posture. The tall blond detective marched by Demetrios, strode directly to the corpse sprawled on the bare wooden floor, and with silent intensity studied the scene.

Even Esther seemed rattled by the detective's ominous aura of authority. As the female detective pulled out a pair of latex gloves and snapped them on, Esther appeared to suddenly remember her assigned duty for the night—to keep the coffeehouse as tidy as possible. Worried the detective would reprimand her for allowing debris to clutter up her crime scene, Esther bent down and reached for the crumpled napkins and tall glass mug that had tumbled to the floor when the fashion editor was first stricken.

"FREEZE!"

The crowd seemed to gasp simultaneously. The detective's latex-covered index finger pointed directly at Esther, whose eyes widened larger than the black glasses framing them.

"Don't touch *anything*."

As Esther shrunk away, the detective's blue eyes played across the scene as if memorizing it. Then she knelt down and touched Ricky Flatt's throat with two fingers.

Throughout the woman's inspection, Ricky's unseeing eyes continued to stare up at the Blend's vintage tin ceiling. Beside the victim, the female detective finally turned her attention to the glass mug near the corpse—the one Esther had nearly disturbed. She drew a pencil from an inside pocket of her trenchcoat, carefully touched the interior of the glass with the tip of the eraser, then lifted the writing implement to her nose and sniffed it. Finally, she rose and faced Officer Demetrios. They spoke softly for a minute or two, too softly for me to hear them over the still pounding music. It looked as if the woman was giving Officer Demetrios instructions, because he nodded occasionally, face nervous. Then the woman turned to address the crowd.

"Okay, what happened here?"

Four

∿∿∿∿∿∿∿∿∿∿∿∿∿∿∿

A dozen voices spoke at once, mine and Matteo's among them.

"Quiet!" the woman barked. "One at a time."

Matteo stepped up to her, taking on the police woman directly. I was suddenly afraid my ex-husband's inbred antagonism toward authority figures in general and members of the law enforcement community in particular was about to assert itself. I was right.

"Look, lady, I don't know what you *think* happened here, but nobody was poisoned."

This isn't the right approach, Matt, I silently wailed. Then I stepped between them—while attempting to push Matteo backward with my elbow. Given that he was over six feet and all muscle, and I was under five-five with zero weight training, the effect was nil.

"Hello," I said, extending my hand. "My name is Clare Cosi. I'm the manager of the Village Blend."

"Detective Rachel Starkey," she replied, ignoring my proffered palm. Then she eyed Matteo behind me. "And who's the big bohunk behind you?"

Bohunk? Who talks like that?

"He's Matteo Allegro, my—"

"Business partner," Matteo finished for me with a glance at Breanne Summour.

"Okay, Mr. Allegro. *My* partner here will get your statement, while I speak with *your* partner here, and the rest of her staff."

I realized as I was listening to Detective Starkey that she had the very slight but telling signs of a Queens accent—a drawling of vowels and dropping of Rs. The Blend's private carting company was based in Queens, and I heard that accent at least twice a week because I always invited the sanitation crew in for a coffee break when they stopped by to empty our dumpster.

Like me, it appeared Detective Starkey had cleaned up well, virtually masking her working-class accent and dressing for a slick presentation of authority.

Starkey faced the rest of the room. "Ladies and gentlemen," she said loud enough to be heard over the dance music, "the uniformed officers will take statements from everyone else."

"Excuse me, Detective," declared the Truman Capote wannabe. "But I should think you'd want to talk with me. I saw the whole thing. That poor man was poisoned. His friend said so before he collapsed, too."

A middle-aged woman in a silk pantsuit and tinted glasses placed a hand on her hip. "Well, I saw it, too."

I couldn't believe this crowd was so catty they were jockeying for prime positions at a crime scene.

Detective Starkey seemed unfazed. "Detective Hutawa will take both of your statements," she said.

The heavyset detective's frown deepened as he pulled out a notebook and pen and motioned the short man in the white fedora to follow him to the coffee bar.

Detective Starkey took my arm. "Get your staff together, Ms. Cosi, and let's talk behind the counter."

I turned, waved for Tucker to come forward. Esther and Moira McNeely were already behind the coffee bar, waiting. We gathered next to the espresso machine, and Starkey pulled us all into a tight circle as she fixed her Ice Station Zebra blue eyes on mine. "What happened here, Ms. Cosi? In your own words."

"Well . . . one minute Mr. Flatt was enjoying himself—"

"You call him *Mr. Flatt*?" the detective cut in. "Does that mean you know the victim?"

"No," I replied and chose my next words carefully. "His name was . . . on the guest list."

"I see," Starkey said, eyes unblinking. "Go on."

"So," I continued, "Mr. Flatt seemed fine. Then he just collapsed. A minute later, his friend collapsed, too."

"Were they eating? Drinking?"

Tucker spoke up. "They shared a latte."

Her piercing stare shifted from me to Tucker. "A latte? What kind?"

"Caramel-chocolate," Tucker replied. "That's mostly what we're serving at this party."

"What's in this latte?"

Tucker shrugged. "Espresso. Steamed milk. Caramel-chocolate syrup. Whipped cream. And a chocolate-covered coffee bean on top."

Detective Starkey paused rather meaningfully. "How about Amaretto?"

"Amaretto?" replied Tucker. "In a caramel-chocolate latte? No, Detective, no Amaretto."

"And you're sure about that, Mr . . . ?"

"Burton. Tucker Burton. And, of course I'm sure. I made that latte myself."

A shout interrupted us. "The medical examiner's here, Detective." It was Officer Langley calling over from his post at the door. Two more uniformed officers had arrived as well.

"I'm busy here, Officer. The M.E. knows his job. Tell him to do it," Starkey replied without shifting her gaze from Tucker. Then she reached out and put her hand on Tuck's shoulder. "And do you know who brought Mr. Flatt his beverage, Tucker Burton?"

Wait a minute, I thought. *What's happening here?*

Starkey's intense gaze was holding Tucker like a hunter drawing a bead on an unsuspecting deer. "Tucker, don't answer that!" I blurted out. But it had already overlapped with his—

"I did. I brought it."

"Ms. Cosi, I'm not speaking with you at the moment."

The detective's words were a little too sharp, a little too loud. I didn't care. Tucker was family, and I wasn't going to watch him railroaded. I stepped up to the woman. "Tucker isn't obligated to answer anything."

At nearly six feet, the chic Detective Starkey towered over me like an imposing stiletto, but I didn't care. My façade and vocabulary, not to mention my current address, may have improved as much as hers since my own working-class childhood, but the old ways died hard—and I'd bet a thousand goomba dollars my old neighborhood was ten times tougher than hers.

"He's my employee," I knocked the woman's hand from Tucker's body. "And I'm the one responsible for the drinks served here."

Detective Starkey reacted but not in the way I'd expected. One blond eyebrow arched and she studied me with the detached interest of Mr. Spock examining a strange new life form.

"Clare, it's okay," said Tucker. "I'll answer your questions, Detective. I've got nothing to hide."

"Did Mr. Flatt say anything to you when you served him the latte?" asked Starkey, dispassionately resuming the interrogation as if I'd never existed. "Did he complain about the taste, perhaps?"

I crossed my arms and made unhappy groaning noises. Tucker ignored me. "No, detective, Ricky didn't complain about the latte. And I didn't *serve* the latte to him, Ricky *took it* off my tray."

Starkey's blond eyebrow arched again. "Ricky? That's the victim's first name? So you knew Mr. Flatt?"

Tucker sighed. His narrow shoulders seemed to sag inward. "I . . . I knew Ricky."

"Under what circumstance did—"

"Rachel!" Detective Hutawa keened from across the room. "The doc wants to speak with us, pronto."

Detective Starkey flinched. What she probably wanted to do was curse a blue streak. Instead, she held up an index finger to Tucker. "I'll be right back," she promised. "And, Ms. Cosi? Do me a favor."

My arms were still tightly crossed. "What?"

"Kill that damn music."

I watched the woman saunter across the room, then go into a huddle with her partner and another man in khaki pants and a blue blazer. Beyond them I spied Matteo, with Breanne Summour stuck to his side like an expensively dressed carbuncle. I stepped to the end of the counter and slammed the speaker system's off switch. Everyone looked up as the pulsing electronica pounded its last beat and a funereal silence fell over the coffeehouse. I returned to find my staff in a tight circle. *Wagon trains*, I thought. Tucker was biting his thumbnail in a sudden moment of regret. "Oh, god, Clare. Did I tell that detective too much?"

"That would be a *yes*," said Esther.

Moira's eyes, already dewy, went wide. "That's not funny, Esther. The police are going to arrest Tucker."

Tucker went pale. "My god, I can't go to jail. I just can't . . ."

"Nobody's going to jail," I said.

"I didn't poison anyone," insisted Tuck. "And I didn't want anything bad to happen to Ricky. I mean, after what he did to me, I wanted to kill him, sure. But I didn't want to *kill* him, kill him. That latte wasn't even meant for him. I was supposed to give it to Lottie Harmon."

Moira put her arms around Tucker and hugged him. He buried his face in her shoulder and shook his head in despair.

I knew that latte was meant for Lottie. And other people did, too. *Surely the detectives will pick up on that,* I thought, *after they interview the key witnesses and gather all the facts.* I noticed that another plain-clothes policeman had entered the Blend, or perhaps he was some official from the Medical Examiner's office. Since it was obvious more law enforcement people were still arriving, I scanned the room, hoping against hope that a certain tall, attractively rumpled police detective might show up in the nick of time and put everything right again. But there was no sign of Mike Quinn anywhere.

Then my gaze caught young Officer Demetrios. He was leafing through a worn notebook filled with his bold block letters. I stepped out from behind the counter to confront him. "What's going to happen?"

He looked nervously beyond me, toward the huddle near the corpse. "I . . . I couldn't say, Ms. Cosi."

He tried to push by me, but I refused to be shaken loose so easily. "Why isn't Mike Quinn here?"

"I heard Detective Quinn's on leave."

That explained why I hadn't seen him lately. Some time ago, I'd weaned the man off the stale, bitter swill they called coffee in the average New York City bodega, so I'd been wondering where he was getting his caffeine fix.

"Is there something wrong with Detective Quinn? An emergency? Is he sick or something?" I asked.

Officer Demetrios shrugged. "He's taking lost time, that's all I know. Something personal, I guess."

Most likely marital woes, I decided. Off and on over the past year, we'd spoken of his troubles, of his cheating wife, of his indecision over seeking a divorce, and of all the custody issues that would subsequently involve his two children—

But I put thoughts of Detective Quinn aside. He wasn't here and he wasn't going to be, so it was up to me to focus on the problem at hand. "What do you know about those two?" I asked, gesturing to slick Detective Starkey and her hapless partner Hutawa.

Demetrios's eyes were guarded as he whispered his reply. "You heard of that good cop, bad cop thing—the one they use on television shows?"

"Yeah, I guess so."

"With these two, it's more like bad cop, worse cop. Starkey and Hut don't cut anybody any slack."

"Starkey and Hut? You're joking."

"For chrissake, not so loud, Ms. Cosi. And you didn't hear those names from me," he rasped, then hurried away as if I had the plague and was on fire.

I noticed the huddle by the corpse had finally broken up. Detective Starkey was heading back toward the coffee bar, her face impassive. My staff and I formed our own huddle as we watched the woman approach.

"The Medical Examiner's early conclusions match my own. Richard Flatt was the victim of foul play," Detective Starkey informed us. Her eyes drifted to Tucker. "And since Mr. Burton here denies your latte recipe uses Amaretto—"

"Amaretto?!" Tucker and I cried together, perplexed.

"Ms. Cosi, the M.E. and I both smelled the scent of bitter almond. The victim's skin has a distinctive pink hue, so if it isn't Amaretto in the latte your barista here has been serving up, then it's prussic acid—that's cyanide."

Moira and Esther paled. I felt sick. Tucker stumbled and nearly fainted. Detective Starkey clutched his arm to steady him. When she spoke, her tone was calm but firm. "Mr. Burton, I'm going to have to ask you to accompany me back to the station—"

"No . . . I won't go," Tucker cried, his eyes like a wounded animal's. Two uniformed officers I didn't know, a young one and an older one, stepped up to Tucker's side, took hold of his wrists. "Don't resist, son," warned the older one.

"But I didn't do anything," Tucker protested, struggling. "Please, let me go. . . ."

"Look at me, Mr. Burton," Detective Hutawa demanded, stepping right in front of him. Tucker stopped squirming to stare at the stout detective.

"Can you hear me?"

Tucker nodded.

"I asked if you can hear me, Mr. Burton?"

"Yes, yes, I can hear you."

Hutawa's face was grim as he began to intone, "You have the right to remain silent . . ."

"Oh, god, no." Tucker closed his eyes.

"Anything you say can and will be used against you in a court of law . . ."

"No. Please," Tucker begged.

"This is wrong!" I insisted.

"You can't do this," Moira sobbed. She pushed forward, trying to get to Tucker. Esther Best restrained her.

Detective Hutawa's gravelly voice rumbled on. "You have the right to an attorney. If you cannot afford one . . ."

"Clare! Do something," Esther Best cried as she held Moira.

I searched the crowded room for Matteo. He stood rigidly watching the arrest, frowning in fury, and it seemed to me he was about to barrel across the floor to raise living hell—but the light grip of Breanne Summour was apparently enough to hold him. Her French manicured fingers looked bone white against the fine black material of his Armani-clad arm, restraining him with bloodless insistence. Her glossy lips vigorously formed words, gripping his ear in a rapid whisper.

I turned my gaze from my ex and squared my shoulders. "Tuck," I said in a voice I hoped was calm and reassuring. "I'll bail you out. I'll find you a lawyer. Don't worry, I promise I'll do everything I can."

Which was, at that moment, not a thing. For now, I was forced to stand by and watch as the detectives placed handcuffs on Tucker's wrists and led him through the doors to a parked squad car.

As the police vehicle drove away, two detectives commanded me and my staff to step away from the counter. Then I helplessly watched as they wrapped my espresso machine, sink, and pastry case with fat rolls of police tape—the bright yellow color providing an incongruously sunny backdrop to the death black words that gave my coffee bar its new name: CRIME SCENE.

Five

~~~~~~

One by one, the police questioned the partygoers. Most were sent on their way, but others who'd been standing near Ricky Flatt were forced to stay behind to sign written statements attesting to what they'd witnessed.

Evicted from the coffee bar, my staff and I huddled near the fireplace. Esther Best settled into a morose funk while Moira tearfully wrung her hands. I turned from trying to comfort the sobbing girl and saw the sour-faced Detective Hutawa walking my way.

"Do you have somewhere we can talk in privacy, Ma'am?" he asked.

I nodded. "My office."

I led the detective up the staircase and through the coffee lounge on the second floor to my small, brick-walled office tucked away in a corner. My battered desk chair creaked as he settled himself into it. I pulled up a second chair and tightly crossed my legs and arms.

Hutawa focused weary eyes on me. "Officer Demetrios tells me you're a friend of Mike Quinn's. Met him through another case connected with this establishment."

I blinked in surprise. "Detective Quinn is a regular customer," I said guardedly.

"That I know," said Hutawa. He finally smiled. "Mike tells me the coffee is really great here. Something special."

"Yes, but I've never seen you in here. Why don't you stop in sometime for a cup?"

Hutawa's smile faded. "Never touch the stuff."

I frowned. *So much for attempting to establish trust.* "What's happening to Tucker, detective? When can I bail him out?"

Hutawa sighed and looked away, his eyes scanning the bulletin board on the nearby wall. "He's being processed, Ms. Cosi. His arraignment before a judge will most likely take place in the next twenty-four hours. If bail is set at all, it will be done at the arraignment. But if you really wish to *help* Mr. Burton . . ." Hutawa's gaze met mine, his weary tone now calm and sympathetic, "I suggest you start by answering some simple questions about him."

"Fine."

The detective then proceeded to ask me a lot of questions, most of them about Tucker. I was honest, though not to a fault. When he asked me if I'd known of a prior relationship between Tucker and the victim, I hedged. "If such a relationship existed, Tucker never mentioned it to me." My answer was *technically* honest, anyway—it was Esther who mentioned their affair.

"Would you say Mr. Burton was acting normally today? Was he upset, agitated or angry about something?"

"Of course not. Tucker was . . . well, he was *Tucker.*"

Detective Hutawa was obviously fixated on Tucker and Ricky's previous relationship as a motive. I knew he'd be questioning Esther—so I finally did confess that Esther had mentioned Ricky and Tucker had known one another "socially." He didn't press the matter, simply jotted down that fact in his notebook.

But I was firm in adding another obvious detail. "That latte on Tucker's tray, the one Ricky grabbed and drank, was actually intended for Lottie Harmon, the jewelry designer who hosted this party."

Hutawa stared at me in silence.

"If you're looking for a motive, I suggest that maybe you should have a talk with Lottie."

"That's what you suggest, eh?" He dropped his notebook, folded his hands and stared at me. "So what do you *suggest* I ask this woman, Ms. Cosi? Should I ask her why a barista at the Village Blend was trying to poison her?"

"For heaven's sake, Tucker had nothing to do with the poison in that drink—if there even *was* poison. If someone was intent on murder, then Tucker was as much a victim as Ricky Flatt."

Detective Hutawa snorted. "Look, Ms. Cosi. Police work in this city is no noodle-salad picnic, and the worst part of this job is that I hear the same prevarications every day—nothing but lies and excuses." The detective sighed. His shoulders drooped as if the weight of the world were slowly crushing them. " 'No, no, it wasn't me, Detective, it was somebody else who looked just like me that pulled the trigger.' Or 'I had to kill him, man, because he screwed me in a drug deal or has evil eyes and an *R* in his name.' "

Hutawa paused, shook his head. "So please, Ms. Cosi, spare me the homilies. I understand the urge to protect your employee and your business interests, but don't try to divert my attention away from the real focus of this investigation. The victim is Ricky Flatt, not this . . . this Lottie Harmon. And like it or not, your coffee brewer—"

"Barista."

Hutawa grunted. "Whatever you want to call him, he's admitted he made the fatal drink."

"That doesn't mean someone else didn't poison the latte after he made it," I countered, realizing, after the words were out, how unlikely that scenario would sound to a hardened police investigator.

But Hutawa sat back, folded his arms, and let me talk on.

"Listen, detective, I know that Tucker's no killer. He's

one of the gentlest souls I've ever met. Why, Tuck even tried to help Ricky, he began to administer CPR—"

But Detective Hutawa had heard enough. "We're through here, Ms. Cosi. If you don't mind, I'm going to use your office for a while. Tell the rest of your staff to come up here—and please don't attempt to concoct some phony story with the others because it will become apparent to me. It will only serve to insult my intelligence, and I don't like to be insulted."

Hutawa and Starkey had already made up their dual minds. To them, the case was clear. Tucker was guilty of murder. Obviously, the two detectives were only interested in building a case against him. And no doubt, the crime scene people were also working toward that same goal.

After Hutawa dismissed me, I found Esther and Moira waiting for me at the bottom of the stairs. "He wants to talk to you two next," I said. Esther frowned, Moira paled as I sent them on their way.

When I returned to the coffee bar, I got a nasty surprise. While Hutawa was grilling me, the folks from the Crime Scene Unit had wrecked the entire area. They'd emptied the refrigerator, the coffee urns, and the cupboards. They'd dismantled the espresso machine, rifled the pantry, and even searched through the loose beans in the coffee bins. They had bagged up the garbage beneath the counter—wet coffee grounds and disposable filters mostly, since we weren't using our usual paper cups for the private party.

All this was done, I supposed, in an effort to locate the source of the poison and confirm that no more of it existed. Of course, that was only a guess on my part, because none of the crime scene investigators would tell me a thing—or even acknowledge that I was speaking to them when I politely asked when I could have my coffeehouse back.

Their silence was beyond disturbing, so I drifted to the fireplace and, with all the chairs and tables moved out for the party, simply slumped down on the wood plank floor. I scanned the room for Matteo, hoping for a sturdy shoulder to lean on, but he was gone—either he'd given his statement to the police and escaped, or he'd shown even more attitude than me to one of the detectives and had been hauled off to jail. I doubted this, however, since I noted that Breanne Summour was also missing (gee, what a coincidence). Had they left together? *Is there caffeine in espresso?*

Someone else was also missing from the scene. While I was being questioned, Ricky Flatt's corpse had been carried off to the morgue—only the yellow tape outline on the floor remained to mark the place where the medical examiner had pronounced him dead.

The partygoers were mostly gone, too. I leaned my back against the cold, brick wall. Next to me, the fireplace sputtered with dying flames. I closed my eyes, lamenting the state of my coffee bar and poor Lottie Harmon's roll-out bash, and attempted to mentally process my gentle friend being forcefully hauled away in handcuffs.

Yet the crime, and the charges, didn't make any logical sense—maybe they did to the police detectives, but they certainly didn't to me. I knew Tucker, and I knew he was incapable of murder. Which meant somebody else at this party had to be.

There was no way cyanide could have been placed in any of the ingredients before the start of the party—the milk, the caramel-chocolate syrup, or the coffee beans. If that had been the case, then many more guests would have become ill than simply the two who'd downed Lottie's drink. Someone had to have placed the poison in the drink right before it was served.

He or she must have been in the vicinity of the coffee bar before Tucker picked up that tray to serve Lottie. I tried to recall who was at or near the coffee bar around the time of the incident. Tucker, of course. Esther and Moira. And I was there . . . on and off, until I'd had to descend to the basement steps for soy milk—for Lloyd Newhaven. Okay, so Lloyd was there. And Lottie's partners, Tad and Rena. Others were close by when I'd left the area for the basement, and almost anyone could have stepped up to the coffee bar and dropped something in that glass mug. The only reason Tucker had taken it himself was because the models had all been busy serving.

I would have to quiz Moira and Esther on who else might have swooped in during that time. But, as I saw it, the first step in clearing Tucker of a murder charge would be to prove that Lottie, and not Ricky Flatt, had been the killer's intended target. And that brought me back to the question of why? I could almost hear Mike Quinn's voice coaching me. . . .

Who would want Lottie Harmon dead? Who would gain from her murder?

And those questions led me to another—what did I really know about Lottie Harmon anyway?

Six

～～～～～～～～～～～～～～～～～～～～

I'D met Lottie about a year before, when I'd first returned to managing the Blend after a decade of suburban single motherhood. Madame had arrived one afternoon with Lottie, the two chatting and laughing as they breezed through the coffeehouse door.

"Clare, dear, I'd like you to meet an old friend and a former light of the fashion world," Madame had chirped.

I shook Lottie's hand. "Model?" I asked since, at over fifty, Lottie appeared tall and slim enough to have been one, and with her bold scarlet-dyed hair she obviously didn't mind attention.

"Model? Clare, surely you jest!" Madame chided. "You don't recall Lottie Harmon accessories? Her brand name was magic."

"*Was* being the key word," said Lottie with a laugh. "Once upon a time, back in the early 1980s."

I thought Lottie's comment was funny and self-deprecating, but her laugh made me cringe slightly. It didn't sound as tossed off as the remark—in fact, it sound strained, high-pitched, forced.

"Lottie was the creator of Spangles," Madame reminded me. "You must remember some of those popular pieces like the Spangle tie-bar? She sold millions."

I nodded vigorously as my mind raced back over twenty years to big hair, shoulder pads, skinny neckties, *Flashdance* legwarmers, and New Wave music. "Lottie Harmon Spangles! Of course!"

Spangles jewelry had been a fashion trend used by every glam rocker and drooling fan. David Bowie, Prince, Annie Lennox, Madonna—all of them wore Lottie's Spangles. American magazines did glossy spreads of her line and famous European ads posed models wearing nothing but Lottie's jewelry. Then came the grunge movement, and that was that. Another designer might have tried changing with the times, maybe stuck around to create bling-bling for rap artists, but Lottie Harmon had simply dropped out of the fashion scene.

"Pleased to meet you, Clare," said Lottie. She smiled, then turned back to Madame. "But where is that husband of yours? Pierre? And your son? The last time I saw Matteo he was barely out of college. . . ."

"Well, I'm very sorry to say that Pierre passed away, but my son is the Blend's coffee buyer now, so, of course, he's always jetting off to heaven knows where . . ." Madame's voice trailed off as she led Lottie to a cozy table by the fireplace.

My former mother-in-law had later informed me that Lottie had come back to New York City to reside in Greenwich Village once again after twenty-five years of living overseas. She'd made it a point to look up Madame within a month of her return to America.

Lottie stopped by the coffeehouse at least once a week after that first meeting. Like Madame, I found her to be a person whose energy and enthusiasm belied her age. She wore her scarlet hair loose and long, and her striking deep blue eyes always seemed to be examining the subtlest color or shape of things. She acted as though she were hungry to hear about the latest trends of popular culture, which seemed a bit strange to me, considering her sudden drop from the center of its spotlight so many years before. Nevertheless, she would routinely arrive with an armload of European and American fashion magazines, pile them on a table and spend hours pouring through their pages, all the while casually engaging my staff or the customers in wide-ranging discussions about fashion, film, music, or current events.

It was during one of her visits to the Blend that the formerly "defunct" designer seized on the simple but brilliant idea that would resurrect her fashion career.

"What a color!" Lottie had exclaimed that Friday as she sat beside one of our regular customers. "That looks absolutely delicious. What are you drinking, darling?"

Rena Garcia, a petite Latina with shoulder-length dark curls, full, cocoa-painted lips and laughing dark eyes, tipped her cup in Lottie's direction. "It's a caramel-chocolate latte. I felt the need for some comfort today—and the Blend's the only coffeehouse around here that makes these."

The latte in question was a Village Blend specialty. Because of the extra prep time involved in making the home-made syrup, I placed it on our menu only Fridays through Sundays. The drink had been popular to begin with, but it was lately improved by Tucker Burton's addition of whipped cream with a chocolate-covered coffee bean placed atop it. Since Tucker's tinkering, the drink had become even more popular. Everyone who tried it loved it and came back for more.

"I'll have one of those myself," Lottie declared.

It was a happy coincidence that Rena had been there at all. The savvy, outspoken marketing professional, who was barely out of her twenties, had been fired the day before from her high-powered job at the nearby Satay and Satay Advertising Agency. She was only in the neighborhood to "clean out her desk and say good-bye to everyone," which included the staff at the Blend.

"Stay awhile and let's enjoy our lattes," Lottie insisted after hearing this.

When I set a fresh caramel-chocolate latte in front of her, Lottie seemed transfixed by the hot liquid, the threads of our own homemade chocolate-infused caramel syrup crisscrossing the whipped cream, the single chocolate-covered coffee bean sitting atop the cloud.

"Now that *is* delightful," said Lottie.

Rena regarded her. "But you haven't even tried it yet."

Lottie twirled her finger above the drink. "The white of the whipped cream is the perfect foil for that beautiful caramel-chocolate color of the syrup and the rich brown of the bean."

"Excuse me?" said Rena.

"It's a sophisticated color, too," continued Lottie. "Not like those bubble-gum pinks I've seen far too much of. These colors are classic, not trendy. Subtle, mature, reas-suring . . . colors that dispel the chill of the autumn day. What was the word you used—"

Rena laughed. "Comfort. It's a comfort drink."

Overhearing them from behind the counter, I jumped in. "Like comfort food, right? Chocolate chip cookies or apple pie or mashed potatoes and meatloaf."

Lottie nodded, tapping her chin with her finger, even more intrigued. "And all of those foods are part of the same palette—creams, tans, browns. Look, Rena. See how, as you drink it, the caramel-chocolate swirls in the latte froth . . . see how it would highlight the weave in your sweater."

"It would look good on me as a brooch, then," said Rena, half-jokingly. "Better that than spilled on my sweater. Actually, I haven't found any jewelry that doesn't look tacky on me. Everything's either blah or trying too hard to be faux antique or like some thrift shop rhinestone retro 'find' when it obviously isn't."

Lottie's brow was still wrinkled in thought, then she nodded. "You're right, Rena. It *would* look good as a brooch . . . in fact, it would look fabulous!" Lottie instantly grabbed a dozen napkins and borrowed a pen from me. As she began to sketch, a man stepped up to the coffee bar from a nearby table to join their conversation.

Tad Benedict, a thirty-something, self-employed invest-ment banker, was working some personal stock trades on his laptop computer when he'd overheard the women. It was soon fairly clear that Tad was more interested in Rena Garcia than the unique hue of her beverage, but all three were cordial to each other.

"You said you'd been fired?" Tad asked Rena. "But why would they get rid of someone like you? Don't they need good people over at S and S anymore?"

Rena tossed her dark curls and laughed. "My boss got rid of me because I'm smarter than her," she replied. "I came up with ideas she took, and when I started making noise about a promotion, a raise, or some sort of recogni-tion, she trumped up complaints about my performance. That uptight vampire bitch of a manager only has a job be-cause she's bled young assistants dry one after another then tossed them aside when she felt threatened."

"I'm really sorry," said Tad, "but you know that's a very old story in this town . . . and probably a lot of other ones too, so don't feel bad."

Rena sighed and shook her head. "Wish I could say I don't but I do."

"You're better off. Look, you've just met me, haven't you? And I know some guys on Wall Street who might be looking for someone like you."

Her full lips smiled and she met his gaze. "Like you, maybe?"

As the afternoon wore on, the trio talked while they consumed gallons of coffee and a dozen fresh-baked pas-tries. As the shadows began to lengthen, Rena looked up in surprise, then glanced at her watch. "I should go," she an-nounced. "I still have to clean out my office and I don't want some security guard hovering over me while I do it, which is exactly what will happen if I try to enter the build-ing after five o'clock."

"Forget about that and take a look at this instead," said Lottie. She held out the napkin. On it, she'd drawn a brooch. Text and arrows indicated the colors she'd chosen—colors that mimicked the hue of the Blend's caramel-chocolate latte.

"It's large, but not garish," Lottie explained. "The branches here would be made of white gold, the central filigree coffee-brown enamel. With sculpting I could re-create a froth effect using something like a milky white chalcedony—"

"A what?" asked Tad.

"It's a type of quartz," explained Lottie. "And here, you see, at the center would sit a semiprecious stone like onyx or even a precious one like opal—something that's dark and nutty, like a coffee bean. I could even work with or-ganic material, say, use actual roasted coffee beans and ex-periment with lacquering and setting techniques to create complementary pieces."

"May I see it?" I asked from behind the coffee bar.

Lottie was only too pleased to share her sketch.

"I'd buy this in a heartbeat," I told her. "I can't believe nobody's done this before. When Joy was a little girl, Matt came back from Guatemala with a coffee-bean necklace for her. Down there, they've been making coffee-bean necklaces and bracelets from varnished roasted beans for years."

"Interesting," said Lottie. "So it's a natural for any cul-ture that embraces coffee."

"Makes sense." I handed Lottie back the sketch. "Which means you've got a worldwide market . . . and since spe-cialty coffeehouses have been on the rise in America, I'd say this culture has never been more ripe for it."

Rena Garcia tapped her chin in thought. She reached for the sketch and studied it. "You know, one of the ac-counts my boss managed was the Vardus line. Their stuff was cheap derivative crap compared to this, but it was *my* ideas for the campaign that boosted sales twenty-two per-cent in the first fiscal year. I could market something like this easily."

Tad nodded. "Can't say I know much about jewelry making, but this seems like a lucrative idea to me. Lottie, why in the world did you ever quit the fashion business in the first place?"

Lottie's gaze broke from Tad's. Her expression darkened. "There's a lot of heartbreak that comes with success," she said shortly. Then she forced that nervous, high-pitched laugh I'd heard her use the first day I'd met her. "I mean, look at Rena here. She boosted account sales and was fired anyway."

At the time, I thought nothing of Lottie's response. But looking back now, it seemed she'd deliberately turned the conversation back to Rena to avoid revealing what had happened in her past. I realized that I'd never heard her talk about her early years or the abrupt end to her career back then. Even when asked, she'd only want to talk about the present or the future.

That afternoon, Lottie had continued to sketch out an entire collection of possible variations on her "coffeehouse palette" theme—earrings, necklaces, bracelets, scarves, handbags. In the end, Rena never did make it to Satay and Satay to clean out her office. Instead, she helped Lottie Harmon map out a marketing strategy and come up with a catchy name for the line: Lottie Harmon's Java Jewelry. And before that chance meeting had ended, Tad Benedict had agreed to put up a sizeable chunk of his own money to purchase raw materials and fund the crafting of prototypes based on Lottie's designs.

Four months later—just in time for New York's February Fashion Week—the Lottie Harmon brand name was reborn with an entire line of coffee-bean necklaces of black and brown gemstones, latte brooches, caramel-loop bracelets and rings, coffee-klatch clutches, cocoa-brown scarves dotted with "coffee-bean" beads, and dozens of other pieces.

The additional backing for Lottie's launch came from the legendary clothing designer Fen, who had worked with Lottie through the seventies and early eighties and agreed to showcase her creations on his own models. The Lottie Harmon accessory line had been the buzz of that buying season with fall orders coming in from top retail: Harrods, Saks, Neiman Marcus, Printemps. The phenomenal sales transformed the moribund Lottie Harmon name into a multi-million dollar cash cow.

Fast forward seven months to the current Fashion Week festivities. Lottie, Tad, and Rena were all now very successful and very rich. Tad became a close friend and confidante to both women, and Lottie Harmon began to treat Rena Garcia like the daughter she never had—buying the younger woman expensive gifts, and even an apartment in the East Village.

For the current rollout, designer Fen had once again agreed to use Lottie's jewelry designs. He would unveil his spring clothing line under the Bryant Park tents at the end of the week—which would mean a big boost for Lottie's newest creations. Already, fashion buyers and top editors were writing about what Lottie might be "brewing up." Everyone seemed to love the woman. She was one of the least catty and most generous people I'd met in my limited contact with the fashion world. . . .

So why, I asked myself, would anyone want to poison Lottie's latte?

Seven

∽∽∽∽∽∽∽∽∽∽∽∽∽∽∽∽∽∽∽∽∽∽

FOUR A.M.

I dragged myself upstairs and was greeted by Java, a little female cat with fur the color of a medium roast *arabica* bean and more attitude than a pop diva.

Mrrrroooow!

She hadn't been given her usual late night snack, and she was not amused. "Sorry, girl," I murmured, bending to lift her into my arms. I carried her to the kitchen, scratching under her chin in a cheap a plea for forgiveness. The slow beginnings of a purr told me she was at least willing to extend an olive branch.

For the past five hours, I'd been toiling to restore some semblance of normalcy to the coffee bar, which was due to open in less than three hours for morning business. The Crime Scene Unit had been a hurricane, blowing through with no regard to private property. Esther and Moira had stayed overtime to help, and I'd called in Maxwell, another NYU student and part-time barista, to give us another pair of hands—but at one o'clock, I'd sent them all home and finished the rest myself.

Together, we'd cleaned the floor and counter and hauled the marble-topped café tables back upstairs from storage. By myself, I'd restocked the cupboards and under-counter fridge, and set up the reserve espresso machine—since the Crime Scene Unit had taken the one used during the party. And the entire time, I'd been thinking about Tucker and dreading what he might be going through. I knew he'd need a good criminal lawyer and fast, so the first thing I did, before any of the cleanup, was phone the Blend's attorney, Larry Jacobson.

After an unfortunate accident in the store a year ago, Matt and I convinced Madame it was important to have legal counsel on retainer for any future civil entanglements, anything that could lead to our being sued to within a penny of our existence. But when I called I didn't get Jacobson. I got his answering service, so I left a lengthy message. Then I called the Sixth Precinct for some kind of update on Tucker's situation (which—big surprise—got me nowhere). I even tried my friend Mike Quinn's cell, but it was obviously turned off, and I didn't leave a message. The man had enough stress dealing with his divorce, and I certainly didn't want to force him into any favors with a frantic, recorded plea. If I didn't have some concrete answers from the police by morning I'd resort to trying Detective Quinn again.

As I stepped into the kitchen, I flipped on the lights, lowered Java to the floor, and popped a can of Fancy Feast. As I watched her eat, I turned on the small clock-radio on the counter. The radio was tuned to 1010 AM—the "All news all the time" station. The murder at the Village Blend was the fifth story, dovetailing behind a piece about the opening of Fashion Week festivities. The news item itself was mercifully short—who, what, where, and when, then the announcer moved on to the next story about a water main break in Chinatown. Ricky Flatt's name was mentioned, but not the suspect's. The Blend was referred to as "a popular Greenwich Village institution"—which would have been flattering under any other circumstances.

I flipped off the radio.

Although I was tired, I was too shaken up to go to bed. I didn't have an appetite either. As bizarre as it sounded after the events of the night—particularly the use of cyanide as a secret ingredient—what I was dying for was a cup o' joe. It wasn't completely off the wall considering religious clerics in Yemen had used coffee in their extended prayer vigils for at least five hundred years, and I knew that's what this night was going to feel like, given my worries over Tucker. In fact, I decided a French pressed pot of some newly arrived Mocha Yemen Mattari would be perfect. I fired up a gas burner under a kettle of filtered water, pulled down the tightly sealed canister from my kitchen shelf and began to scoop the dark, oily beans into my electric grinder.

Mattari was hard to obtain year-round (it's best obtained in North America in fall and winter) but it was a rich cup, full of body, incredibly aromatic, and I'd roasted this batch dark, which meant there would be slightly less caffeine. (Customers are often under the mistaken impression that darker roasts, such as French and Italian, have more caffeine than lighter roasts. Not so. The darker the bean, the less caffeine. Which is why Breakfast Blends are usually light to medium "city roasts".)

I was just pouring the boiling water over the ground coffee in my smallest French press when I heard the front door open, the rattle of keys, then heavy footsteps in the hallway. The kitchen door swung wide and Matteo stood there, frozen in his tracks, staring at me in surprise. He was still clad in the black Armani, which, with his tall stature and impressive physique, made him an imposing figure. Kind of like Darth Vader—only less trustworthy.

"You're up early," he said, checking his watch.

"Late," I replied. "Notice the clothing? It's what I was wearing last night."

Not that you had eyes for anyone but that woman from Trend *magazine*, I thought—but was too chicken to say. After all, the man was no longer my husband, and what he did in his spare time was *so* not my business. The fact that

I found myself caring at all was what irritated me more than anything.

Using a wooden spoon, I stirred the grounds with a little more force than necessary and replaced the lid of the French press. (I found that stirring the water and freshly ground coffee nicely kick-starts the brewing process.)

"How are you fixed for staff?" Matt moved to the small kitchen table, removed his suit jacket, and draped it over a cane-back chair.

"It's Esther's regular day and she agreed to come early to help me open."

Matt almost laughed as he sat down. "Good luck with that."

Esther had slept through her alarm so often, I'd finally restricted the girl to afternoon and evening shifts only. But she seemed willing, and I was definitely desperate. "It'll take me a day or more to juggle the schedules. I was relying on Tucker for so much, but at least his friend Moira agreed to cover for him." I sat down opposite my ex-husband and stared.

He knew the look. "What?"

"I could have used your help last night. The investigators from the Crime Scene Unit didn't leave the shop until after eleven. The place was totally wrecked."

"Sorry, Clare, but I thought Tucker needed my help more."

"Tucker?" I sat back. "You . . . you were helping Tucker?"

My shocked tone seemed to offend him. "Of course I was helping Tucker," he said. "Where the hell did you think I was?"

Sleeping with Breanne Summour, what else? I thought, but what I said was—

"How did you even know where to find him? I called the precinct, but no one would answer my questions or return my calls. Around one, a desk sergeant finally informed me that Tucker was 'being processed'—exactly the same vague crap I got from Detective Hutawa."

Matt sighed and rubbed his neck. "Tucker spent the night on suicide watch inside Rikers Island jail—"

"Suicide watch!"

I think the blood must have drained from my face because Matt's expression went from simply tired to suddenly alarmed. "Clare, it's okay. He's okay. It's just a ploy."

"A ploy? What do you mean 'a ploy'? What are you talking about?"

"Suicide watch means he'll be isolated from the general hardened prison population and presumably safe from . . . interference."

It took a few seconds for this notion to sink in—that a "suicide watch" could, in any way, be a good thing. But it finally registered, and a perplexing question came with it: "Matt, how in the world did you even know about suicide watch? Or arrange to get Tucker that status?"

"I didn't," he replied with a stifled yawn. "It was Doyle Egan."

The name was vaguely familiar, but I couldn't place it. "Who is—"

"Detective Egan is a former New York undercover cop who cracked that big Mafia case years ago, the one that led to the mob graveyard in Queens. He retired from the force, got his law degree, and is now practicing with a big firm."

I nodded, recalling old headlines as mob victims from decades past were unearthed. "But how do you know this Egan person?"

"I don't. Breanne Summour does. Egan writes a monthly column for *Trend*."

"What would a man like that write about for a fashion magazine?" I asked. "The aesthetics of pinkie rings and prison tattoos? How to dress like a Wise Guy?"

"Breanne's magazine doesn't just cover fashion. It publishes all kinds of articles," he replied, a bit too defensively, I thought.

"All right, okay. So . . . what about bail?"

"If the judge sets bail, it will be sometime this morning.

Tucker is most definitely going to be arraigned for the murder of Ricky Flatt—that's the bad news. But the good news is a top-notch criminal defense lawyer will be there to represent him."

"Thank God. I tried Jacobson, but only got the service."

"Clare, come on. Larry Jacobson's not a criminal lawyer. We have him on retainer for civil matters."

"I know that! I just didn't know who else to call for a criminal lawyer recommendation!"

"Well, I worked it out."

"I'm glad you did. Believe me, I'm grateful."

"His name is Walter Tanner. He won a few high profile criminal cases. He agreed to represent Tucker as a favor."

"A favor?" Matt had made a lot of connections over the years with his world travels, but I couldn't recall him ever mentioning knowing a high-powered criminal lawyer. "A favor to you?" I prompted.

Matteo shrugged, looked away at the French press. The hot, filtered water was now clear as mud.

"Oh, I see . . . another favor for Breanne Summour."

My ex didn't answer. He simply checked his watch, then reached across the table and pressed the French press's plunger. The flavors had been extracted from the grounds and now they were forced downward, all the way to the bottom. The beans had been chopped, drowned, and now they were being shoved out of the way. The entire process seemed very violent to me, all of a sudden, and through my exhausted gaze, the plunging action seemed to go on forever in surreal slow motion.

"That Mattari smells heavenly," said Matt.

I grunted in reply.

It remained quiet after that, though silence between Matteo and I was not unusual, having been together—and apart—so much in our lives. Matt stood and retrieved two mugs from the cupboard and a pint of cream from the fridge. The cream was a gesture. He always drank his coffee black. After pouring both cups, he splashed cream into mine and set it down in front of me.

"Nice crop this year," he said. "Sweet, fruity, nice depth."

The Mocha Yemen Mattari was a single-origin coffee; that is, it was unblended with any other bean and simply came straight from its country of origin, in this case the country of Yemen and the region of Mattari. The "mocha" aspect of the name referred not to "chocolate" as in your average mochaccino, but the port from which the coffee was originally exported. If you mixed these beans with Java *arabicas*, then you'd have Mocha Java, the oldest known of the coffee blends.

I took in the piquant aroma, the warmth, the earthy richness, but none of it was reviving me.

"So," sighed Matteo, breaking another long silence. "Why do you think he did it?"

"Who . . . did what?"

"Come on, Clare. Why do you think Tucker poisoned that guy? A lover's quarrel? I never thought of Tucker as all that tempestuous. But you never know, I guess."

"You can't be serious."

"What?"

"Do you really believe Tucker Burton is a murderer?"

Matteo sat back in his chair. "If not Tucker, then who?"

I set my mug down hard enough to rattle the small table. "That's what I intend to find out."

Matteo closed his eyes. "Oh, please, Clare. Not again."

"Not *what* again?"

"You know. That Nancy Drew thing of yours. This time would you please call that Irish flatfoot, . . . what's his name? Flanagan?"

"Quinn!"

"Fine. Call Quinn."

"I did already, but he didn't answer his cell and he's not even in the city. He's on leave. Family trouble."

"Oh."

"Matt, I can't believe you could think Tucker would do anything like this. Why did you help him if you think he's a killer?"

"I . . . I don't know. Tucker's a nice guy, and he works

for the business my great grandfather started—my family's business—and for that I feel like he's part of the family. And everyone has a right to a fair trial."

"But you *do* think he's guilty."

For a full minute, Matteo just sipped his coffee and mulled over his response. Finally, he sighed. "I'm sorry. I know you don't want to believe it yourself, but yes, Clare, I think Tucker is guilty."

EIGHT

TWO hours later, I was stunned when I came downstairs. Esther was there. She'd used her key to get in, and had already opened the pastry case in anticipation of the morning bakery delivery. Though she seemed her old cynical self, Esther's face was pale and her thick glasses could not hide the redness behind them.

Moira arrived fifteen minutes later. She looked delicate in the harsh morning sun and I suspected she'd had as sleepless a night as Esther and I. When she complained of a headache but declined any aspirin because of an allergy, I knew I should send her home—but I needed the help. She was carrying the morning edition of the *Post*, the only paper that had put the murder on the front page—the others had placed it on inside pages. "Lethal Latte" was the headline on a sketchy story stating "a suspect had been detained but not yet charged." I knew that would change later in the day.

After we looked over the paper, I sat Moira and Esther down. Over coffee, I told them what Matteo had told me—that Tucker spent the night in jail and would be arraigned later today with a lawyer present. Of course, I left out the fact that my ex-husband thought Tucker was guilty.

"How could this have happened?" Esther moaned.

"That's what I want to figure out," I replied. "We were all here when it happened. Let's try to recall exactly what took place and who was present."

I rose and stepped to the customer side of the coffee bar. "I was standing here. Then I walked around the counter and checked the fridge for soy milk. When I didn't find any, I went downstairs to bring some up from storage."

Esther stepped up to stand next to me. "Before you left, I was standing next to you."

"And after I left? What did you do?"

"I hung out a little longer. Then I went back out on the floor to collect more used mugs and napkins."

"Moira?" I asked. "What do you remember about that time?"

"Well, Ms. Cosi, I was behind Tucker, who was pulling espressos. There was a whole line of them right here on the counter, in the tall glass latte mugs." She pointed to the space. Moira, Esther, and I exchanged glances. We were all thinking the same thing.

"Those mugs were in easy reach. Anyone in this area of the coffee bar could have tampered with one of them," I pointed out.

"A lot of people moved by that area," said Esther.

"Then anyone could have done it!" Moira cried.

"Hold on, calm down," I replied. "Let's try to recall who was at the bar during the specific time when Tucker was making that latte. Think. Who did you see sitting or standing here between the time I went downstairs and came back up."

"That Lloyd Newhaven character," said Esther. "That's the reason you went downstairs in the first place—to get soy milk for his latte."

"Right," I said. "Wait." I ducked into the pantry near our back door and grabbed an inventory checklist, then I returned to the counter, pulled a pen from my pocket, and wrote Lloyd's name on the blank back. "Okay," I said. "What else do you two remember?"

"After you went downstairs," recalled Moira, "a woman came up to talk with Lloyd."

"What did she look like?" I asked.

"She was tall, had long black, straight hair—really long, like down to her hips. And she was all in violet. I think she was Asian."

That sounded to me like one of the women whom Lloyd had escorted into the party. "Did you happen to notice if she had violet eyes, too?" I asked.

"I think she did," said Moira.

"She did," said Esther. "I came back and forth to the counter while I was collecting dirty mugs. And I saw her, too."

"She's a friend of Lloyd's," I told them, jotting down a few more notes. "That much I know, but not much else because she came as Lloyd's guest, and his was the only name on the invitation. Who else do you remember coming up to the coffee bar?"

"There was a male model type," said Esther.

"And what did he look like?" I asked.

Esther closed her eyes. "Dyed white-blond hair . . . crew cut . . . white T-shirt, black leather jacket and pants, bike chains, a wristband with studs—"

"Excuse me? Did you say studs?"

Esther opened her eyes and nodded. "He had this whole Billy Idol thing going."

"Billy Idol, that's right!" I cried. "I remember seeing him in the crowd. How old would you say he looked?"

"Oh, young," said Esther. "Maybe twenty. Eighties retro is the new trend."

"Oh, geez," I said, scribbling away. "The twenty-year cycle continues."

"What's that?" asked Esther.

"When I was in high school, the fifties had made a come-back . . . you know, with *Laverne and Shirley* and *Happy Days*."

"Happy what?" asked Moira.

"It was a TV show," Esther informed her. "Ron Howard was in it."

Moira's brow wrinkled. "The movie director?"

I sighed. "Okay, do either of you remember anyone else?"

"Well, there was that man and woman," Moira said. "The ones who work for Lottie Harmon."

"You mean her partners, Tad Benedict and Rena Garcia?" I clarified, but I'd already remembered them and didn't consider them suspects. After all, they had no motive. What was there to gain from killing off your golden goose partner?

"You know what?" said Moira, eyes widening. "*Tad* was the one who asked Tucker to make that latte in the first place."

"Tad was?" I asked, intrigued. "You're sure?"

"I'm sure," said Moira nodding emphatically.

"Yeah, that's right." Esther agreed.

I whirled. "You heard it, too?"

Esther shrugged. "I thought you were there for that."

I shook my head. "No, I must have still been downstairs. Tell me exactly what you remember."

"Well," Esther began, "it was so crazy that people were taking the lattes before the trays could get more than a few feet beyond the coffee bar and Tad said that Lottie looked like she could use some caffeine. And then Tucker sort of announced he was going to make a latte for Lottie."

"That's right," said Moria. "That's what I remember, too. Tad touched Tucker's arm and said something like, 'Sorry to pressure you, but could you see that Lottie gets one? She could probably use another shot of caffeine to get her through the final hour.' Then Tucker said something like, 'One very special caramel-chocolate latte for the guest of honor coming up.' He announced it very theatrically, you know?"

"Well, that's nothing new for Tucker," I pointed out. "But it does mean anyone nearby would have been aware the drink was going to Lottie . . . I just wonder why Tad didn't take the latte to Lottie himself?"

Moira shrugged. "I don't know."

"Neither do I," said Esther. "By that time, I was back doing my clean-up rounds."

"So Tad asked for it to be made, but didn't take it to Lottie . . ." I murmured.

"You think Tad poisoned the latte with arsenic?" asked Moira.

"Cyanide," I corrected. "And I'm not saying that at all . . . it's just . . . interesting."

"You mean suspicious," said Esther. "Sounds that way to me."

Only if Tad had a motive, I thought. What could he gain by killing Lottie? Her designs made him a wealthy man—well, a wealthier man, anyway. Why would he murder his meal ticket? Could it be a war over control of the designer label? That didn't seem to make sense because the label wouldn't be worth half as much without Lottie's designs behind it.

"Ms. Cosi? . . . Clare?"

I blinked, finally hearing Moira's voice break into my thoughts. "Yes . . . what is it?"

Moira and Esther exchanged a look. "The bakery van is here," said Moira. "Didn't you hear the knocking?"

"Oh," I said and rose to unlock the back door. I was surprised to find Theresa Rosario standing there, in jeans and a sweater, her long brown curls tied back. Next to her stood the regular delivery person, Joey, a good-looking Italian kid attired in his usual baggy jeans, backwards baseball cap, and Yankee jacket.

Theresa was the youngest baker in her large Italian family. Like the Village Blend, the history of the Rosario Bakery stretched back over a century. A small storefront in Little Italy had led to a second shop on First Avenue in the East Village, then to two more on the Upper East and West sides of Manhattan.

"I brought over more Ricciarelli," Theresa told me as

she and Joey carried in boxes of pastries and deposited them in our pantry area near the back door. "We had so many almonds on order, I just whipped up another big batch."

Joey had delivered the special order of pastries for Lottie's bash the night before. The little diamond-shaped almond cookie with powdered sugar on top was a delicious rarity, so I wasn't complaining to hear she'd included them in our standard daily delivery, too.

"The guests practically inhaled them last night," I told her. "And I'm sure my customers will love them today."

"Last night, right . . . you know, I heard *something* on news radio about your party," she said. "Was there some kind of trouble?"

I met Theresa's intense, gossip-hungry brown eyes and suddenly realized why she'd shown up to help with deliveries, today of all days. "Oh! You know, I think I hear the first customers of the day knocking!" I cried. "I'll tell you all about it later, okay? Gotta go!"

Then I shooed Teresa and her delivery boy out the back door and darted off to open the front.

nine

∾∾∾∾∾∾∾∾∾∾∾∾∾∾∾∾∾∾∾

THE morning rush was typical of a weekday, a welcome surprise considering the *Post*'s headline. The bulk of my regular clientele hadn't heard or read about the poisoning—not yet anyway. Or, at least, they didn't mention it to my face.

A few, however, were most definitely whispering about "that thing that happened here last night." And one young businessman actually took a swig from his cup, then grabbed his throat like he was dying. His colleagues practically doubled over with laughter.

"What a card," I muttered.

Meanwhile, I was waiting for a lull to duck out and have a talk with Lottie Harmon. I had to warn her that she might be in danger, though I wasn't quite sure how I'd break that news to her—or if she'd even accept it. Fortunately, I knew exactly where to find her on this particular Wednesday morning. Weeks ago, she'd handed me a pass to view a special display showcasing her work from the vintage designs of the 1970s to her label's current renaissance in the new century. The embossed invitation, sent to magazine editors, newspaper reporters, and wire service correspondents, stated that the designer herself would be on hand from 11:00 A.M. to 3:00 P.M. "to answer questions from the domestic and foreign press." I'd kept the pass in my office, not really intending to use it. But after the murder last night I decided it was my ticket to paying Lottie Harmon a visit.

It's my personal philosophy that nothing says "I'm sorry" like a double-tall mocha latte—so when the Blend's early morning rush slid into its usual mid-morning lull, I took off my apron, slathered on some lip gloss, and took extra care in whipping up the drink to present to Lottie. After I sealed my masterpiece in a Village Blend thermal mug, I spoke to Esther and Moira.

"I'm going up to the Fashion Week tents to speak with Ms. Harmon. After last night, I need to find out if she still wants us to cater her runway show with Fen on Sunday—a long shot by any stretch."

"You're bearing a caffeinated gift, I see," Esther noted. "Good idea."

I held up the latte. "Yes, a frothy bribe. You and Moira hold the fort until I get back."

"Let me bag that up," said Moira, taking the hot cup.

"Thanks," I said.

"Well, if you're trying to bribe her, why don't you throw in a couple of those Ricciarelli the baker brought this morning?" said Esther. "Didn't Tad say something last night about Lottie loving them?"

"Good idea," I noted and sighed with relief as I left to find my jacket on a hook in my second floor office. Esther had always been a reluctant worker, but she was really rising to the occasion now and I was grateful. A few minutes later, Moira handed me two paper bags, and I stepped out to a brisk fall day—not cold, but with a distinct chill in the air.

The sky over Hudson Street, pristine and cerulean blue, offered a vista only possible near the ocean. Coupled with a cool breeze off the water a few blocks away, this particular autumn morning reminded New Yorkers of a fact they often forgot—that their fair city was also a port, and the salty waves of the Atlantic Ocean lapped at her shores.

I caught a cab on Hudson and listened to Bollywood music on the cabbie's sound system as the Sikh driver raced uptown. Traffic was light and I was soon climbing out of the cab in front of the New York Public Library's flagship building on Forty-second Street. The pair of immense stone lions that guarded the cathedral-like front entrance stared impassively as I paid the fare and followed the wide sidewalk to the back of the massive structure, where a lovely patch of green sat nestled among the skyscrapers just one block east of Times Square's blinding neon and crazy congestion.

Although this midtown space has been called Bryant Park since 1842, the area itself has endured a checkered history. In the 1970s, for instance, when Times Square was a haven of prostitution and pornography, Bryant Park was a blighted site of muggings and drug deals. But a decade-long effort begun in 1980 has totally transformed the space and redeemed its fallen reputation. A refuge of peace and calm, Bryant is a true urban park, full of historical monuments, gravel paths, green chairs, and even a jaunty carrousel.

Bordered by the Main Library to the east, the modern Verizon Building to the west, and a brace of skyscrapers north and south, this emerald rectangle—named after the poet William Cullen Bryant in honor of that man's tireless efforts to create large garden parks in New York City—has, since its renovation, become a midtown mecca for nature-starved urban dwellers seeking sunshine, the feel of grass under their feet, the sounds of a free concert in spring and summer, or the glamour of Fall Fashion Week in early autumn.

I entered the park along a gravel path which paralleled one of the three flower beds bordering the shady north lawn. Along both the northern and southern sides of the park were twin promenades lined with tall London plane trees—the same species found at the Jardin des Tuileries in

Paris. The long trunks and delicate leaves of these one-hundred to one-hundred and twenty foot trees lent the place a distinct European character—the illusion completed by the towering stone backdrop of the New York Public Library, standing in for the Louvre.

Because of Fashion Week, the entire south and west sides of the park were dominated by several huge white tents, the largest of which appeared sizeable enough to house an airliner. Along Fortieth Street, which had been closed to vehicular traffic for the duration of Fashion Week, large mobile homes lined the curbs, all of them brightly painted, and decked with signs and the logos of the designers who used them.

The sidewalks were crowded with people. Many were obvious fashionistas—designers, wardrobe specialists, makeup artists, and young apprentices—beautiful and vacuous-looking enough to be aspiring models themselves. They were easy enough to identify by their bright blue T-shirts with the Spring Fashion Week logos, and their identity badges hanging from yellow cords around their necks. As I passed a trailer marked Malibu Bitch Swimwear, a door opened and out came a poised thirty-something woman in a conservative business suit. She waved a clipboard and stepped onto the street. Like chicks following a mother hen, five tight-bodied models in the skimpiest of bikinis cat-walked across Fortieth Street behind her. They strolled through the park and into the largest tent.

With the warm Village Blend bags still in hand, I fumbled through my purse for the invitation. The location of Lottie's display was "Plaza—Bryant Park, Sixth Avenue between Fortieth & Forty-second Streets." I was here, but where was the "Plaza"?

I corralled one of the young women wearing a Fashion Week badge. "Is there a plaza around here?"

"There are three venues in Bryant Park," she said by rote. "The largest tent is the Theater, the tent next to it is the Bryant. That round tent in the middle is the Plaza."

"Thank you."

A guard insisted I show my invitation at the door. He glanced at the card, smiled when I asked for directions.

"The Lottie Harmon exhibit is in the second wing. Go through the lobby, past the photo display, then make a right. There's a sign at the door."

The interior of the tent was as spotlessly white as the exterior—even the plywood interior sections that parceled out the space under the canvas were painted the same virginal color as the tent's walls and ceiling. Massive fans circulated air, sending the canvas rippling. That movement, combined with the gentle rush of cool, fresh air, made the white tent feel as light and dreamy as the interior of a cloud.

The middle of the Plaza was dominated by a large display on portable standees—a photographic retrospective of past Fashion Week styles, divided by year. Though the tent was crowded, few of the guests were viewing the exhibits. Most were heading toward one of the four wings that radiated out from the central exhibit area, a security guard at each door.

I spied the familiar Lottie Harmon logo—the stretched L and H, tiny handwritten letters spelling out the rest of the brand name. The designer label was still using its original logo, created from Lottie's own distinctive handwriting a quarter century ago. Inside the white-walled area, I spied Lottie herself, posed within a space filled with hundreds of photographs, large and small.

She'd traded her chocolate brown evening wear for a champagne colored blouse and pants. The outfit was completed by an elegant tawny "maxi-jacket" with cream stitching that fell to her calves. Her bright scarlet hair was piled on top of her head and around her neck hung a glistening necklace of semiprecious stones polished to look like rich, darkly roasted coffee beans.

Lottie was speaking quietly with a Japanese man, whose wizened face was framed by iron-gray hair. The man looked prosperous, a fine pinstripe suit, of the kind tailor-made in London, hugging his compact form. His interest in Lottie's words was obvious, and he respectfully bowed each time she answered a question. When I entered, Lottie waved to me, but did not excuse herself. A few moments later, the man bowed deeply, then strolled back to the lobby.

Lottie hurried forward to greet me.

"Clare, I've hardly had time to breathe, but I so wanted to call."

No doubt to deliver bad news, I thought. *There goes the Blend's big runway catering gig.*

"We still have so much planning to do for the big runway show Sunday. But I'm *counting* on the Village Blend to serve lattes to the crowd. After your troubles last night, I wanted to make sure you can still do it because, really, there's just no better way for them to understand the inspiration for my Java Jewelry than if they're sipping one of your fabulous coffee drinks!"

Lottie laughed just then. It was that high-pitched, forced laugh she sometimes used. I didn't know if it was a tick to cover her nervousness or something else entirely, but it never failed to unsettle me.

I tried to summon a reassuring smile. "I'm very glad you still want us there, considering all that's happened . . ."

Lottie frowned. "Oh, yes, it *was* terrible. At first, I thought the man was having a heart attack or something."

"I was looking for you afterwards," I replied. "I wanted to apologize for ruining your party, maybe hurting the reputation of your accessory line."

Lottie waved her arm. "Don't be silly, Clare. In the fashion business, any publicity is good publicity. Back in 1980 . . . or was it '81? . . . a well-known lead singer of a superstar band overdosed on stage during a concert. He was wearing one of my Spangle pieces—you could see it clearly in the photos of the man being rushed to the hospital. After that night, I couldn't keep that piece in stock!"

"So you weren't . . . troubled?"

"Last night? Not at all. After I spoke with the police, Tad and Rena whisked me away. No problem."

Lottie gave that high-pitched laugh again. "Let's go sit down," she suggested, leading me to a pair of folding chairs set up in the corner. "I'm so tired, and I've been dreaming of one of your invigorating lattes."

I held out the warm bag. "Dream no more. Still hot and fresh in a thermal mug—and I brought along some of those Ricciarelli you said you liked last night. The baker made this batch fresh this morning."

Lottie clapped her hands, then opened the bag and sniffed the contents. "Clare Cosi, you're a life saver! I didn't have anything to eat for breakfast—nerves, you know?"

"Are Tad and Rena around by any chance? I was hoping to talk to them."

Lottie sipped the latte and sighed contentedly. "Oh, you just missed them, dear. They brought me a watercress sandwich and some salad. I wolfed it down not ten minutes ago—right before Mr. Kazumi arrived. But I'm still so hungry."

"Mr. Kazumi?"

"That man I was speaking with when you came in. Otomo Kazumi of the Kazumi department store chain. His Tokyo store is a real marvel. Twenty stories, more lights than Broadway, more bells and whistles than a Las Vegas casino. Stores in Osaka, Singapore, and Riyadh, Saudi Arabia, too—probably the most upscale and expensive department store chain in the world. He's been buying my accessories since my heyday in the 1980s. A wonderful man and a delight to see again after all these years."

We chatted pleasantries while Lottie sipped her latte and nibbled on a Ricciarelli, licking the powdered sugar off her perfectly lined lips. As gently as I could, I steered the conversation toward Lottie's business partners.

"So where has Tad gone? And Rena? Shouldn't they be here helping out?"

"Oh, they *said* they had some last minute arrangements

to make before the show." Lottie arched an eyebrow—as if she suspected them of something.

"So where are they then?"

She waved a hand and shook her head. Again the strained, high-pitched laugh. When she didn't offer any other theories, I started fishing. "You know I still remember the day when you three first met," I said. "I never asked you. What exactly was the business arrangement you all worked out?"

"Oh, Tad and Rena each own twenty-five percent of the label. Fen has a few points, too."

"So, you're the single largest stakeholder, but if you put all their stakes together, they actually own over fifty percent?"

"That's right. But it's not as if they're going to use that against me." Once more, Lottie laughed nervously. "We're all friends. And I'm not only the head designer, I'm the only designer. They can't get a thing done without me."

Just then, two young men appeared in the doorway. One was laden with photographic gear, the other carried a clipboard and an over-the-shoulder tape recorder.

"Oh, the folks from *Paris Match* are here and I promised them an interview. I have to go now, but we do need to discuss some of the changes I made to the show, which will mean some changes to the coffee menu. Can you stay for a while?"

"Of course," I replied. "I'll wander around and we can talk in a half-hour or so."

While Lottie chatted with the French journalist—the photographer circling the pair and snapping pictures the whole time—I perused the fashion designer's photographic retrospective. It was easy to see why Lottie's accessories had returned to the forefront of fashion. Some of those clothing designs, hair, and makeup styles from the early eighties did appear contemporary again.

I recalled a discussion Moira and Tucker had had one night at the coffee bar . . . Moira, a fashion student at Parsons, had explained that fashion style was cyclical because of two things: imitation and class distinctions. The rich emulated the fashion of the poor who in turn emulated the styles of the rich. This theory of fashion evolution explained why every decade or so the same fashion trends would tend to reemerge.

"Sounds crazy," Tucker had said.

"My professor explained the theory using the example of that fashion trend from a few years back," Moira had explained. "The hip-hop look, where guys sported baggy pants and shoes without laces. That look actually started among impoverished urban African-American youths in the late 1970s. The ill-fitting pants were hand-me-downs—even bell bottoms that had fallen out of fashion by then. The shoes without laces were the result of criminal behavior—they take your shoelaces away in jail so you don't hang yourself or something. Soon the look became cool among urban kids, then gangster rappers. From there, the style moved to MTV, where it was mimicked by affluent rich kids, who were in turn emulated by the young in the middle classes. Voila, within a decade or so, everyone's wearing baggy pants and shoes without laces."

The memory of that conversation made me shiver. I wondered if Tucker had surrendered his laces before being sent to Rikers . . . or if he would become so depressed and desperate he really would do himself harm. I glanced at my watch, wondering if Tucker had been arraigned down at the courthouse yet. I decided to call the Blend and see if they'd heard any news—Matteo had promised he would keep me updated. I found a green park chair inside the billowing tent and used my cell. The phone rang nine times before it was answered.

"Yo, Village Blend," said a harried voice.

"Esther. It's me. I called to see—"

"Jeezus, Clare. When can you get back?"

I sat up. "Bad news? Is there a problem?"

"It's a mob scene here. Must be some special event in the neighborhood because we've got double the lunch crowd than normal."

Some noise erupted in the background, and Esther shouted a garbled reply.

"Gardner just stopped by to pick up his paycheck and I corralled him to work lunch. Hope that's all right with you."

"Sure, if you think it's all that crowded."

I heard voices, Esther calling something out in reply. Then she came back on the line. "Sorry, boss. Gotta go."

"But—"

Too late. Esther had already hung up. But I guessed that if she'd heard something about Tucker's plight, she would have told me. I chalked up her description of the lunchtime rush as typical Esther Best hyperbole, but decided I'd better get back as soon as possible anyway. I glanced at my watch, saw that forty minutes had passed, and decided to find Lottie and jot down her menu changes, talk to her about my worry that she had been the real target for last night's poisoning, then say farewell and get back to the Blend.

When I returned to Lottie's display room, I found her alone, sagging like a rag doll on her chair. She looked up as I approached. I nearly gasped when I saw her pale face. I hurried to the woman's side.

"Lottie, are you all right?"

"I don't know," she stammered. "After the reporters left . . . I suddenly got weak. My ears started to ring, and I got dizzy. I . . . think I need to lie down."

I looked for a place for Lottie to rest, but all I saw were two more chairs. I grabbed them and shoved them together, seat to seat, next to her chair so Lottie could stretch out across them. But as I reached to help her over to the makeshift cot, Lottie moaned. "Clare, I . . ."

Then she pitched forward and slumped to the floor.

Ten

~~~~~~

"Lottie! Lottie!" I cried, falling to my knees at her side. I thought the woman had fainted, but Lottie opened her eyes again and focused them on me. I could see confusion there.

"God, Clare . . . I felt dizzy . . . lost my balance."

"Here, let me help you up."

I reached for the woman, but she shook me off and rose under her own power. "I feel sick . . . cramps. Probably nerves."

My first thought was poison. Not cyanide or she'd be dead already. Perhaps a slower acting substance—

"We'd better get you to a doctor."

But Lottie waved that idea aside. "I need to sit down, that's all. I'm sure it's just nerves . . . exhaustion. So much is riding on this rollout. . . ."

But I was not convinced. "What are your symptoms, exactly?"

"I feel dizzy . . . my ears are ringing. There's some nausea."

"Maybe it was something you ate?"

Lottie laughed. "I probably haven't eaten enough. Just that sandwich and salad that Tad and Rena brought me. I don't think I had a decent meal last night, either."

I plunked Lottie down on a chair, sat opposite her.

"I'm fine, Clare . . . really."

"Well I'm not going anywhere until I'm sure you're okay."

Lottie touched my hand. "Thanks for caring. Last year I was a wreck for the rollout, but I survived—mostly because I was out of the business for so long I didn't even *know* half the things that could go wrong."

"You exaggerate, I'm sure. You've been in the fashion business before."

"But so much has changed over the years. The rollouts are bigger, there's more media, everything costs more. The stakes are much higher now that more people have brand awareness."

"But not everything's changed. You told me so yourself—said you've known Mr. Kazumi for decades."

"Oh yes. Otomo is a good friend, and so is Olaf Caesara at the Caen department stores. And of course Fen. I don't know what I would have done without Fen. He never forgot Lottie, even after two decades."

Odd to hear Lottie call herself by her own name, I thought. But I guess that's what happens when you and your business have the same name.

"Has this ever happened to you before?" I asked. "Getting sick like this . . . so suddenly?"

To my surprise, Lottie nodded. "Oh, when I was young, I used to get panic attacks. I was so afraid of everything. My knees would get weak, I would feel dizzy and sick to my stomach. And I did have these same symptoms a few weeks ago, the night we all sat down in your coffeehouse and planned the party."

"Have you sought help?"

"I saw the doctor the next day and he couldn't find anything wrong—said it was probably nerves. Asked me if I wanted to try Prozac." She shook her head.

I recalled the evening, about a month ago, to which Lottie was referring—in fact, it had been the arrival of Lottie, Tad, and Rena that had sparked Tucker's and Moria's cyclical fashion discussion.

I'd taken Lottie and her partners to the coffeehouse's second floor and we sat in overstuffed chairs around the fireplace, drinking lattes and eating pastries while we talked. Could Tad or Rena have tampered with Lottie's food or drink that night? It was possible—there were trips to the rest rooms and I'd taken Lottie downstairs and back up again at one point to have her decide whether the ground floor's tables should be taken out for the party.

"And you haven't felt sick like this since then?"

Lottie shrugged. "No. Not until today."

I wanted to ask Lottie many more questions. How often did she eat or drink with Rena and Tad? Had she narrowly avoided an accident of late, or had a close brush with death? But for the life of me, I just couldn't think of a tactful way to do it.

"You do know all the details about what happened in my coffeehouse last night?" I asked. "Someone was poisoned. Died. My barista was arrested for the crime. I believe he'll be charged today with murder."

Lottie frowned. "It's so terrible. You must feel awful."

I met Lottie's gaze. "Tucker, my barista, said something before the police arrested him. He told me that the latte he had on that tray was supposed to be for you."

Lottie seemed genuinely surprised. "Are . . . are you sure?"

"Tucker told me Tad asked him to make one for you, specifically. The victim snatched the cup off the tray while Tucker was carrying it to you."

Lottie's expression darkened. She brushed an errant strand of scarlet hair away from her face and stared at me. "Are you saying someone tried to kill me?"

"I can't say that," I replied. "Not honestly. The poisoning could have been random. Or—"

"Or your barista could be lying. Trying to hide the fact that he's guilty."

I shook my head. "That's not possible."

Lottie reddened. "No, you're right. I shouldn't have said that, Clare, and I'm sorry. But really, think about it. Who would want to get rid of me?"

I shrugged, not wanting to reveal my suspicions just yet because they could possibly hurt Lottie in the same way her remark about Tucker wounded me. In any case, accusing Lottie's business partners of trying to murder her without a shred of evidence to prove it would not convince her—I wasn't even sure I was convinced myself.

"Maybe a business rival?" I suggested after a pause.

Lottie tossed her head back and laughed that strained laugh of hers. "I've been out of the fashion scene for twenty years, Clare, and only back into the muck for a year. Believe me, it takes a little longer for your rivals to want to kill you in this business—though not *much* longer, I grant you that."

"Maybe a crazy stalker? Or someone from your past?"

Lottie smiled sympathetically. "Look, Clare. I understand why you're searching for answers, for someone to blame. Something terrible happened in your coffeehouse, and one of your employees was arrested. I can see why you'd want to get to the truth, and you probably will, eventually. But I can't think of anyone who would want me out of the picture for any reason."

Then Lottie grinned, rose, and pulled herself together.

"I feel much better now," she said. "The cramps have subsided and my ears aren't ringing anymore. I'm sure this episode was just a bout of nervous tension, just like my doctor told me."

ELEVEN

~∾∾∾∾∾∾∾∾∾∾∾∾∾∾∾∾∾∾∾∾∾

After saying goodbye to Lottie, I hopped into a cab going west on Forty-second Street. Traffic was not as light as it had been on my way up and it took nearly forty minutes to drive less than two miles.

As I exited the cab one block from the Blend, I noticed two things. The first was a television crew doing a live interview on Hudson. The subject was a twenty-something woman with so many tattoos and pierced body parts that her round, pretty face resembled a pin cushion, her neck a brightly colored tapestry. In her hand, she clutched a Village Blend take-out cup. The interviewer's earnest face and photogenic smile looked vaguely familiar and I assumed it was because I'd seen her on one of the local channels.

The second thing I noticed was a crowd loitering on the sidewalk in front of my coffeehouse, and I simply assumed Esther's guess had been correct, when we'd spoken on the phone earlier, that some special event was taking place in the neighborhood.

I jostled my way through groups of people and clouds of tobacco smoke to the front door of the Blend. Inside, customers packed the main floor. It was so crowded, in fact, that some of the people had taken it upon themselves to open a few of our French doors for air and space, and they were flung wide despite the autumn chill.

At the bar alone, a line of at least twenty men and women were waiting for coffee drinks. As I threaded my way to the counter, Esther spied me, relief evident on her tired face.

Moira was behind the counter, too, along with Matteo. With his sleeves rolled up to reveal muscled forearms, he looked to be pulling espressos as fast as the Blend's exacting standards would allow (because, if you pull an espresso too fast, i.e., if the liquid does not flow slowly out of the spout like syrup, what you've made isn't espresso but brewed coffee).

"I thought Gardner was here," I cried over the noise.

Matteo looked up, face sour. "He had a dentist appointment. Left a half hour ago. I had to take over for him."

It was obviously not something my ex wanted to do.

"Nice of you to pitch in," I said without a trace of sarcasm (for once). Then I slipped behind the counter, donned an apron, washed up, and replaced Moira at the espresso machine.

"What's with the mob scene?" I asked. "Is there some event going on? A new tourist attraction?"

Matteo stared at me as if I'd cluelessly suggested we start serving instant coffee crystals. "Don't you get it? *We're* the attraction, Clare."

I blinked. Still clueless.

"Just look around, take a look at the customers . . . especially the ones who've just been served their drinks."

I watched a young man collect two take-out cups, slip one to a young woman hovering over an occupied table. The man opened the top of his cup, sipped his first taste, then he grimaced and made a face as if he were in his death throes. The woman slapped his arm playfully.

"I see," I muttered.

Matteo shrugged. "I suppose it's better than being shunned."

Realization dawned. "That reporter . . . out on the sidewalk . . ."

"She's from New York One," said Esther Best, bringing more cups in from the pantry.

"Yeah, I ran the camera crew out of here a half hour ago," Matteo said, fuming. "I can't believe they're still stalking our customers."

"Have you heard anything about Tucker?" I asked.

Matt glanced at the Breitling on his wrist. "We should hear something in the next two hours. Breanne promised she'd call as soon as she spoke with her lawyer about the case."

"So Breanne hears everything first."

Matteo ignored me as he finished pulling another espresso, dumped the caked grounds, and reached for the coffee bin only to find it empty. "Hey, we're out of our house espresso blend," he complained.

"I haven't had time to prepare any this week," I told him. "*You* took over the roasting room, remember?"

Matt grunted. Which I still didn't consider a reasonable explanation. When he'd *first* arrived back home from Ethiopia, he'd hardly said two words to me before vanishing into the Blend's basement roasting room for hours. Holed up with three fifty-pound canvas bags of green coffee beans delivered from Kennedy International Airport customs, he interrupted the store's roasting schedule in order to roast those beans. When he was finished, he divided up the entire batch into twenty-five pound, vacuum-sealed bags, carried all the bags up to his room, and locked them inside—singularly odd behavior, even by Matteo's diminished standards. I'd pressed him for an explanation but he'd refused to answer.

"Use the French roast Mocha Java," I advised him.

For the next two hours the flow of customers was practically nonstop. Then, around four thirty, a semblance of calm descended. We still had a big crowd—bigger than normal—but it was manageable. Matteo was taking a caffeine break himself when the cell phone in his pocket rang.

He checked the display, then, turning on the charm in

his voice, said "Hello, Breanne." I figured the call was about Tucker, and intended to stay close and eavesdrop, but their conversation seemed to steer dangerously toward the intimate and Matteo turned his back to me and crossed the room to an empty table a discrete distance away.

They talked awhile, and it was clear from his smiles that Tucker's fate wasn't the only topic of conversation. Finally, about the moment when I was ready to scream with impatience, Matteo closed the phone and caught my eye. I hurried to his side with Esther at mine.

"Tucker's lawyer postponed the arraignment another twenty-four hours," Matt announced.

"Why?" I asked, outraged. "Detective Hutawa told me Tucker can't be bailed out until he's arraigned."

Matteo frowned. "Clare, you better wake up and smell the java. The judge isn't going to set bail on a case like this."

"Why the hell not?"

"Because it's poisoning, and we don't exactly keep cyanide in a canister next to the sugar, so it wasn't in any way an accident, which means it was premeditated, which means Tucker is a danger to the public and will be kept off the street until his trial."

"But that could be months!"

"The lawyer's doing his best. He got the case postponed as a procedural tactic. He told the judge he'd just joined the case and didn't have adequate time to interview his client. He actually asked for a seven-day adjournment, but the judge refused." He sighed. "At least Tucker's name hasn't been leaked to the press—not yet, anyway."

I shot Esther a not-so-subtle look. She got the message and obediently returned to her duties. I sat down across from Matteo at the coral-colored, marble-topped café table.

"This is so terrible," I sighed.

"Bad for Tucker. Fortunately not bad for the Blend, which seems to be more popular than ever."

"And what's that about?" I cried, rather too loudly. Matt raised an eyebrow and I lowered my voice considerably. "Someone was poisoned here. We're lucky the health department hasn't shut us down. Instead we have more customers than ever before. I know this city drives people crazy on a daily basis—but have they *completely* lost their minds?"

Matteo shrugged. "I suspect it's the fugu effect."

"The *what* effect?"

"Fugu. Japanese blowfish. It contains deadly poison in its organs, a tiny, near-microscopic sliver can be fatal if ingested. Preparing it is so dangerous the chefs have to have a special license to serve fugu in Japan. Yet despite the risk, fugu dishes—especially blowfish soup—are considered great delicacies."

"Are you feeling all right? We're talking about coffee here."

"No, we're talking about human nature. The sudden appeal of our coffee has nothing to do with the coffee. With fugu, it isn't the taste, either. It's so delicate it borders on nonexistent—yet it cost over two hundred dollars for a single dish the last time I was in Shimonoseki, which is the fugu capital of Japan."

"I don't know what you're getting at."

Matteo shook his head. "All those years you were married to me and you still don't understand, do you Clare?"

"Do tell. *What* don't I understand?" I was in no mood for one of Matteo's "my wife never understood me" lectures—that act might get him a night of casual sex from some impressionable bimbo, but it made me want to run screaming from the room (which, given the past twenty-four hours, was highly likely at this juncture).

"There's an expression in Japan that translates, 'I want to eat fugu but I don't want to die.' We don't have that exact sentiment in America, but think of that saying as a combination of our 'wanting our cake and eating it too,' and 'you can't make an omelet without breaking a few eggs.' "

"Are you speaking Japanese?" I was so tired from my lack of sleep and the events of the last twenty-four hours that nothing was making sense to me anymore.

"Clare, the attraction of fugu doesn't have anything to do with eating the stuff. True connoisseurs will tell you it's surviving the meal that gives you the thrill. What could be more intense? You and your companions sit down to a perfectly prepared meal that tastes delicious and just might result in a slow and agonizing doom . . . It's aesthetics and death combined like, bungee jumping or mountain climbing—"

"Or casual sex with strangers? Maybe a cocaine overdose? Are you talking about anyone I know?" I'd had enough of Matteo's condescending tone.

Matt threw up his hands. "Okay. You win. Let's drop the subject."

We sat in fuming silence for a moment. "You're right. Let's drop the subject," I said at last. "I have something else I want to talk to you about anyway."

I told him my theory that Tad or Rena, or maybe Tad *and* Rena, might be responsible for the poisoning, and the real target may have been Lottie herself. To my annoyance, my ex-husband didn't even pretend to entertain the possibility that my theory might be correct.

"Oh," I cried. "So you're so certain two complete strangers are innocent and Tucker is guilty?"

"I'm not saying that," he replied.

"But that's what you think."

"Never mind what I think."

"Listen, Matt—and try to keep an open mind—I sense Lottie herself has doubts. I could hear it in her tone. Even Lottie is a little suspicious of those two for some reason."

Matteo scratched his chin. "If she's suspicious, what exactly does Lottie think is going on with her partners?"

"I don't know."

"Well, if Tad's gone missing today, I can explain that myself," said Matt. "Tad's working on his second business—"

"Second business?"

"Tad's still an investment counselor. He's sponsoring an investment seminar tonight and tomorrow. When I told Tad about my kiosk idea, he suggested that something called quick-turnover investing might be a way to raise capital fast—"

"Wait just a minute. Back up. What kiosk idea?" Then I remembered. Tad had mentioned something about kiosks during Lottie's party—he'd even claimed it was the reason Matt had been chatting up *Trend* magazine editor Breanne Summour.

"I didn't want to get into this with you until it was off the ground," Matt warned.

"Into *what* with me?"

"Any potential arguments."

I narrowed my eyes. "Spill."

"Okay, but don't discuss it with my mother. When you two start talking, I'm always the odd man out."

I crossed my arms and sighed with theatrical patience. "Fine."

"Good." Matt leaned forward and lowered his already low voice. "My goal is very simple. I want to duplicate the success that Starbucks has had in placing cafes in Barnes & Noble by opening Village Blend coffee bars—or kiosks, if the venue is large enough—in exclusive clothing boutiques and department stores. New York, L.A., London, Paris, Rome, Rio, and Tokyo are my 'wave one' rollout cities. Tad suggested to me that some of his potential clients might want to invest in my kiosk start-up. I'm going to his seminar tonight to pitch my plans to a small select group."

Matt fished around in his wallet and pulled out a card printed on silver-gray parchment paper. He handed it to me and I read:

INVESTMENT OPPORTUNITIES

A three-hour seminar sponsored by renowned
Wall Street investor Thaddeus P. Benedict,
formerly of Pope, Richards, and Snyder.
Learn about young, fast-growing companies
and exciting start-ups. A rare opportunity to meet visionary
entrepreneurs. Potentially double, even triple your assets.

Join us aboard the *Fortune*,
Pier 16 at Forty-ninth Street, 8:00 P.M.

The dates on the card—tonight and tomorrow night, as Matt had said—placed Tad's seminars right in the middle of Fashion Week, one of the busiest and most stressful weeks of the year for Lottie.

"Don't you find the timing odd?" I asked.

Matt gave me one of those looks that I translated to mean, "Uh, *no*."

"Look," I pleaded. "I'm a bit suspicious of Tad. And Rena, too. Even if you don't believe me, we owe it to Tucker to try to find the real culprit—you know we can't rely on those Starkey and Hut characters to do that. And besides, you said it yourself, this morning. Tucker Burton works for this business. He's like family, Matt."

Despite my ex's flaws—which had more permutations than the coffee drinks on our menu—Matt did have a conscience, and he hated when I appealed to his better angels, mostly because he usually relented. His expression appeared pained. He sighed and looked down.

"Clare, you've got to understand how important it is to me to get this kiosk idea off the ground. I . . . I'm . . . getting older . . ."

My god, I thought, *he's actually admitting it.*

"I can't be trekking around the world looking for coffee forever . . . I've been planning this for a year now . . . and no matter what you suspect him of, Tad is helping me approach investors this week. I did what I could to help Tucker. Now it's up to his lawyer, Clare. Not me . . . and not you."

I let Matt see the hurt and disappointment on my face.

"Oh, all right," he said at last. "You can come with me if you want to. Snoop around, find out all you can. Just don't mess up my presentation, okay? Or my relationship with Tad."

"But if I start snooping around Tad's investment seminar, asking all kinds of questions, then Tad's bound to get suspicious—especially if he really is guilty of something." I shook my head. "No, I can't do this myself. What I need is a potential investor. A complete stranger who won't arouse any suspicion. . . ."

Matteo snorted. "Maybe you should wear a disguise then. Sounds like the perfect Nancy Drew move."

"Maybe I will. But even then, I won't go alone. I'm going to bring the perfect candidate along with me. Someone who obviously looks like she's made of money—old money—and is itching to throw it into risky ventures, win or lose. The last sort of individual Tad Benedict would suspect . . ."

Matteo sat back in his chair and crossed his arms. Now it was his turn to sigh with theatrical patience. "And who might this perfect candidate be?"

"Why, Matt. I'm surprised. Have you forgotten your own mother?"

TWELVE

‿‿‿‿‿‿‿‿‿‿‿‿‿‿‿‿‿‿

I phoned Madame from the coffeehouse and told her I was on my way over to see her.

"I hope this is a social call," she replied. "My maid told me you rang me up last night."

"It's business, I'm afraid."

I could almost feel Madame tensing on the other end of the line. "Well, let me warn you, dear," she said after a pause. "If it concerns those monthly financial reports you insist on sending me, I haven't read a one of them."

"We'll talk when I get there."

A brief, brisk walk brought me to Washington Square Park. The large square appeared luminous in the long, golden rays of the waning September day. Students from the surrounding New York University occupied the benches or sat in clusters in the grassy areas, with dogs, squirrels, and children romping around them. I circled the fountain and followed the paved paths.

Finally I passed under the seventy-seven-foot marble arch that dominated the northern end. Built in 1895 to re-place a wooden structure that had been erected by architect

Stanford White for the Centennial celebration of George Washington's inauguration, the white marble arch has served as a rallying point for labor unrest, civil rights marches, antiwar protests, feminist bra-burnings, socialist gatherings, and anarchists riots for generations. The irony is that Fifth Avenue, a central Manhattan artery running north from the arch, where the most affluent of the New York City old guard resides, geographically begins at this site of repeated antiestablishment rebellion.

Madame occupied an opulent penthouse capping one of Fifth Avenue's exclusive residential buildings near the arch. The imposing structure boasts a concrete moat, a spectacular view of the city, and a doorman dressed like an eighteenth-century European naval officer. My mother-in-law had moved into that building when her late second husband, Pierre Dubois, insisted she give up what he felt was Madame's "rather small" West Village duplex above the coffeehouse—the elegantly furnished space where I now live.

Of course, Madame's world was not mine. She'd been raised an aristocrat before being forced to flee Europe during the Second World War, finding herself in America with very little to her name. After her first husband—Matteo's father—died, a life of great wealth followed through her second marriage to the late Pierre. Even though the bulk of his assets had been willed to the children from his first marriage, Madame retained ownership of the fabulous penthouse where she now lived, as well as a modest trust fund for her living expenses.

Coming from solidly working-class roots, I was admitted to Madame's world through marriage to her son. And through the rocky marriage and divorce, the birth of my daughter Joy, and the move to the New Jersey suburbs and back again, Madame and I had only grown closer. Part of our bond was having more in common than superficially appeared—my own immigrant grandmother had raised me with the same values Madame had come to embrace through the hardships that Nazi-occupied Europe had in-

flicted on her and her family. The other part was our mutual
love of Joy. And, if questioned under torture, I suppose I'd
admit that sprinkled in there somewhere was our common
affection for Matteo.

When I arrived at the front door, Madame's personal
maid ushered me into the matriarch's dark, brocaded sitting room, rich with a heady aroma. Coffee had been
freshly pressed, and the scent of it nearly knocked me over.
I had recently smelled something vaguely similar.

A filigreed tray containing a silver coffee service and
petit fours had been laid out on a table of Italian marble,
beside an original Tiffany lamp. I no sooner dropped into
one of the leather chairs than Madame appeared. Today
she was clad in a white silk pantsuit, her silver hair in a
French twist, held by an ivory comb.

Madame poured the coffee into delicate china cups.
Normally, I would stain the black with a bit of cream, but
the scent of this offering was too intriguing. I sipped the
rich, hot brew, and looked up, astounded and amazed. I
didn't know exactly what it was—I only knew what it
wasn't.

"This isn't your usual Jamaica Blue Mountain."

Madame smiled. "No." She raised an eyebrow in challenge. "Can you guess?"

For a moment, neither of us spoke as we continued to
savor the flavor of this absolutely remarkable coffee, brimming with kaleidoscopic nuances of fruit. The taste was
clean and sweet, yet densely rich with hints of blueberry,
wine, and spice. It was bright and spirited yet at the same
time deeply resonant and balanced. A coffee this complex
and alive with fruit almost had to carry a very slight fermented tinge, and it did, but to care would have been like
criticizing Da Vinci because he left a stray stroke of paint
on the Mona Lisa's frame.

"Is it Ethiopian?" I asked.

"You're guessing?"

"To be perfectly honest, the aroma is familiar only because Matt roasted a top secret batch of whatever this is af-

ter he came back from Ethiopia, but I'm still not sure what it is. Of course, your son wouldn't tell me squat."

"It's Harrar. Wet-processed."

"It can't be."

"Oh, but it is."

Grown on small farms in the eastern part of Ethiopia, Harrar was one of the world's oldest and most traditional coffees. Unlike its more elegant and high-toned wet-processed cousins in other regions of the country—Ghimbi and Yirgacheffe (a.k.a. Sidamo)—Harrar was traditionally a *dry-processed* coffee, meaning the coffee cherries were picked and put out in the sun to dry, fruit and all, as they had been for centuries.

Such simple dry-processing (or "natural") methods emphasized bold fruit notes. But the fruit taste could come off as overly wild and fermented. Here, however, the wild fruit character had been tamed. The taste was more balanced, with a longer lasting body than a typical Harrar. And it was far more aromatic. The floral and fruit notes remained intact from the first sip through the last (a real trick in a dark roast). And, as the cup cooled, these flavors assembled themselves differently with each taste. It was a complex and beautifully structured cup, a coffee for those who wished to sip rather than gulp. A coffee worthy of contemplation.

"A coffee like this," I mused, "used in our espresso blend, would be spectacular."

"Yes, my dear, just imagine the fine aromatics in the crema."

I nearly swooned. "More, please."

As Madame poured, she explained to me that Matteo had personally presented her with five pounds of these beans so that he could explain what he'd secretly been working toward. He and a small Ethiopian farmer he'd befriended had together attempted to experiment with processing methods other than the traditional dry method the farmers of Harrar had used for hundreds of years. No easy feat.

The Ethiopian coffee industry, like many others in the Third World, depends mainly on the work of small-holding farmers with virtually no access to technology and a limited infrastructure. Most Ethiopian farmers still carry their coffee to the mill on their heads. Dry-processing is used in regions where rainfall is scarce and there are long periods of sunshine.

In wet-processing, water is used to remove the four layers surrounding what we know as the "green" coffee bean—the part of the cherry that we roast, then grind and brew. There are other methods, like natural pulping and an experimental process called "repassed" or "raisins," where the cherries float because they have dried too long on the tree before being collected; then those floaters are removed from the rest and then "repassed" and pulped.

The bottom line, however, is this: while microclimate and soil are contributing factors to the profile of any coffee, processing is usually the single largest contributor to the coffee's flavor characteristics. The differences between a washed and dry-processed coffee from the same region can be more distinct than two wet-processed coffees from different regions.

Madame spoke up again. "Matt would like to call this the Village Blend Special Reserve."

I nodded. "And did Matt tell you what his plan was for this Special Reserve?" I asked carefully, thinking this had to be part of Matt's big kiosk plan: an exclusive coffee for his exclusive settings. *Not bad, Matt. Not bad at all.*

"Plan?" said Madame, perplexed. "What sort of plan? He plans to sell it at the Blend, of course, what else?"

Again I nodded, this time with nervous indulgence. Obviously, Matt hadn't told her the rest of his tale—only the "Once Upon a Time" part. I didn't blame him for breaking the kiosk plan to her slowly, getting her on board with the Special Reserve idea first. Madame had never expressed anything but loathing for the idea of franchising the Village Blend or commercializing its name—the most recent attempt being the rather shady business deal proposed by

Eduardo Lebreaux, the Eurotrash importer who had tried to sabotage the landmark coffeehouse after Madame had rejected his offers to purchase it. Madame always believed there should be one Village Blend and only one—or, as she's been known to say, "There's only one Eiffel Tower, dear, only one Big Ben, only one Statue of Liberty. . . ."

Although Madame's employment contracts with Matt and I gave us increasing equity in the business over time, she was presently still the owner. She could shut Matt down with one simple syllable, which was why I wasn't about to say another thing about it. Frankly, it was up to Matt to inform his mother of his plans, not me.

As our conversation continued, Madame got around to telling me about her date to a major charity function the previous night (lucky her, she was still seeing Dr. Mc-Tavish, an oncologist at St. Vincent with the sex appeal of Sean Connery), and I slowly realized Madame wasn't bringing up the subject of Tucker and the Blend because she hadn't yet heard about it.

I broke the news as delicately as I could, telling Madame about the Lottie Harmon party which she'd missed, the murder of Ricky Flatt at the coffeehouse, and Tucker Burton's arrest.

"A flagrant miscarriage of justice," Madame declared. "We both know Tucker is innocent of this terrible crime."

Her faith in the Blend's barista cheered me considerably. Before her comment, I'd felt pretty much alone in my crusade to free Tucker. Madame's next words did more than cheer me up. They gave me hope.

"What can I do to help?" she asked.

I told her about Lottie's partner Tad Benedict. Although I hadn't discussed *motive* with Matt, I now voiced my suspicion that Tad was maneuvering to take control of the label—a strategy that might just involve murder. I mentioned Tad's seminar on investing—a suspicious action, coming on the heels of the attempt on Lottie's life. Then I dropped the other shoe.

"I was hoping you would attend that seminar tonight, try

to find out what Tad Benedict's up to, whether the business ventures he's representing are legitimate or not. Snoop around, find out what you can."

Madame's eyes lit up brighter than Radio City. "How exciting!" she exclaimed. "What time do we leave?"

"Unfortunately, I can't go. Tad knows me and might get suspicious if I show up. But Matteo will attend. He's pitching . . . a . . . um, a new business venture."

"Then perhaps Matteo can do the snooping," suggested Madame.

"That would be helpful. But he says he can't. He's determined to find funding for his business, and that's his priority—he claims Tad promised him results."

"What is Matteo so fired up about?"

I shrugged.

"Perhaps he's looking for more monetary backing for the Ethiopian wet-processing?" Madame fished.

I smiled. "I'll let him tell you about it."

I could see she was quite curious now, but she didn't force the issue. "I want to help," she said. "But I wouldn't know how to snoop around, or what to look for. Clare, I think you'd better come along, too."

I sighed. "Matteo actually suggested I wear a disguise, but I'm sure he was being snide."

Madame clapped her slender, graceful hands. "A disguise! What a perfectly marvelous idea."

"But that's crazy! I'm no undercover cop. And . . . I'm not very good at deception."

"As I recall, you did a pretty good job of bluffing your way into that Meat No More fundraiser a few months ago."

"That was a desperate situation. I thought my daughter was in danger."

"Don't you see? This is a desperate situation, too. Think about Tucker, what that poor man is going through. Sitting in a jail cell, accused of a crime he didn't commit."

"Look, I'm doing all I can. But in this instance what can I do? Wear a wig? Dark glasses? It doesn't matter anyway.

I don't have the poise or the attire to trick anyone into believing I'm a wealth investor."

"Bah," she cried. "Poise comes with the proper attire, and that's a problem easily solved."

She set down her china cup and stood. "Come with me. I'm sure we can find something suitable from my own wardrobe."

Madame led me down a long hallway lined with statuary and through the door to her boudoir. The corner room was bright and spacious, with ivory lace curtains pulled back to admit the afternoon sun. Passing the mirrored dressing table, Madame flung open the cream-colored doors to her walk-in closet and stepped inside.

She stared, clucking at the array of fine clothing hanging there, then shook her head. "No, no, no . . . these clothes just won't do."

Madame moved deeper into the closet, to an ornate armoire made of dark teakwood. When she opened its doors, my eyes widened. The armoire was packed with vintage clothing sealed in clear plastic—a fabulous array of textures, a cascading rainbow of colors. An Oleg Cassini evening dress in shell pink, silk-georgette chiffon beside a Givenchy dress and jacket in deep-pink wool bouclé. An elegant two-piece linen suit in blazing red, a la Chez Ninon. A pale blue Herbert Sondheim sundress. Black cigarette pants with matching black-and-white striped jacket. Pillbox hats. Capri pants. A-line skirts. And there were vintage accessories, too. A Gucci hobo bag. Real crocodile shoes. Belts. Handbags. Gloves. Jewelry. Even several pairs of oversized tortoise-shell sunglasses.

"When I was your age, these were the clothes I wore," Madame said with a note of pride, as she pulled out piece after piece.

"They're . . . marvelous. Simply spectacular. These clothes are thirty years old, yet they seem so contemporary."

"More like *forty* years old, my dear. But it does not matter one whit. Elegance is timeless."

"And your taste is impeccable. I like this black number. . . ."

"The crepe minidress with the pleated hem ruffle? It's Mary Quant. A lovely dress, but all wrong for this occasion. You must wear light colors to blend in with the rich and powerful. . . ."

"Light colors?"

"If for no other reason than to demonstrate to the world that you can afford the dry cleaning bills."

"That's ridiculous."

"That's the rich. Ah, let's try this Christian Dior skirt and jacket, perhaps with this white cashmere sweater. Or would this Andre Courreges A-line shift dress be more appropriate? No, no, the hemline is much too short. . . ."

I soon realized that much of Madame's wardrobe mimicked the style of a highly public figure of that era, a woman known for her impeccable taste in fashion—an arguably effortless feat with all the top-tier designers of her day scrambling to dress her. Well, who could fault Madame for that? After all, what woman of Madame's generation didn't try to dress like Jackie O?

We decided on a Coco Chanel wool suit in a creamy beige—jacket, skirt, and coordinating blouse. The fit was pretty good. The overall ensemble elegant and flattering. Unfortunately, at five-two, the skirt's hemline hung too far below my knees, but Madame called in her maid and the two women were soon fussing and pinning and promising to have the hemline lifted up for the event.

"When that suit was new, I would wear it with a pair of high-heeled pumps and this hat," said Madame, holding up the hat.

Uh-oh, I thought, seeing the signature Jackie pillbox with the lacy veil. *I think we're going a little too far on the time warp.* "I'll lose the hat and go with calf-high boots," I told her gently. "It's a more contemporary look."

"Oh, yes, of course." She tapped her chin. "I suppose the white gloves are out too?"

I smiled indulgently and nodded. Then I gazed at my reflection in the floor-length mirror, amazed at the transformation. Even without the hat, I looked like a different woman—elegant, ageless, timelessly fashionable. I also appeared affluent, wildly so. In these clothes, even my personal style changed from practical to poised. I stood straighter, my movements seemed graceful. I felt nearly as confident as I looked. But there was one problem—my head. My face and hair still gave away my identity.

"Try this." Madame handed me a hat box containing a shoulder-length, straight-styled natural hair wig in a color at least three shades darker than my own natural chestnut brown. The wig, and a pair of oversized Oleg Cassini tinted glasses, completed the ensemble.

We fumbled with my hair for a good ten minutes before we got it bundled tightly enough to place the wig on my head, but with the addition of the dark hair and bangs and the glasses, the illusion was complete.

"My god!" I cried. "I . . . I look just like . . ."

Madame smiled, patted my hand. "I know, dear."

THIRTEEN

~~~~~~

As I followed Madame out of the cab in front of Pier 18, Matteo was waiting on the sidewalk. He spied his mother, then did a double-take.

"It's Jackie O!" he cried.

"We're calling her Margot Gray, this evening," Madame whispered. "You remember Margot and her husband Rexler, from Scarsdale? We saw a lot of them when you were a teenager."

Matteo grinned. "I remember their daughter much better."

"You are incorrigible," his mother replied. She took her son's arm. As darkly handsome as ever, he had abandoned the black Armani tonight for a more approachable look—a cream V-neck sweater outlined his athletic, broad-shouldered torso beneath a caramel-colored camel-hair jacket and chocolate brown pants.

"Son, tell me about this business venture of yours. *Margot* has been quite evasive about the subject."

Matt's uneasy gaze attempted to find mine through the oversized tinted tortoiseshell glasses.

"I haven't been evasive," I protested. "I haven't said a word."

"I was hoping you'd be surprised by my presentation, mother," he said smoothly, "pleasantly surprised." He glanced at his watch. "Maybe we'd better get to the dock. We wouldn't want the boat to leave without us."

We moved through a sheltered space to the dock area where signs directed us to Tad Benedict's seminar. At the gangplank, a table was set up to greet potential investors. A blond woman in a Fen pantsuit and one of Lottie Harmon's coffee swirl brooches on her jacket lapel took our invitations and wrote down our names and addresses.

"Margot Gray of Scarsdale," I said in a nasal drone that I thought sounded suitably snobbish. The woman wrote down my name and fictitious address, then handed me a spiral bound prospectus. On the cover were the words "TB Investments." Perched on the lettering was a spot of art that looked like a butterfly—or was it a moth?

"Welcome aboard the *Fortune*," Clipboard Lady said in a faux-friendly tone. "When you go up the gangplank, make a right. In the main ballroom cocktails are being served."

The *Fortune* was a dazzlingly white seventy-five-foot pleasure yacht transformed into a Hudson River sightseeing and party boat. The entire superstructure below the boxy pilot house was glass-enclosed, offering a panoramic view of the New York skyline. From the deck, the view was impressive. The sun had already set, and the lights of midtown Manhattan reached into the clear evening sky. I'd had to push my dark glasses down to the tip of my nose just to make it out.

The grandly named main ballroom was basically a carpeted space approximately the size of a two-car garage—a crowd circled a table of hors d'oeuvres and a well-stocked bar, where a young bartender deftly mixed adult beverages to order. I asked the man for a Long Island iced tea (for courage), which I sipped judiciously as I moved among the group.

The forty or so people were mostly in their fifties and

sixties and mostly paired up. Many of the older men were displaying, on their arms, young, blond trophy wives (Tom Wolfe's "Lemon Tarts"); a good many older women were chatting in small clusters; and two gay May/September couples had gravitated to each other. A few quite elderly investors had come, as well, including a rather imperious man in a wheelchair who seemed to take pleasure in ordering his nurse to fetch him drink after drink.

I saw no sign of Tad Benedict, but the chic, faux-smiling blond who'd signed us in appeared with her clipboard under her arm. I watched her tap Matteo on his shoulder, then crook her finger and lead him through a bulkhead door behind the bar, which was where, I presumed, the entrepreneurs with start-ups to pitch (i.e., the debutantes of this gala) were probably being prepped by Tad.

I began my snooping with a study of the people in the room. The rich, to paraphrase F. Scott Fitzgerald, are very different from us ("they have money"), and that legendary observation held true for this affluent flock. In my experience, any other social gathering of this size—even one packed with total strangers—would become somewhat lively as copious amounts of expensive liquor were being consumed. But not this bunch. Even as they imbibed, the group wondered about, leafing through Tad Benedict's prospectus, looking a little lost.

"They're all so quiet," I whispered to Madame.

"Yes, my dear. Well, some people are just used to letting their money speak for them, and in my opinion, money alone has absolutely nothing to say." She smiled, leafing through Tad's prospectus. "Look at these obviously high-risk investment opportunities: a new restaurant, an independent film. Why do you think these people are here, Clare? Not for money. They have that. What they don't have is excitement. They're bored, you see. These start-ups are the kind of thing that makes them feel they are participating in the world."

I couldn't fault Madame's slightly disdainful attitude—because I knew where it came from. She may have married a wealthy second husband, but she'd spent decades running the Blend—initially with Matt's father and then by herself. It was hard, disciplined work running any business, rising at dawn every day, tracking and checking up on thousands of details, wrangling employees. And, over the years, Madame had done much more than simply roast and pour coffee for the people in the neighborhood. She'd become intimately involved in the lives of many of the people who'd come through the Blend's door—the actors, artists, writers, dancers, and musicians who'd always populated Greenwich Village—giving them the Blend's second floor couch to sleep on when they'd been evicted from their cramped studio apartments, pouring black French roast for the borderline alcoholics, holding the hands of emotionally fragile souls who'd come to one of the most brutal cities on earth to peddle their talents. So, it didn't surprise me that Madame wouldn't think much of a group of people who simply wanted to throw money at a business to feel as though they were a part of it. In Madame's experience, blood, sweat, and tears made you a part of something, not simply placing ink on a check.

I felt the deck rumble under my heeled boots as the engine roared to life. Then the yacht bumped, sloshing the drink in my hand, and a moment later, a deckhand cast the mooring lines aside and we pulled away from the pier. The boat moved along the Manhattan skyline, its towers of lights shimming in the Hudson's dark waters.

Speakers crackled, and an amplified voice filled the room. "A million lights. A million stories. A million opportunities for those who know how to find them, use them. My name is Tad Benedict, and I can show you how. You can participate in a number of ways—put a little bit down on every opportunity I will offer tonight. Or you might want to invest only in a single start-up . . . that's up to you. There are no losers here, I assure you. The amount you gain depends on how aggressively you choose to invest. . . ."

The interior lights dimmed, and everyone turned to face

Tad Benedict. The stocky man with the elfin face stood in the center of a white spotlight, microphone in hand.

"Thank you all for coming," he continued. "I thank you now because I can afford to be generous. Why? Because I know you are all going to thank me later."

Then Tad launched into a spiel that was one third Tony Roberts can-do optimism, one third Wall Street get-rich-quick pep talk, and one third awkward metaphors—basically a lot of drivel about flames and moths being drawn to them, which explained the logo on the prospectus, at least. I had always found Tad Benedict likeable, but the result of this bizarre combination was bullish—and not in a good way.

"Madame," I whispered, "this sounds like nothing but bull—"

Madame touched my arm. "A lady does not use such language, Margot. Hogwash will suffice. To tell you the truth, the only thing that really bothers me are his constant references to flying insects."

Tad continued speaking another twenty minutes or so. Finally, he directed everyone's attention to his prospectus while he began a Power Point demonstration featuring logos and growth charts of the investment opportunities represented there. Suddenly, the distinctive stretched *L* and *H* of the Lottie Harmon logo appeared.

"TB Investing holds fifty percent shares in the phenomenally hot Lottie Harmon accessory line," said Tad. "Lottie Harmon is a resurrected designer label that has seen over two hundred percent growth in the last year, a tiny caterpillar that's come out of its cocoon, unfurled its wings, and really flown. . . ."

Tad moved on to other names and logos, but I hardly paid attention. How could it be, I asked myself, that Tad Benedict is touting a fifty-percent share in Lottie Harmon stock if he owns only twenty-five percent?

Lottie had told me herself that only she, Tad, and Rena were shareholders—with a tiny percentage going to Fen—

because that's the way she'd wanted it. Lottie had waited decades to be able to express herself through creative designs, and maintaining control of her own label meant more to her than money. So either Tad was lying, or he had managed to gain control of either a portion of Lottie's shares, or all of Garcia's stock.

Finally, Tad wrapped things up.

"After a short break, I'll be introducing several clients of TB. These visionary entrepreneurs are here to personally offer potentially lucrative shares in their start-ups and to answer any questions you might have. This is a rare opportunity to get in on the ground floor of exciting new businesses—a soon-to-be hot restaurant, two new magazines, a theatrical production, a coffee bar franchise, two designer clothing labels, a shoe boutique's expansion, and an independent film are among the dozens of opportunities about which you're going to hear. Rarely are investors offered a chance to board a train before it even leaves the station, just before it takes off for the wild blue yonder—"

Madame sighed. "These mixed metaphors are annoying me."

"Yes, Madame." I whispered nervously, secretly glad Madame's eyes had glazed over enough to have apparently missed Tad's mention of a "coffee bar franchise" start-up.

"Meanwhile," Tad continued. "I'm going to circulate among you. Please feel free to approach me at any time with questions, or offers. . . ."

I huddled with Madame as we formulated a plan. A few minutes later, as Tad mingled with his potential clients, Madame strolled up to him.

"I so love Lottie Harmon's designs," she began. "I wonder . . . would it be possible to make a block purchase of that stock?"

Tad turned on the charm. "Of course, Miss . . ."

"*Mrs.* Dubois. And this is my friend, Margot Gray."

"So delighted you've come," he said, taking my hand. Behind my wig and tinted glasses, I held my breath, praying Tad wouldn't recognize me. He didn't. He simply turned and faced Madame. "Of course, the shares of Lottie Harmon are not cheap, Mrs. Dubois."

Madame waved her hand. "Money isn't a problem. But I don't want to be selfish. I'm only interested in twenty or thirty percent. . . ."

Tad Benedict nearly choked on his sparkling water.

"Of course, if the stock is reasonably priced, I might be convinced to purchase more."

Tad set his water glass down and took Madame's hand. "Please follow me, ladies," he purred. "I'd like to handle the details regarding this transaction personally."

Fourteen

~~~~~~

WITH Madame on his arm, Tad Benedict led us across the packed ballroom. He threaded through the crowd so fast I had trouble keeping up. Fortunately, Clipboard Lady stopped him near the busy bar.

"Should I start the presentations?" she asked.

Tad looked around, nodded impatiently. "Yeah, let's get the show on the road. Bring out one presenter at a time— and hold everyone to a five-minute limit. We're due back at the pier in a little over an hour."

Clipboard Lady's brow wrinkled with concern. When she spoke, her whisper was loud enough to reach my ears. "There's kind of an issue backstage about who gets to go on first. Two men are arguing . . . It's getting out of hand."

He waved the woman aside. "Do the job I pay you for."

"But—"

"Send them out alphabetically, the way their names are printed on the roster. Who can argue with that?"

For a moment the pair huddled in conversation. I managed to pull Madame aside.

"This is so thrilling. What do we do next?" she asked.

"Press him," I whispered. "We need to find out how many shares of Lottie Harmon stocks he's willing to part with. If it's more than the twenty-five percent I know he owns, then there's something fishy going on."

Suddenly the Clipboard Lady hurried away and Tad reached for Madame's arm once more.

"I must apologize for the interruption. There's just so much to do, and I only have a few associates here to take care of things."

Tad said this over his shoulder as he hustled us through a door, and into a wood paneled hallway. We passed three other doors, one obviously a bulkhead that led outside to the deck. Tad opened a door at the end of the narrow hall. On the other side there was a small stateroom with a wall-sized window that offered a spectacular view of Manhattan's towering lights, bordered by dark water and black sky.

Tad directed us to chairs, and when we were both settled he sat down across a narrow table from Madame and I. Behind him, a computer rested on a small desk. On its monitor, a screen saver with the stylized logo of TB Investments flickered. Tad smiled at us both and leaned forward.

"So, Mrs. Dubois, you're interested in purchasing a large block of Lottie Harmon shares?"

"That's right, Mr. Benedict," Madame replied, quite convincingly I thought. "I own shares in several large concerns, most of which I patronize in my daily life. You see, I believe in that old adage—one should only invest in businesses and products one would patronize or understand. I do purchase high-end fashions, so when I heard the Lottie Harmon name . . ."

"Of course," Tad said smoothly. "But I must warn you that this is a special offering. Shares in Lottie Harmon are in great demand."

"I was not aware Lottie Harmon was a publicly traded label."

Tad shifted in his seat. "TB Investments is the only firm authorized to trade Lottie Harmon shares, and only in limited amounts."

Madame feigned excitement. "An exclusive offer! Now I am enthusiastic . . . I do hope the amounts are not *too* limited."

"Well . . ."

"Oh, I don't want to be selfish. I'm not interested in taking over controlling shares in the company. I just want to make a substantial investment in the concern—perhaps thirty percent . . ."

Tad didn't even blink. "I'm sure that amount could be secured, unless some of the other investors have beaten you to the punch."

Then Tad shifted his eyes to me.

"So, Ms. Gray? Has any facet of TB Investment's prospectus piqued your interest?"

I adjusted my tinted, tortoiseshell, Jackie O glasses and sighed theatrically. Up to this point I'd kept my conversation to a minimum in front of Tad, fearing the sound or cadence of my voice would somehow reveal my identity. I knew my disguise had been effective so far—I didn't even recognize myself in the reflection on the plate glass window. Behind the wig even the shape of my face was obscured, and no one could see my eyes because in anything less than a brilliantly lit room like this one, the tinted glasses rendered me nearly blind, so who could see in? But as much as I wanted to pump Tad Benedict for more information, I was forced to remain silent due to my fear of exposure. Instead, I sighed, shook my head solemnly as I waved my hand in a dismissive gesture.

Tad put his arms on the desk, leaned closer. "Surely there's something here to entice even you, Ms. Gray?"

I felt him watching me, waiting for a reply. I cleared my throat, preparing to unleash the nasal drone I'd used on Clipboard Lady.

"Well—"

Suddenly the door burst open without a knock. Clipboard Lady was there, hair windblown, face flushed.

"You've got to come . . ." she stammered. "Trouble on the deck."

We heard the voices a moment later. Loud, angry voices—one of them familiar—Matteo.

Tad was on his feet and out the door. This time he didn't even excuse himself. I rose and followed him into the hall, Madame close behind. A blast of cool night air was streaming into the passageway, the dank river smell potent. I noticed another door was ajar. Through it I spied a large stateroom were several men and women milled around in various states of shock or surprise. All wore Wall Street attire, their pie charts, graphs and Power Point machines at the ready. In the middle of that room, a table had been upset. A chair, a broken laptop computer, and a shattered pitcher of water lay on the floor.

The draft was pouring in from the bulkhead door, now flung wide. From outside, on the deck, the angry voices continued.

"Don't they teach you the alphabet in Europe?" Matteo was barking. "I thought your educational system was supposed to be better than ours. Or did they do the ABCs backwards, like everything else in the Old World?!"

As I hurried to the door, I could hear Tad Benedict trying to restore calm. "Listen, gentlemen, this can be resolved—"

"Perhaps *after* you toss this . . . this *cowboy* over the side."

The voice that interrupted Tad was dripping with arrogance, sarcasm, and contempt—so much so that I recognized the speaker even before I stumbled onto the chilly deck.

Eduardo Lebreaux.

In his late fifties, Lebreaux was the kind of oily Continental who would have been at home in *Casablanca*, angling how to cheat at cards in Rick's Café American. He had dark brown hair, thinning on the top and a little too long at the back, a mustache, and a pensive look to his pale green eyes. No wrinkles but the sort of blotchy skin acquired from drinking and smoking to excess. His evening clothes were well tailored, of course—what little I could see of them, because he was presently standing behind a wall of well-dressed, thick-necked flesh that was his bodyguard.

"I'd like to see you *try* and throw me off this boat," replied Matt, fists balled. "With or without your rented thug."

Matteo was referring to Thick Neck, of course, who stood impassively, eyes on Matt, hands raised but open. There were, I noted, a lot of muscles crammed into the guard's open-necked white shirt and blue blazer. I wondered if Matteo could really take on the man standing between him and Lebreaux.

The amoral European importer-exporter used to work for Madame's second husband, Pierre, and had been a thorn in Madame's side since her husband's death. Matteo had always had an instinctive negative reaction to Lebreaux, and he'd been right. Lebreaux wasn't someone you could trust. In fact, some of his tactics bordered on the criminal.

Just then, I noticed a woman on Lebreaux's arm—and recognized her. It was Violet Eyes, the tall, strikingly beautiful Asian woman who had accompanied Lloyd Newhaven to Lottie's party. Her face appeared placid, impassive even in the face of this outrageous scene.

Before I had a chance even to consider the meaning of Violet Eyes's presence, others instantly appeared on deck. Several of the presenters scrambled topside to watch the conclusion of the heated melodrama they'd seen ignited in their stateroom. To my shock, I spied another familiar face among them—the male model who'd attended Lottie's party. His platinum blond Billy Idol crewcut was unmistakable, even through my tinted glasses.

My mind raced. While the presence of Violet Eyes might have been mere happenstance, meeting another person who'd attended that fatal party—*and* was near the coffee bar at the time of the poisoning—was at least one coincidence too many for me.

Matt glared at the bodyguard, then tried to step around the man and return to the stateroom. A ham-sized palm slapped the middle of Matt's chest, stopping him. Matteo glared up at the man. When he spoke, his voice was surprisingly calm: "I'm going inside to make my presentation. Look, Eduardo . . . tell your hired help to get out of my face and out of my way."

Lebreaux looked around and spied Madame standing next to me. His lips twisted into a cruel smile and he bowed in her direction. "I see you are not yet untangled from your dowager mother's skirts, Matteo. Was franchising the Village Blend's brand name Madame Dubois's idea? Perhaps an act of financial desperation?"

At my side, I felt Madame stiffen.

I saw Tad's expression, too. There was surprise at hearing that Mrs. Dubois was Matt's mother.

Matteo exploded. "You son of a—"

He launched himself at Eduardo's throat. The European fearfully stumbled backwards, almost knocking Violet Eyes overboard in his haste to escape. Matt didn't get far before Thick Neck stopped him cold. There was a flurry of movement, loud grunts, and the sound of fists striking flesh.

"Wait! Wait!" Tad Benedict cried.

But events had gone too far. Everyone backed away and watched helplessly as Matt and Thick Neck grappled for a moment, stumbling across the deck. The struggle continued until both men tumbled over the rail, their fiery confrontation finally getting doused in the cold, churning waters of the Hudson River.

Fifteen

∞∞∞∞∞∞∞∞∞∞∞∞∞∞∞∞∞∞∞∞

THE *Fortune* received an official police and fireboat escort all the way back to Pier 18. The Coast Guard even arrived to lend a hand.

After Matteo and the bodyguard had splashed into the water, the sailors aboard the yacht went into action, fishing the two men out and depositing them back on deck in record time. Unfortunately, one of the guests on board had panicked and dialed 911 on his cell. Just about every agency responsible for river safety—with the possible exception of Homeland Security—responded with an appearance.

The excitement aboard ship interrupted the flow of presentations. The rest of the seminar was cancelled and the *Fortune* returned to port. Meanwhile, there were so many blinking red lights on the water that by the time we approached the pier, a crowd had gathered to see what all the fuss was about.

The *Fortune* bumped into its berth, and the crew lowered the gangplank. Like rats fleeing a sinking ship, the affluent passengers crowded the exit. Matteo, dripping wet and smelling like stagnant water, accompanied his mother as they joined the exiting throng. I hung back, however, hoping to catch a glimpse of Tad or one of his associates, even Clipboard Lady.

I slipped into the ballroom, saw the bartender tidying up while a pair of women wearing aprons collected glasses from around the room. I went back outside and circled the deck, to the other side of the ship. My booted toe bumped against a rope stand, and I nearly pitched over. With a moan of frustration, I ripped the tinted glasses off my face and stuffed them into the Gucci purse.

The view was nice from this portion of the deck. Ships were approaching Manhattan, or moving out to sea. Far in the distance, the Statue of Liberty was lit in a brilliant glow. At the rail, I gazed at the vista for a moment, then heard a door open around a corner from me. A man and woman stepped out of the light, and up to the darkened area near the rail. I recognized the man—Tad Benedict. The woman's back was turned so I couldn't see her features. I stepped back, against the bulkhead, not daring to breathe. They were so preoccupied with each other, they failed to notice me in the shadows, listening to their conversation.

"We didn't sell enough," the woman said. Her tone seemed desperate, her voice familiar. I tried to lean my head just a little bit closer.

Tad snorted. "Sell *enough*? We didn't sell a damn thing."

After a moment of silence, the woman spoke. "I just want out, Tad."

"We'll get out," he said with conviction. "We'll buy our way out if we have to. I know I can raise the money. Enough money to make the payoff, and still have something left for the both of us to make a life for ourselves, free of . . . you know . . ."

His voice trailed off and he rubbed the woman's shoulder. She turned to caress his hand, but her face remained in shadow.

"We're running out of time," she said.

"Don't worry," came Tad's reply. "I can fix this."

Finally she turned to face him. As their lips met, the

woman moved into the light. I recognized her instantly: Rena Garcia, Lottie Harmon's partner and marketing and publicity manager.

The kiss broke, and Tad, escorted her back inside. When they were gone, I hurried around to the other side of the boat. At the gangplank I joined the last of the passengers disembarking. Out on the street, I found Madame standing alone on the sidewalk, looking out at the river. Matt was waiting on the taxi line by the curb.

"I'm sorry, Madame," I said. "I probably should have told you what Matt had in mind. I know it's not what you'd do with the business."

"Yes," she replied. "Perhaps you should have told me. But it really doesn't matter now. It's water under the bridge—" She gazed at her sopping wet son in the taxi line. "—so to speak."

Madame faced me. I was surprised to find her eyes bright, her expression buoyant. "In any case, my dear, how I've done things in the past is not the point any longer. The Blend's future belongs to you . . . and Matteo. In a way, I'm happy."

"Happy?"

"My son is finally showing genuine interest. In the business. In the future."

She touched my arm. "Perhaps he really has changed, Clare."

Then she turned and walked to the waiting cab. She and Matteo spoke briefly as he held the door for her, then he closed it and the cab sped off. Matt immediately hailed the next car in line and we climbed inside for the silent trip back to the Blend.

WHEN we arrived, I pitched in to help Gardner, the evening shift's barista, while Matteo ran upstairs to shower the river stench away and change into dry clothes.

Gardner Evans was an easy-going African-American composer, arranger, and jazz musician (sax, piano, guitar, bass—the guy was amazing). He'd moved to New York from the D.C. area a few years before, after finishing college, and had immediately started playing the clubs and hotel lounges with a small ensemble.

His group, Four on the Floor, had an excellent sound—I'd seen them live a few times and they'd put out two CDs, which we often played in the evenings at the Blend, along with CDs he'd bring in from his own impressive collection. For my money, however, the best thing about Gardner being a musician was his affinity for night hours. He was always alert and alive in the evenings when he arrived for barista work, which was pretty much any night his ensemble didn't have a gig.

I hadn't yet changed out of my Jackie O disguise, and the customers obviously found it amusing. As I served up a *doppio* espresso and a skinny vanilla lat with wings (i.e., a double espresso and a vanilla latte made with skim milk and extra foam) Gardner shook his head and said, "I swear, C.C., you should wear that get-up for the Village Halloween parade."

"Don't laugh at your boss, Gardner, it's demoralizing. Besides, don't you think I'm just a little bit credible as a Jackie O type?"

He responded by laughing harder.

I raised an eyebrow. "You know, mister, you're treading a very fine line. Maybe you should start restocking the cupboards—that should dampen your levity."

But as he turned for the pantry, his chuckles failed to fade.

Matteo returned just then, still toweling his hair dry. "My shoes are ruined. Italian leather. I could strangle Lebreaux for that alone." He dropped into one of the tall swivel chairs at the coffee bar.

Behind the espresso machine, I dumped the cake of used grounds and rinsed the portafilter, packed more of our freshly ground Mocha Java inside it, tamped it, clamped it, and began to draw two new shots. I poured each into a cream-colored *demitasse*, added a twist of lemon for my ex-husband, and a bit of sugar for myself.

After a fortifying hit of caffeine, I finally asked, "Matt, what was that fight all about exactly?"

"Fight?" Gardner asked, returning to the counter with an armload of cups, lids, and heat sleeves. "Did I hear the word 'fight'?"

Matt made a sour face. "It was just a scuffle—"

"You were trading *blows* with the guy," I pointed out. "And in front of your mother, too."

Gardner lifted his eyebrows and gave Matt a closer look. "Really?"

"Yes," I said. "Really."

"Cool," said Gardner, sounding impressed.

"No. Not cool," I said.

Gardner shrugged and went to work restocking.

"But, Clare," said Matt. "Lebreaux insulted my mother—"

"No," I pointed out, "he insulted *you*."

"You weren't even there for most of it."

"That's why I asked you to enlighten me," I said.

"Remember when Lebreaux was pushing my mother to franchise the Blend label? Well, after she shut him down and we exposed his little scheme to take over this coffee-house, Eduardo apparently gave up coffee and went to Asia. He hooked up with a Chinese tea concern. Now he's importing and marketing specialty teas in partnership with a very wealthy family in Thailand."

I took another sip of my espresso. "Nothing wrong with that. Does he want to open tea shops?"

"More like kiosks within existing businesses—specifically upscale department stores and high-fashion boutiques. *Sound familiar?*"

Replace tea with coffee and it was the very concept Matt was proposing. "It's a wonder you didn't murder Le-breaux on the spot."

"Instead, I was very mature about the whole thing. I mean, Tad could have warned me, but when I thought it over, I realized he'd included two magazines in tonight's invest-ment presentation like-up and two designer labels. Each had their own business plan and unique approach, and when he first scheduled the seminar, he actually thought Lebreaux and I had distinct enough products—tea versus coffee."

"That's crazy," I replied. "You're both going after the same real estate to set up shop."

"Yeah, well, we weren't at first. Lebreaux's initial prospectus had mentioned nothing about kiosks. He was seeking investments for straightforward importing only—to supply existing tea shops and specialty gourmet food stores with his imported Asian teas. But one week ago, he changed his business plan to include 'tea kiosks inside high-end department stores and clothing boutiques.'"

"One week ago!"

"Clare, obviously, he stole my idea and meant to go head-to-head with me. When he started to make a stink about making his presentation first, he was told we'd go on alphabetically. That's when he blew his top. Made threats. Accused me of stealing *his* idea, which I suspect was his plan all along—to discredit me in public. That's when I had a few words for him—words, I swear, only words—and his hired thug dragged me out onto the deck . . ."

I sighed. "I believe you, Matt. Lebreaux is an expensively dressed snake. And his bodyguard was the one who got physical first, so I doubt he'll try to file any charges."

"His man wouldn't cooperate anyway. The guy was tough, but he couldn't swim to save his life." Matt shook his head. "I ended up keeping him afloat until the crew dragged us aboard again."

"You're kidding."

"He actually thanked me before we got ashore."

I smiled. "Well, at least someone in this place avoided prosecution this week." My remark began as a joke, but it reminded both of us of Tucker's plight and brought us down again.

"Doesn't matter," he replied. "I saw Mother's face before I went overboard, so maybe it's for the best. The Blend still belongs to her."

I was about to tell him what Madame had told me—that

she was actually pleased her son was finally taking an interest in the future of the business, even taking it to a new level, though it was not where she would have chosen to go with it. But I stopped myself from saying a word. I assumed Madame herself would want to break that news to her son—and that Matt would prefer to hear it directly from his mother instead of through his ex-wife.

We finished our espressos without saying anything more, just listened to a smooth, almost melancholy number by Four on the Floor, which was currently playing over the Blend's sound system. Suddenly, a noisy group of late-night revelers came through the front door, chatting and shrieking with laughter as they approached the counter.

"Oh, god," I muttered, checking my watch.

Matteo took one look at my overwrought expression and said, "Let me pitch in, Clare. Go upstairs, change, relax. I'll close up."

With that, Matt rose from his seat, and came around the counter to begin taking drink orders. As I turned to go, I heard him add with an edge to his voice—"It's about time I did something useful around here."

That's when I hesitated. *Should I have told him?* Tad's investment seminar wasn't all that important in the scheme of things. Matt didn't know that now, but he would soon realize that Madame was with him instead of against him. Once she discussed her feelings with him, I knew she'd help him secure all the investment money he might need from her late husband's business contacts.

I turned back to tell Matt not to worry. To assure him that Madame did understand what he was trying to do—what he needed to do as a man—and she was sure to help him now. But when I stepped back to the coffee bar, the new customers were already swarming the counter and shouting out their drink orders. Resolving to wait up for Matt instead, I turned once more and headed for the back staircase.

My ex and I had been over a lot of bad road together, but that didn't mean I didn't care about him. *No one*, I thought, *especially my own business partner, should have to go to bed thinking himself a failure.*

Sixteen

~∾∾∾∾∾∾∾∾∾∾∾∾∾∾∾∾∾∾∾∾~

"CLARE!"

The voice was familiar, but I couldn't see the person calling my name. Darkness surrounded me, my legs and arms were buoyed, and the rhythmic sound of waves lapped against my ears. The lights of Manhattan towered above me, and I realized I was floating in the Hudson River.

"Clare! Help!"

Nearby, the rank water began splashing back and forth like the agitation cycle in a washing machine. Not more than twenty feet away, Tucker was flailing around in the river. He was drowning!

"Clare, help me!"

I swam toward him, but a thick fog suddenly descended, obscuring the monumental towers of light. I peered into the dark mist. "Tucker, where are you? I can't find you!"

"Clare, hurry! Please!"

I swam forward again, tried to cut through the fog. Finally, I saw his face ahead in the water. His eyes were fearful, his expression panicked. He was going under! I lurched forward to take hold of him, but suddenly I couldn't move. My arms felt weighted, my legs paralyzed. Now I was sinking too.

"Tucker, hold on!" I tried to shout, but my mouth slipped below the surface and the foul smelling river water swallowed my words.

"Hi, cupcake!"

My father, the short, wiry Italian with the manic energy of an excited terrier, rowed by on a dinghy, chewing the stub of a cigar. Forward and back, forward and back, he leaned with carefree ease, pulling the oars that glided him along right past me.

"Just remember what I told you, cupcake. Before they try to scam you—and they always will—stick it to 'em and twice as hard!"

"Dad!" I cried.

"Gotta, go, cupcake. Another day, another half dollar." Then he was gone, rowing right along, disappearing into the fog.

"Clare!"

The voice was male but not my father's or Tucker's. I looked up from beneath the water. Above the undulating surface of the river, the foggy night had magically turned into blazing day. A large yacht drifted nearly on top of me. Standing on its deck, Matteo wore a white suit and bow tie. His hair was neatly trimmed, his face closely shaved, and his smile nearly blinding. But after he spotted me in the water, his brilliant smile faded.

"Clare, sweetheart, hold on! I'm coming!" he cried.

He was about to climb over the rail and jump in with me when Breanne Summour, head-to-toe in a hot pink night-gown, the color of Ricky Flatt's corpse, strode up and whispered in his ear.

He nodded, then laughed and swung his leg back, behind the rail. Suddenly, Joy was there on the yacht's deck, moving up to the rail, squeezing in between them. "Bye, Mom! See ya!" she called, waving happily in her white sundress.

As I sunk deeper and deeper into the river, I watched all three of them wave, then turn from the rail and disappear, laughing and raising glass latte mugs. I closed my eyes, devastated beyond words . . .

I opened my eyes—

Matteo's face was next to mine. His jawline was no longer clean-shaven but shadowed with dark stubble. His brown eyes appeared tired.

"What the . . ." I murmured.

"You were having a bad dream," Matt informed me. "You were moaning."

I was also still floating, I realized, but not in water.

"Where am I?"

"On your way to bed."

I blinked again and saw that Matt was carrying me with ease in his muscular arms. He was cresting the short flight of carpeted stairs and heading into the duplex's master bedroom—my own. Matt had his own, smaller room at the other end of the short hall, for his infrequent layovers in New York.

On and off since I'd moved into the Blend duplex, I'd tried to get Matt to see reason and stay in hotels for the ten or so days a month he came back to New York. But he balked, claiming the cost was an outrageous expense that would bust his budget, especially when he had legal permission from the duplex's owner (his mother) to reside here for free. He suggested that if I didn't like it, I could always move out. But I couldn't afford to live anywhere near the Blend without taking on roommates—and at my age, I wasn't about to go back to collegiate living. Neither did I want to give up my residential right to the duplex or end up driving any great distance to do the sunup to sundown job of properly managing the business. So Matt and I agreed to be French about the whole thing and try to make the arrangement work by giving each other our distance and our privacy.

At the moment, neither was in play. I was wearing nothing more than a white cotton nightgown, beneath which were slight lace panties and no bra. I was small but my breasts weren't, and the intimate grip of my ex's hands was quickly having an unwanted effect on them.

"Matt, it's okay," I told him gently. "You can put me down."

He did, on the four-poster bed of carved mahogany— part of Madame's exquisite antique bedroom set. Then he sat down beside me, sinking into the white cloud of a comforter. I shifted into a sitting position, pressing my back against the gaggle of goose feather decorative pillows piled up against the headboard, and yawned, aware my ex-husband was no longer wearing the Good Humor Man white suit and bow tie from my bizarre dream. His faded blue NO FEAR—CLIFF DIVE HAWAII T-shirt stretched across his hard chest, gray sweats covered his legs.

"You're okay then?" he asked.

"Sure . . ." I rubbed my eyes and sighed, trying to remove the lingering images of Tucker drowning, my father rowing, and Matt and Joy laughing as they carelessly waved *ciao* to me. I even glanced around the room to get my bearings.

Like the rest of the duplex, Madame had decorated the master bedroom with her romantic setting on high. The carved ivory-colored Italian marble fireplace was not original to the room, neither was the gilt-edged French mirror above it, or the fleur-de-lys medallion in the center of the ceiling, from which hung a charming chandelier of hand-blown, pale rose Venetian glass. The walls had been painted the same pale rose as the imported chandelier while the door and window frames echoed the same shade of ivory as the silk draperies pulled back from the floor-to-ceiling casement windows.

My favorite aspect of this room, however, wasn't the furnishings, the fireplace, or the draperies. Hanging on practically every inch of free wall space were priceless original oils and sketches from artists my former mother-in-law had known over the years—including Jackson Pollack, whom she'd attempted to sober up more than once with hot, fresh pots of French roast, and Edward Hopper, one of my all-time favorites, who'd sketched this very coffeehouse for Madame on one of the marble-topped tables three floors below.

"I found you passed out in a living room chair," Matt informed me. "Java was curled up in another. You both looked too cute to disturb, but I figured you'd be pretty sore in the morning if I left you in that position. Java can fend for herself."

"I didn't mean to pass out." I yawned again. "I didn't get much sleep last night."

"You didn't get any, Clare." He smiled. "I didn't mean to wake you."

"It's okay . . . I was actually trying to wait up to talk to you—"

"What did I do now?"

He'd cut me off before I could mention the kiosks. But it didn't matter anyway. Something more important had come up before I'd dozed off.

I shook my head. "Not you Joy."

Matt's body stiffened: aloof to anxious in less than sixty seconds. It didn't surprise me. Even when we were married, Matt's focus on Joy had been hyper-protective—when he'd been around, that is. When he'd been off on his coffee buying and brokering expeditions, an entire week could go by without even a call. For that, it had been hard to forgive him.

"She's fine, Matt. At least . . . I think so."

"What do you mean, you *'think so.'*" His tone was censuring, but I overlooked it. When it came to extreme sports, my ex-husband had no fear. When it came to our daughter's well being, however, dread was his middle name.

"Take it easy," I said gently. "When I first came upstairs, it wasn't that late—just after eleven. I called her home phone and she didn't answer. Then I tried her cell . . ."

"And?"

"And an obviously drunk boy answered."

Matt stiffened again.

"After a number of tries, I got out of the boy what was going on. He was a friend of Joy's. Apparently, she'd left her bag at the bar at some dance club and went to the restroom with a few people in their group. I asked how long she'd been gone—and he said a half hour or so but that was no big deal because, as he put it, 'Joy obviously didn't go to the restroom to rest.' Then he hung up."

"*Which* club, Clare?"

"He wouldn't tell me. I tried calling her cell again, but the boy must have turned off the phone because I just got her voice mail for an hour after that. And before you ask, I left messages on her cell and her apartment phone, demanding that she call me no matter the hour."

Matt stood up, rubbed his neck, began to pace the polished hardwood floor in his bare feet.

"What are you thinking?" I asked.

"I'm thinking she's doing drugs. What else?"

"I thought about that, too, but it just isn't Joy. For one thing, where would she get the money?"

"Clare, you're so naïve. The club scene revolves around young professionals with money to burn. They drink and do drugs because things are good, and they drink and do drugs because things are tough. Joy's an attractive, outgoing young woman and she has a lot of friends. It would be easy for her to fall in with a crowd that would share their recreational drugs with her. She wouldn't need money for that."

"I know my daughter. She's too smart for that. We had long talks about this stuff when she was in high school. She has her head on straight. Besides, she saw what . . ."

Matt stopped his pacing. "What? Saw what?"

"Nothing."

He folded his arms and his biceps swelled, obscuring the NO part of the NO FEAR scrawled across his faded tee. "Saw *what*?"

"You. What the cocaine did to you. To us."

Matt's expression faltered. "I thought she was too young to . . ."

"Children, even young ones, pick up more than you know." I was ready to point out that if he'd been around more, maybe he would have noticed how very perceptive his young daughter had been, but I'd made that point so much and so often over the years, Matt had to be sick of hearing it—and I was certainly weary of repeating it.

He uncrossed his arms, sat back down on the bed, met my eyes. "After rehab, I never did drugs again, Clare. You know that, don't you?"

"I know it was hard for you. I know you're straight now. I just pray you stay that way."

"Junkies don't need a reason to start. But they definitely need one to stop . . . I had more than one reason. I had two." Matt's hand came to rest on my leg. I felt the warmth seeping beneath the nightgown's thin layer, warming my thigh.

I swallowed uneasily, trying not to react to his touch. "Matt . . . I . . ."

The phone startled us both as it rang at my bedside. I reached for it. Matt was faster.

"Hello."

"Daddy?"

I leaned a little closer to hear Joy's end of the conversation. Matt didn't appear to mind. In fact, he angled his own body, making the proximity even more intimate.

"Joy, where the hell are you?" he asked, taking the words right out of my mouth. "What's going on? Are you all right?"

"I'm fine. I'm home. You and Mom should get a life. I'm over eighteen and I was out with friends, that's all. Relax, okay?"

Matt sighed. "Muffin, we're just worried. Your mother told me a drunk boy answered your cell phone and—"

Joy began to laugh. "That was Tommy. He's so crazy. He also should have told me you called. I didn't get Mom's message till I got home."

"Ask her about the restroom!" I hissed.

"Is that Mom?" snapped Joy. "Is she listening in?"

"Your mother is understandably worried, Joy. That boy gave her a heart attack. She thinks you're doing drugs."

"I'm not."

"And why should I believe you?" Matt demanded.

"Because I'm your daughter and I totally don't lie." She sighed. "Look, I have a few friends who like to do it for fun in clubs sometimes. I hang with them, but I never do the drugs, okay? So, listen, it's late and I'm really, really tired. I'm going to bed. Okay?"

"We'll talk about this again," Matt promised her.

"Fine, but not at one in the A.M. Please, Daddy? Good night."

"Good night, muffin."

Matt hung up. Then he and I stared at each other in silence for at least thirty seconds. This whole over-eighteen thing was definitely uncharted waters.

"What do you think?" he finally asked. His expression, usually confident and cocky, was so lost and helpless that I nearly burst out laughing.

"I think I'm relieved Joy called us back tonight," I told him. "And because she called, I do believe she's telling us the truth."

"But she's hanging with friends who do drugs," Matt pointed out, "which is why I'm going to have a long, straight talk with her."

"That's a very good idea. She'll listen to you."

Matt grunted and rubbed his eyes as if he were trying to ward off a monumental headache.

"She worships you, Matt, you know that, don't you?"

Matt stopped rubbing his eyes and looked up. "I've never heard you say that before."

"Sure you have."

"No, Clare. What I usually hear is how I wasn't around enough for her, which was completely true. And I honestly can't see why Joy would want to listen to her old man when he's just an ex-drug addict . . . a fuck-up."

"Matt, stop. Of course she worships you. You're her father—her exciting, larger-than-life, super-cool, globetrotting, *no-fear* father. I reached out and underlined those very words on his shirt. He caught my hand.

"Matt . . ."

"Are you just saying that because I'm so pathetic?" He brought my hand to his cheek, kissed my palm. "I mean, did you hear me on the phone?" He lowered his voice to a ridiculous octave. " 'Your mother is *understandably* upset.' "

I smiled. "That's the thing about parenthood. No matter how cool you think you are, you are doomed to one day channel Ward Cleaver."

As I spoke, his lips moved, touching the inside of my wrist and elbow. Then he shifted closer on the bed, pulling my arm around his waist, he angled in to nibble my throat, my ear, my jawline . . .

I sighed. It felt good. Too good. "Matt," I said softly. "I don't think—"

"Clare, sweetheart," he whispered into my ear, "please . . . don't think."

Then his lips were on mine, warm and gentle, like an espresso, relaxing and rousing at the same time. The weight of his body pressed me farther into the sea of pillows. I closed my eyes, and I was floating once more. It felt like a dream, but not a bad one . . . and I let it carry me away.

Seventeen

~~~~~~~~~~~~~~~~~~~~~~~~~~~~~~~~~

The dawning sun streamed in with a blinding vengeance. I yawned and arched my back, wondering why I hadn't drawn the drapes. Beside me Java trotted across the clean, white sheets and arched her back, too, then she butted her coffee-bean colored head against my arm in her usual demand for attention. As I petted the silky length of her, a Technicolor scene from *Gone with the Wind* flashed through my sleep-addled brain. I saw Scarlett awakening and stretching like a cream-fed feline the morning after Rhett carried her off to bed.

Now what brought that to mind? I innocently pondered. Then my hand stilled on Java's fur.

Oh, god.

I sat up, the sheet fell down. I was naked.

"Good morning, sweetheart!"

A bare-chested Matteo strode through the master bedroom door as if we were still married. I snatched up the sheet to cover my naked breasts and realized with an appalling jolt that what had happened between us last night hadn't been a dream.

Oh, no, I thought. *No, no, no!*

Matt wore gray sweats and nothing else. In his hands were two mugs of freshly brewed coffee. The aroma told me at once he'd broken into his special reserve Harrar for what he undoubtedly presumed was a "special" occasion.

He set the mugs on the rosewood nightstand, dropped onto the bed beside me, and immediately began to nuzzle my neck. "Mmmm, Clare, sweetheart . . . it's been so long . . ."

"Y-yes."

"You've changed, you know . . ."

"Changed?"

He pressed closer, the heat of his naked chest penetrating the thin layer of sheet between us. "You were so . . . different last night . . . ."

"Different?"

"Less inhibited . . . more open . . . passionate . . ." He continued to nuzzle my neck, my ear, moved to brush my lips. "You even taste different . . . like vanilla . . ."

I squirmed. "Must be the new shampoo and body wash. It comes in comfort food flavors. Strawberry ice cream, butter rum, gingerbread . . ."

"Mmmhmm . . . good to know . . . I like variety . . ."

I closed my eyes at that. Matt may have changed in some ways, but I knew he would never change in others. *That's always been our problem, Matt,* I thought. *You like variety a little too much.* I touched his chest. As gently as I could, I pushed him away. "You made me your special reserve, didn't you? I can smell it."

He nodded, reached for one of the mugs and handed it over. As we sipped in silence, enjoying the incredible flavors, I tried not to panic.

Giving in to Matt had been a big mistake. Huge. And I should have known better. Notwithstanding the fact that our getting back together was something his mother had wanted for years—as well as our daughter—I had been through the mill too many times with my ex to want to risk getting my heart ground up again. Besides which, our relationship was changed now. We were business partners in the Blend, and I didn't want that disturbed. Matteo was the best coffee buyer and broker in the business as far as I was concerned, and the Blend couldn't lose that.

Stupid, stupid, stupid, I railed at myself. My resistance to Matt's physical charms had failed only a few times since our divorce over a decade ago. Usually, I could rely on one of my memories of Matt's extracurricular sexual romps to break "the mood" more effectively than an icy spike through my spine. But last night I couldn't see Matt as a betrayer, only as a father and, shockingly, as a maturing man. He'd been hurting and open and unbelievably vulnerable. I wasn't used to seeing him like that, his cockiness stripped away, his need so raw. It got to me . . . that and the fact that this mattress hadn't seen any action for quite some time.

"Might as well enjoy the Harrar while you can," Matt said, interrupting my thoughts. "Since my kiosks are a bust."

"Oh, god, Matt. I'm so sorry—"

"It's not your fault, Clare. My mother's a stubborn old bird, and I obviously screwed up the presentation by going after Lebreaux—"

"No! Listen to me," I told him. "The reason I'm sorry . . . I was waiting up to tell you, but then the whole thing with Joy at that nightclub happened, and then we . . . you and I . . ."

"Wait, back up," said Matt. "What slipped your mind?"

"Your mother confided in me last night, while you were waiting on the taxi line. She thinks the future of the Blend is ours to decide, not hers. She understands what you're doing and why. She's not going to stand in your way."

"Jesus, Clare. Why didn't you tell me that last night!"

"Because at first I thought *she* should be the one to tell you, in her own words, but when I saw how hard you were taking it, I knew it was something you shouldn't have to wait to hear—and then I . . . I got distracted. I'm sorry. But, Matt, I know she thinks your work in Ethiopia is phenomenal. And I do, too, by the way."

His outraged tone softened. "She told you about the Harrar wet-processing?"

"Yes, and it's just astonishing. You know, your mother

will help hook you up with investors. She's kept in touch
with all of Pierre's old contacts. You won't have to go it
alone or trust Tad to . . ."

My voice trailed off. The mention of Tad brought back
all the things I'd witnessed on the *Fortune* the night
before—not to mention my dream of Tucker drowning.
And I realized with a sickening stab of guilt that while I was
enjoying amazing coffee in the luxury of an elegant bedroom, my good friend was alone and afraid in a Riker's Island jail cell.

I threw off the covers and got out of bed. I was totally
naked, and I felt Matt's eyes on me as I darted around the
room, dressing for the day. But I didn't care. I didn't have
time to.

"Listen to me, Matt," I said as I pulled on a pair of panties and hooked on a bra. I told him all about Lottie Harmon's business arrangement with Tad Benedict and Rena
Garcia, and about the intimate moment they'd shared together on the dark deck—a moment I had secretly witnessed from the shadows.

"Sounds like they're desperate to sell," said Matt,
scratching his chin as he leaned back against the four-
poster's headboard and continued to sip his coffee. "And I
doubt Lottie is in a position to buy them out."

"Yes, but she obviously has no idea they're selling."

"It doesn't matter. Together, Tad and Rena control exactly half the business and they can sell fifty percent of the
stock if they want to. It's their right, Clare."

"Yes, but I'm sure they were trying to sell even more.
Tad didn't even blink when Madame said she wanted thirty
percent. Instead, he pressed me to buy some, too."

"That doesn't make sense," said Matt. "Why sell more
stock than you own? You're bound to get caught."

I thought it over as I zipped up my jeans. "Selling more
stock than you own was a great scam in *The Producers*. Do
you remember that Mel Brooks movie?"

"I thought it was a play."

"Only lately. It was a movie first—"

"A movie *first*?" said Matt. "I thought they made movies out of plays and not the other way around."

I waved my hand as I jerked open one of the deep drawers of the mahogany dresser and rifled through my sweaters. "You've been out of the country too often. With the exception of *Chicago* and *Phantom*, it's often the other way around now, which is why Tucker is always bemoaning the state of the American musical."

"*Anyway*—"

"Sorry. Anyway, in *The Producers* the two crooks sell shares in a Broadway musical to dozens of investors, figuring on a flop, so they can secretly keep the extra capital. It would have worked, too, except the show was a hit and they get stuck owing lots of people lots of money."

"That's a stretch."

"No. That's it!" I cried. "And Tad's plan can only work if Lottie's line is a flop. With Lottie dead, it's game over—no wonder he tried to kill her."

"Clare, you are really getting carried away here," said Matt, watching me button on a pale yellow sweater, a suggestive little smile on his lips. "You would have to be pretty desperate to do something like that."

"But that's what I'm trying to tell you," I said, striding back to the closet. "They both sounded desperate. Tad and Rena talked like they were in some kind of trouble and needed a lot of money fast."

"What kind of trouble?"

I shook my head. "No clue."

"Well, I have a different theory about Ricky Flatt's poisoned latte—"

I gritted my teeth. "Not that stuff about Tucker being guilty again—"

"It's Lebreaux."

"Oh, Matt, come on. You're just royally pissed at the guy."

"No, listen. Lebreaux's idea would be even more lucrative if he served both tea and coffee. And he has a vendetta against us, don't forget. What if he hired someone to sabotage the Blend's reputation by making it look as though our coffee was killing people?"

"I suppose you could be on to something," I conceded. "But who did he hire—" I stopped dead in the middle of pulling on a low-heeled half-boot. "Violet Eyes," I murmured.

"Who?" asked Matt.

"Violet Eyes," I repeated. "There was an Asian girl with Lebreaux," I explained. "She was tall and—"

"Had violet eyes. Long, straight, black hair, down to her hips. Legs that went on forever."

I raised an eyebrow. Put a gorgeous girl in a room and Matteo Allegro would have her measurements calculated faster than an M.I.T. mathematics professor.

"She was at Lottie's party," I informed him as I finished pulling on my boots. "I greeted her at the door myself. And Esther and Moira said they saw her come up to the coffee bar in that critical window of time when Lottie's latte must have been poisoned."

"I'd call that pretty incriminating, Clare."

"Unless it was just a coincidence. I mean . . . she and Lebreaux could have met for the first time tonight on the *Fortune* for all we know."

"No," said Matt. "She was with him the entire time in the yacht's 'backstage' stateroom where all of us presenters were waiting to go on. She came with Eduardo Lebreaux, Clare. And she never said two words to anyone but him."

"Okay, but I still say Tad is acting way too suspicious not to question."

"I think you're wrong."

"I think I'm right."

"So what are you going to do?"

"Not me, Matt. It's what *you're* going to do."

"Oh, please, Clare, don't involve me again—"

"I just want you to set up a meeting with Tad downstairs. Invite Rena over for coffee, too." I checked my watch.

"Speaking of which, I have to get my butt down there and open."

As I grabbed the thick set of keys from the top of the dresser, Matt crossed his arms and narrowed his eyes. "Why?"

"Why? Because we're in the business of serving coffee and it's time to open."

Matt smirked at me. "Clare, why do you want me to set up a meeting with Tad Benedict and Rena Garcia?"

"Because," I replied with a smirk of my own, "that Detective Starkey isn't the only broad around here who can weasel a confession out of a suspect."

EIGHTEEN

∿∿∿∿∿∿∿∿∿∿∿∿∿∿∿∿∿∿

As it turned out, Tad was too busy with his second *Fortune* seminar to meet with Matt any sooner than Friday morning. Consequently, Thursday came and went in a blur. From dawn till dusk I served customers, then spent most of the evening in my office juggling schedules, balancing books, finalizing the payroll—and, frankly, hiding from Matt.

After helping Gardner close, I quickly slipped upstairs to the master bedroom, firmly shut the door, and prayed my ex-husband wouldn't come barging in. He didn't. In fact, I didn't see my ex again until Friday morning.

I was behind the coffee bar, tidying up after the morning rush, when Matt's strong hands came down on my shoulders and began a slow massage. I jumped under Matt's touch, not accustomed to—and not wanting—this new round of physical intimacy.

"I looked in on you late last night," he rasped against my ear, "but you were already sleeping so soundly, I didn't have the heart to wake you, even though I was tempted . . . and, honey, was I tempted."

I closed my eyes and silently cursed. I had no one to

blame for this but myself, and it was now up to me to delicately redraw the lines that I never should have allowed to be erased in the first place. I didn't want to hurt him, or our working partnership, but it was time I gathered my courage and opened my mouth, which I was about to do when Matt added—

"Tad's here."

I looked up, spied the paunchy, balding, elfin-faced man at the front door, and knew the subject of my relationship with my ex would have to be put on hold.

"Take him up to the second-floor lounge," I told Matt. "I'll be up in a minute with coffee."

Matt greeted Tad and they shook hands, then my ex led our guest upstairs. I looked for Rena, too, but there was no sign of her. I put a service for four on the tray anyway, added a few muffins, a carafe of freshly brewed Breakfast Blend.

"Back in a little while," I told Esther.

Her jaw dropped. "It's just Moira and I as it is," she complained.

"I'm doing this for Tucker," I whispered over my shoulder as I hefted the tray and climbed the stairs.

I found the two men seated in the circle of overstuffed chairs situated next to the now-cold fireplace. Matt was grinning and chatting amicably. If there were any hard feelings about the overboard incident on the *Fortune* Wednesday night, I couldn't see them. When I arrived, Tad rose to greet me while Matt took the tray and set it on the table. I poured and served.

"I brought Matt some good news," said Tad, offering a self-satisfied smile. "Someone read his prospectus and expressed his wishes to invest in the kiosk idea. Apparently this individual is a real fan of the Village Blend."

"I really appreciate this, Tad," said Matt.

"And my way of apologizing for the . . . incident with Eduardo Lebreaux," Tad replied.

"Forget it," said Matt with a wave of his hand.

"No, really. I didn't want you to think I was some kind

of idiot," Tad insisted. "Lebreaux's prospectus came in two months ago and I figured one's tea and the other is coffee so why not include them both . . .".

Tad shrugged sheepishly. "Then without my knowledge, Lebreaux withdrew his old prospectus and submitted an 'updated' one last week to my people."

"Oh, really?" said Matt.

"The first deal involved importing exclusive teas from an eastern producer. The second prospectus was quite similar to yours, except the retail ideas were for marketing tea instead of coffee. . . ."

Matt shot me his *didn't I tell you* look. Tad noticed the exchange. "Anyway," he continued. "It's obvious that you and Lebreaux have a history."

"I'll say," muttered Matt.

"I should have caught the bait and switch, but between the TB Investments seminar and Fashion Week, Rena and I have been running around like crazy."

I spied an opening and jumped in. "How is Rena?" I asked, reluctant to confront Tad without Rena present. I was hoping she might still show.

Tad glanced at his watch—a Rolex, I noted—and a shadow of concern crossed his round face. "Actually, Rena should have been here by now. I called her early this morning from my office—several times—and left messages on her answering machine and cell. She should have picked up or called back by now, but some last minute crisis with Lottie probably has her hopping. I told her to meet us here if she possibly could."

There was a pause. Tad added cream to his coffee, tasted his cup, and gushed about the quality of the brew. He tried to appear normal, but I could tell there was an undercurrent of concern—no doubt he was wondering why we asked him here. I pressed for time, but ten more minutes passed without a sign of Rena. Tad shifted impatiently and glanced at his watch once again. I decided to pounce before he bolted.

"Matt tells me you were selling stock in a number of fashion lines," I began.

Tad nodded. "There was an offering for a very promising start-up. Designer Wylbur Watley left Martyrdom to start his own label, Sentinel Hill. I think we got some nibbles for him."

"I heard you were selling Lottie Harmon shares as well . . . a *lot* of shares, in fact."

An uncomfortable silence descended. Tad looked at Matt, who shifted in his chair, suddenly fascinated by tiny dust motes floating in the late morning sunlight pouring through the windows.

Tad set his cup aside, met my gaze. "What are you trying to say, Ms. Cosi?"

I dropped all pretense. "I know for a fact that you and Rena are closer than you let on—"

"My relationship with Rena Garcia is none of your concern—"

"Except when you and she form some kind of clandestine partnership to sell Lottie Harmon's business out from under her."

Tad's face flushed red, and I thought he was going to jump down my throat. Instead he slammed his fist on the table. I winced, and Matt sat up straight.

"You don't know what you're talking about," Tad cried. "Lottie Harmon made Rena and me both very wealthy— and she treats Rena like the daughter she never had. We would never do anything to hurt Lottie."

"Then why sell the stock?"

"I'm doing it to *protect* Lottie, Ms. Cosi," Tad replied. He stood up to go, but I stood right in front of him. I wasn't letting him get away without some answers.

"I have it on good authority that you and Rena are in desperate straits. That you need money in a hurry, and have to sell your shares in Lottie Harmon to raise it. Tell me. Are you bankrupt, or is it blackmail?"

I expected more anger and outrage. Instead Tad's shoulders sagged. He slowly sat back down.

"Why do you want to know, Ms. Cosi? Why do you care?"

"Because my employee . . . my *friend* . . . is sitting in

jail right now, because someone tried to murder Lottie Harmon and used my coffeehouse to do it."

Tad's eyes were suddenly haunted. "You mean the poisoning?"

I nodded. "With Lottie out of the way, you and Rena would become the sole owners of her label."

Tad shocked me by laughing. "You are so wrong," he said, shaking his head. "So off the mark . . ."

"Enlighten me then."

Tad took a swallow of air, then a gulp of coffee. When he spoke again, his voice was quiet, guarded.

"Over a year ago, when the label was just getting launched, Lottie somehow got Fen on board. It was a real coup—a miracle, really. Fen dropped his long-standing relationship with Verona accessories to take Lottie on. Anyway, Rena had been working for months for practically no salary. Her savings were gone and she was borrowing from friends. There was no guarantee that Lottie's label was going to catch on, and she was starting to get very nervous about her financial security. She was feeling desperate . . ."

Tad gulped more coffee, black this time. "Anyway, Fen sent over patterns for some of his fall line, so Lottie could design the accessories. . . ." He glanced at his watch, looked in the direction of the empty staircase. "Someone approached Rena pretending to be an international knockoff merchandiser. He offered her seventy-five thousand dollars for copies of Fen's designs. Like I said, she was desperate, owed money. So Rena took the deal. She copied the designs and traded them for cash." Tad snorted. "Turned out to be a set-up. Fen himself sent an employee to make the deal—"

"Wait a second," I interrupted. "Let me get this straight. Fen stole his own designs?"

Tad nodded grimly. "The man Fen had sent to Rena made the exchange in some hotel room on Eighth Avenue. A private surveillance firm taped the whole thing. Then, about three weeks ago—around the time Rena and I became engaged—Fen approached Rena and told her the truth. He threatened to go to the police and expose the crime to Lottie. I think Rena was more concerned about what Lottie would think than any jail time she was facing. The two women had become close."

"What were Fen's demands?" I asked. "All blackmailers have demands . . .".

"Rena's shares in Lottie Harmon . . . and mine. After Fall Fashion Week is over and Lottie is finished with her major presentation, he wants us to trump up a reason to want out of the business, and tell Lottie that we're selling him all of our shares. Fen wants to buy our shares and control Lottie's business."

"I don't understand," said Matt, who'd been pretty quiet up to now. "Why try to sell the Lottie Harmon shares at the seminar after Fen threatened you and demanded you sell the stock to him?"

"Rena and I don't want to hurt Lottie," explained Tad. "And we don't want any trouble from Fen. We're hoping if we divest fast, before the end of the week, Fen will have no hold on us. The shares he wanted will be dispersed among other investors, and Lottie will be safe—she'll be able to retain the largest percentage of stock—and control of her business." Tad met my stare. "Like I said before, Ms. Cosi. I was just trying to protect Lottie. I—"

The conversation had become so intense that we didn't notice we were no longer alone until a shadow fell across the table. I looked up, stunned to see Detective Mike Quinn standing there, his sandy, windblown hair longer than usual. He had a five-o'clock shadow despite the fact that it was not even noon yet, and his face appeared gaunt, but his shoulders were as broad as ever. Only after his piercing blue eyes met mine did I notice Quinn was flanked by two policemen in uniform, neither of whom I recognized.

Quinn nodded silently in Matt's direction, then faced me. The ice in his eyes momentarily warned. "Good to see you, Clare."

"Hello Mike," I said softly.

Matt glared, but Quinn didn't seem to notice. His gaze smoothly shifted from me to Tad, turning glacial again as it focused on the paunchy man squirming in the overstuffed chair.

"Are you Tad Benedict?" Quinn asked.

"Yes, I'm Benedict." Tad eyed him suspiciously. "What do you want?"

"I'm Detective Michael Quinn." He flashed his badge. "I need to speak to you in private, Mr. Benedict."

"No," Tad shot back, defiant and worried at the same time. "We'll talk right here. What's this all about, anyway?"

"Do you know a Rena Garcia who resides at the Continental Arms Apartments?"

"Yeah. Sure. She's my fiancée."

I saw the uniformed cops exchange glances, and with a sick jolt of dread I sensed what was coming next.

"When was the last time you saw Ms. Garcia?" asked Quinn.

"Yesterday afternoon before my financial seminar . . . why?" Tad rose to his feet. "Listen, what's going on here. Where's Rena? Do I need to call my lawyer?"

Mike Quinn put his hand on Tad's arm, squeezed it solicitously as he met the man's gaze squarely. "I'm afraid I have some bad news for you, Mr. Benedict—"

Tad froze. "Rena . . . has something happened to Rena?"

"I'm sorry to inform you that Ms. Garcia was found dead in her apartment early this morning."

"No, no!" Tad cried. "It's a mistake!"

Quinn shook his head, reached into his natty trenchcoat, pulled out a Polaroid photograph, and showed it to Tad. I could just make out the face of a woman, raven-dark hair splayed like a crown around her head, her flesh cartoon pink against a blue background that could have been either a carpet or a bedspread.

Tad choked, sagged. Quinn and a blue suit grabbed his arms to keep him from sinking to the floor. "What happened?" Tad groaned, his face pale.

"That's what we're trying to establish, Mr. Benedict," said Quinn. "To do that, we need a statement from you."

Tad's lower lip trembled, his eyes misted.

"You are not a suspect, and you may have a lawyer present at any time," Quinn continued. "Can you accompany us to the precinct right now?"

Tad grunted an unintelligible reply. Quinn nodded, then passed him to the other officers.

"Take him down to the car," Quinn told the uniforms, who led Tad to the stairs.

I expected Quinn to follow them; instead, he turned to face me. I stood and walked over to him. I could see he wanted to say something on a personal level, but the situation was obviously awkward, especially with Matt's eyes boring into my back.

"There was a homicide here the other night," Quinn began. It was not a question.

I nodded. "Someone was poisoned . . . cyanide, they said."

Quinn's eyes held mine. "We believe Rena Garcia was poisoned, too."

I found myself ringing my hands. "Look, Mike . . . something's going on . . . I'm pretty sure—"

"Not now."

My temper flared. "*When* then?"

"Later."

"But I've got to tell you—"

Quinn raised his hand to stop me. "Listen, Clare. I trust your judgement, and I want to hear what you have to say. But I have to take care of this situation first. I'll come back later, okay? We can speak in private?"

This time it was a question. His chin went up, indicating Matt behind me. I didn't turn need to turn. I knew my ex-husband's eyes were on us.

"I'll be here until closing," I said quietly.

Quinn nodded, then headed for the stairs. Matt moved to my side, curled his arm around my waist. Quinn looked back just then, saw the intimate gesture. He frowned and looked away.

"The cop's not staying?" Matt said a little too loudly. "Didn't Rosario's deliver any donuts this morning?"

"Give it a rest, Matt," I said and slipped out of his grasp.

* * *

THE rest of the work day was long and busy. The younger customers never stopped coming. Even the usual lulls between rush hours were nonexistent. I'd told Esther Matt's theory about the appeal of our so-called poisoned coffee and she began calling our patrons "Fugu thrill-seekers."

At four o'clock Esther headed for home, and Moira agreed to stay on. She'd worked until nine the evening before, and agreed to work the extra hours again tonight. I told her how much I appreciated her help. "Don't mention it," she replied. "I want to help Tucker any way I can."

When Gardner Evans arrived with some new jazz CDs from his collection, Moira finally departed. Not until ten did Detective Quinn return. He strode through the front door and approached me at the coffee bar.

"Have a seat," I told him as I foamed up a couple of lattes (his favorite). Quinn took a quiet corner table by a window and I joined him there. He sipped the drink, his blue gaze steady over the rim of the glass mug, never straying from my face.

"I meant what I said this morning, Clare," Quinn began. "It is good to see you again."

Oh god. A caffeinelike jolt that had nothing to do with the shot of espresso in my latte was rocking my metabolism. I counseled myself to keep my mind off Quinn's incredible blue eyes and on the business at hand.

"What happened to Rena Garcia?" I asked.

Quinn sighed and finally broke his stare, looking down into the frothy cloud in his tall glass mug. "That's a police matter—" he tried to tell me, but I was ready for him.

"Don't you clam up on me now, Mike Quinn."

My tone wasn't teasing and it wasn't warm. I'd waited for hours for him to get around to talking to me again, and I swore to myself that he wasn't leaving this coffeehouse until I knew as much as he did.

Mike, who could obviously see I meant business, rubbed his stubbled chin, then took another sip of his latte, a long one. Foam clung to his top lip and he wiped it away with the easy brush of two fingers. He leaned close, lowered his already low voice.

"This morning the supervisor in Ms. Garcia's apartment building received some complaints about loud music coming from the apartment. He knocked, and when he didn't get a reply he used his pass key to enter the premises. That's when he found the victim. The Medical Examiner estimates she'd been dead for ten to twelve hours."

"You said she was poisoned."

Quinn nodded. "Cyanide was used. Forensics examined the dregs of a coffee Ms. Garcia consumed, found traces of poison . . ." The detective paused, locked eyes with me. "It was a Village Blend take-out cup, Clare. That's why I asked you about the poisoning that took place here the other night."

I told Mike about that night. About Detectives Starkey and Hutawa, and Tucker's arrest. He listened quietly to my theory that Lottie had been the original target, and I told him what Tad had admitted to me earlier today—about Fen and the blackmail threat.

"Benedict never mentioned blackmail to me," said Quinn, clearly annoyed.

"He's trying to protect himself," I concluded. "One way or the other."

"What do you mean?"

"If the truth gets out about his involvement with something as shady as Rena's theft of Fen's designs and Fen's subsequent blackmail, it could ruin Tad's investment business. On the other hand, maybe he didn't tell you about the blackmail because he killed Rena himself—"

"No," said Quinn quickly. "Benedict's not a suspect. He has a rock-solid alibi from seven o'clock last evening until almost four this morning."

"What?"

"First he and his staff were conducting some kind of investment seminar on a boat called the . . ." Quinn pulled a worn leather-bound rectangular notebook from the breast pocket of his trenchcoat. "*Fortune.*"

I nodded, recalling Tad's seminars had been scheduled for both Wednesday and Thursday nights.

"After that," Quinn continued, glancing at his notes, "he and his staff traveled together to their investment firm's office and spent most of the night working with Tokyo counterparts on Nikkei stock sales."

"So when did Rena drink the poison?"

"Between nine and eleven o'clock in the evening. And the body wasn't moved. She drank that poison in her apartment."

I thought that over. Could Tad have handed Rena a poisoned cup of coffee before he'd boarded the *Fortune*? It made no sense on the face of it. Who would carry around a cup of coffee for hours without drinking it?

I tried to make the pieces fit another way. "Could Tad have *hired* someone to poison her?" I pondered out loud.

Quinn shook his head. "I don't think so."

"Why?"

"First, my gut. I've seen enough trumped-up versions of shock and grief to judge when it's genuine, and Benedict's reaction to his fiancee's death was as real as I've seen. Second, my background work today showed that Tad Benedict put down substantial nonrefundable deposits on a Hawaiian wedding and honeymoon package, and a realtor was handling the sale of his one bedroom and the purchase of a two bedroom in the same building. The realtor said Benedict was getting married next month and wanted more space."

"And you don't think he could have set all that up to make himself look innocent?" I pressed.

Quinn shook his head. "If Tad Benedict had wanted to kill Rena Garcia for financial gain, he would have married her first before killing her. Then he would have inherited her shares of Lottie Harmon after her death."

"Okay," I said. "Then what if he was simply trying to dump Rena because Fen was blackmailing her? What if he wanted to be free of the entanglement?"

"Why not just cut and run? Why not just break off the engagement, go to Lottie and tell her everything, and let Rena take the fall? No . . . there's no logical motive for Benedict

killing his fiancee. With Rena dead, life gets very compli-
cated. As it happens, Rena has no will. Her shares will be going to her closest living relative, not Tad and not Lottie."

I sighed, agreeing—for the moment—that Tad didn't
look very good as a suspect in Rena's murder.

"But it's good you told me about the blackmail, Clare.
This gives me an in."

"An in? With whom?"

"Starkey and Hut aren't exactly forthcoming, and I
don't want to horn in on their investigation of the Blend
poisoning. But this Rena Garcia murder, it's a separate
case that may be connected so they can't complain."

"Demetrios called them bad cop, worse cop," I said.
"Are Starkey and Hut really that terrible?"

"They're not bad cops. They just have bad attitudes."

"Well, I think you should go after the designer Fen.
Have a talk with him."

Quinn's lips twitched and one eyebrow arched. "Thanks
for the advice, Detective Cosi. He's the first on my list."

I shrugged. "Just making sure you're dotting your *I*s and
crossing your *T*s, Detective."

We sipped in silence for a moment, then I carefully
broached another subject. "I tried to reach you a few days
ago . . . Demetrios told me you were out on leave."

Quinn frowned. "Personal matter . . ."

I was going to let it drop, but Quinn obviously felt he
had to explain. "My wife took the kids on a little
vacation—without telling me. Wait, that's not entirely ac-
curate. She left a note."

"Jesus, Mike, what happened?"

"We had a fight one night. Next thing I know, I come
home from a double-shift and she's gone—took the kids
and hopped a plane to Orlando for a week. I come home to
a note, you know? Needless to say, I panicked. One of her
old boyfriends works at the Disney World resort, and I
thought she'd decided to snatch the kids and leave me."

For many months now, Mike had been confiding in me
about his bad marriage. He'd gone back and forth many

times on the issue of divorce. Finally, for the sake of his young kids, he'd decided to try marriage counseling.

"I thought you said the counseling was helping?"

"I thought it was. But she was obviously acting out. . . ." He sighed in disgust. "When I got down there, it was passive aggressive central. She acted like it was some carefree family vacation that we'd planned for months. For the sake of the kids, I went along." He shook his head. "She pulled the kids out of school, terrorized me, ran up our credit cards on first-class tickets . . . I left cases hanging, victims' families . . . I could have strangled her."

"I'm sorry, Mike."

"I've consulted two lawyers. The estimates for a contested divorce and custody battle . . ." He shook his head. "You can't imagine."

"Believe me, I can," I assured him. "Although I was lucky. Matt never contested my getting Joy."

"That wouldn't happen with me."

"The rewards of full-time parenting outweigh the expenses."

"Maybe so. But those attorneys still need to put their fat fees on a low-carb diet."

"Well, look on the bright side. Lots of lawyers patronize this place. Ultimately, you'd be helping my bottom line."

I smiled. Quinn's grim demeanor cracked, and he laughed out loud. I laughed too, and squeezed his hand. I was about to pull it back, but he held on, caressed my fingers gently with the rough pad of his thumb. I met his eyes. What I saw there made my limbs weak.

Across the room, a throat loudly cleared. I looked up. Matteo was standing there, glaring at us. Quinn noticed. He released my hand, finished his coffee, and rose.

"I've got to go," he told me. "But I'll check back with you after I talk with this Fen character."

"I'd appreciate that," I whispered.

Then Quinn touched my arm. "Don't worry, Clare. With a second murder using the same modus operandi, I predict Tucker will be out of jail in no time. . . ."

I closed my eyes, praying he was right. "Thanks, Mike."

Quinn gave me one last small smile. Then he was gone.

As I bussed the table, Matt approached. "What did the flatfoot want? Did he tell you he threw Tad in jail?"

I ignored the jibe, carried the cups to the coffee bar. Matt followed me behind the bar and pinned me to the counter. He tried to hug me, kiss me. But his gestures weren't simple affection as much as raw possessiveness. Once again, I regretted the other night.

"Want to have dinner after we close up?" Matt asked. "There's a new late-night Thai place on East Seventh."

"Matt, I . . ." My voice trailed off when I noticed a scarlet smudge on my ex-husband's collar. Lipstick, in a garish hue I would never wear.

Matt followed my eyes, found the smudge.

"Jesus, Matt," I snapped, "we just slept together two nights ago—"

"Take it easy, Clare, this lipstick is Joy's—"

"Joy was never here."

"No, I ran into her on the street, an hour or so ago."

I crossed my arms. "And I suppose you had that little talk? About Joy's questionable friends and their drug use?"

Matteo looked away. "I didn't have time. She said she was running late . . .". He could see the doubt in my eyes. "Clare, honestly, I can explain—"

"Forget it."

"Come on, it's almost closing time. Give me a break."

"I was stupid to have ever thought you'd change," I shot back. But I didn't really think myself stupid. I'd been smart—smart enough to have protected my heart from Matt. Smart enough to have already guessed this would happen.

"Clare!" he called as I strode away. But I just kept walking.

ƞINETEEN

~~~~~~~~~~~~~~~~~~~~~~~~~~~~~~~~

THE next day was Saturday. I opened the shop, greeting the baker's Yankee-jacketed delivery boy and my first customers of the morning in a near-robotic state. I couldn't stop thinking of Tucker. I had run out of leads. Even worse, my own decidedly less than brilliant theory about Tad and the late Rena Garcia being the guilty parties now lay on the ash heap of history. I could not have been more wrong about the ill-fated couple, who were not suspects, but victims.

The morning rush came and went, the mail arrived, and I pulled espressos, mixed lattes and cappuccinos by rote. By eleven, Detective Quinn was too busy to return my calls—presumably because he was diligently tracking down the elusive fashion designer Fen. Matteo was off and running on his coffee kiosk planning. And Rena's killer was still on the loose. Then, as I was preparing for the early lunch rush, a bicycle messenger arrived with a hand-delivered package.

"Are you Clare Cosi?"

I nodded and he offered me a clipboard. "Sign here . . . and print your full name here."

I scribbled my name, then wrote it out in block letters. The man handed me a manila envelope; the return address read "Tanner and Associates, Attorneys-at-law." The address was on Madison Avenue. Noting the delivery, Esther Best appeared at my shoulder.

"What is it? Good news I hope."

"Something from Tucker's lawyer, I think."

I ripped into the envelope and found a letter and another envelope inside—this one from the Deputy Commissioner of Corrections, the New York City Department of Corrections.

"Be advised that this authorized pass allows Ms. Clare Cosi and Mrs. Blanche Dreyfus Allegro Dubois to visit prisoner #3244798909, Mr. Tucker Burton of—"

I ceased reading because Esther Best was whooping and *woofing* (a hip-hop generation thing) and drawing the attention of several patrons. "When are you going?" she cried.

"As soon as I can," I said, closing my eyes in grateful relief.

I quickly climbed the back steps and entered my small, second floor office to call Madame. I had been trying without success to arrange a visit with Tucker since his arrest, never imagining how difficult it could be to visit someone once he was incarcerated in what amounted to America's only penal *colony*. Unless you're a relative, it's nearly impossible to visit a prisoner on Rikers Island, and even then you can only see the inmate if they've put your name on an official list kept at the prison. For everyone else, save legal council or members of law enforcement, a request for a visit must be sent to the Deputy Commissioner of Corrections, who receives between 1,500 and 2,000 such requests every month. Typically it takes weeks to receive a reply, usually in the negative.

I'd mentioned the problem to Matteo, who passed the

information on to Breanne. Somehow Ms. Summour's lawyer had managed to cut through the mountain of bureaucratic red tape and the authorization magically had appeared. Though I was no fan of Breanne Summour, at the moment, I was truly grateful for the pass, and I knew Madame would feel the same.

I dialed her number and Madame answered on the second ring. "It's the maid's day off, my dear," she explained. I told her the wonderful news and Madame was as ecstatic as I was.

"I'll be over in an hour," I told her.

Fifty-two minutes later, I flagged a cab on Hudson, climbed in, and told the driver my destinations. "First I need to pick up someone on Fifth near Washington Square Park. Then we'll be going on to Rikers."

The driver did a double take, his dreadlocks flying as he turned his head. "Rikers? Mon, you mean the prison?" he said in a lilting Caribbean accent. He shook his head, his dreads taking flight again. "Lady, I don't even know how to get there. It's in Queens, no?"

"Yes, it's on the north shore of Queens—in the middle of the East River."

"Well, lady, this cab, she don't float. So I'm gonna have to call my dispatcher." While the driver headed over to Washington Square, I pulled out my cell and rang Madame.

"Apparently, cabbies don't know how to get to Rikers Island," I explained.

"Never mind, dear. I'll call my own car service. I'm sure Mr. Raj can help us out."

I informed the cab driver I'd be getting out at Washington Square, and to forget the trip to Rikers. He seemed relieved. On Fifth, I found Madame waiting for me on the sidewalk in front of her building. She was wrapped in an elegant belted, pecan brown coat with faux fur trim on the cuffs, lapels, and turned up collar.

"Mr. Raj insisted on driving us himself. He's made the trip before."

My eyebrows went up. "Did he tell you why?"

She waved her hand. "I did not ask and he did not offer."

A few minutes later, a black late-model Lincoln town car with bright white Taxi and Limousine Commission plates pulled up to the sidewalk. A diminutive middle-aged man with cocoa-brown skin and a thick iron-gray moustache stepped out and opened the door for us.

"*Bonjour*, Mr. Raj," said Madame sweetly.

"*Bonjour*, Madame," he replied to my French-born ex-mother-in-law. Smiling behind his moustache, he wore a well-tailored suit and a deep blue turban.

The ride out of Manhattan was fairly uneventful. We headed uptown and through the Queens Midtown Tunnel, then onto the Grand Central Parkway. As we approached LaGuardia Airport, however, the driver swerved onto a rarely used ramp marked Nineteenth Avenue. The ramp led to a narrow two-lane bridge, the only route to Rikers Island without a boat.

The bridge, largely unknown to most New Yorkers, stretched more than a mile across the East River. As we drove across the fast-moving water, a deafening roar sounded around us and the silver wings and fuselage of a United Airlines plane appeared over our heads. It rapidly descended, flying so low its roaring engines rattled our car windows and I could almost make out passengers in their upright and locked positions. For a moment, my heart stopped—I was certain I was witnessing a passenger airplane crash. Then I noticed the pier on our right displaying a huge sign directing pilots to LaGuardia's runway 13-31. Seconds later, the jet smoothly touched down.

I sighed and sat back. Outside the car's tinted windows, the sunlight played on the rippling waters of the East River. The route over the bridge was a lonely one, patrolled by officers in cars and on foot. Along the way, posted signs warned passengers that firearms, cameras, and photographic devices, tape recorders, beepers and cell phones, and a host of other items were not permitted inside the prison and would be confiscated; that proper identification would be required; and that all visitors were subject to a physical search before entering the sprawling island compound.

During the drive from Manhattan to Queens, I read to Madame from some papers the lawyer had provided, learning the information myself as I read. Apparently the island was named after the Rikers family, who'd sold the giant piece of rock rising from the East River to New York City in the 1880s. The city initially used the land as a dump. Over the next forty-plus years, the size of the land mass quadrupled, a result of the thousands of tons of refuse deposited there. By 1935, the dump was closed and the garbage barges halted as the first jail opened. The Rikers Island Correctional Facility is now one of the largest prisons in the world, comprised of *ten* jails spread across an area half the size of Central Park. There are nine jails for men and one for women, and the entire place has a daytime population of close to twenty-thousand people including prisoners, employees, and visitors.

Two-thirds of the inmates were in the same boat as Tucker—detainees who were legally innocent and waiting for their cases to crawl through the criminal justice system, stuck there because they could not produce bail, or bail was denied them by a judge because of various circumstances. The other third of the inmates on Rikers had been convicted and sentenced already and were waiting for an empty bed in an upstate prison. A smattering—all with sentences under twelve months—actually served out their entire incarceration on the island.

With its own schools, clinics, chapels, grocery stores, barbershops, a bakery, a bus depot, even a ball park and running track, Rikers essentially has become a small town.

After driving through the security gates, we were stopped by a pair of armed guards who recorded our names and asked us the nature of our business. I showed them the official letter from the Deputy Commissioner of Corrections, and we were directed to the Control Building. On the way, the town car nosed its way through a quiet and seemingly deserted two-lane street that was lined by ultra-modern modular buildings erected between aging jails of brick and mortar built half a century ago. Everywhere I looked, fences loomed, twelve-foot-high steel mesh walls tipped by razor-wire.

At the Control Building we were compelled to pass through metal detectors, then I slid the official pass from the Deputy Commissioner of Corrections under a thick, bulletproof Plexiglas window to a bored-looking desk sergeant. He checked our identification—my New York State driver's license, Madame's United States passport—and we were handed off to two female prison guards. They took us to another area, scanned us again, this time with metal-detecting rods and a relatively new machine called an Ionscan, which was capable, we were told, of detecting drug residue in much the same way an airport scanner can detect the residue of explosive materials. One of the chattier female guards told us the year before over three hundred *visitors* were arrested on Rikers for attempting to smuggle contraband in to prisoners—drugs, weapons, bullets, etc.

Finally, we were frisked. The women worked silently and efficiently without meeting our eyes. We were asked to empty our pockets and purses, and our cell phones were confiscated, to be returned at the end of our visit. A few minutes later, another armed guard presented us with plastic identification cards.

"Don't lose these," he warned. "You will be subject to arrest if you do not display these badges at all times."

I didn't doubt it.

Our pass from the Deputy Commissioner must have put us on some kind of VIP track, because we were immediately taken outside by a young Hispanic guard and escorted across the street and down the block to a modern modular building.

I expected the kind of thing you see in the movies—a long table with chairs, bulletproof glass separating you from the prisoner on the other side, a telephone on the table, through which you talk to your loved one. Instead we were placed inside a small windowless room—a cell, really—with a heavy steel door, fluorescent lights, and insulated brick walls thickly slathered with institutional green paint. Madame and I sat on green plastic chairs until the door opened a few minutes later.

We looked up as Tucker entered, a burly uniformed guard twice his size leading the lanky young playwright and actor by his thin arm. I rose to give my friend a hug, but the look of pain and embarrassment on Tucker's face gave me pause.

"Lift up your arms," rumbled the guard.

Only then did I notice Tuck's hands were folded behind his back—and handcuffed. The guard drew a key from his belt, removed the cuffs. Then he acknowledged our presence for the first time.

"Thirty minutes," he said. "If you need me sooner, bang on the door."

The guard turned on his heels and left. The door slammed with a loud clang. Tucker, pale and thinner than I'd ever seen him, rubbed his wrists where the cuffs had chaffed them. His beautiful mop of floppy brown hair was gone—replaced by a crewcut. He looked like a shorn sheep, but despite his obvious torment, Tucker stared at us through grateful eyes.

"God . . . Clare, Madame . . . thank you . . . for . . ." His voice broke as he sat in the green plastic chair beside me, and I took him in my arms. He sobbed, his shoulders heaving.

"I'll get you out of here, Tucker. I swear . . ."

Tucker wiped his cheeks with his hands, nodded, but his face was a mask of doubt and confusion. "How did this happen?" he moaned.

Madame leaned forward, "Are you getting good legal council?"

"The lawyer . . . Mr. Tanner . . . he's doing his best. Says that since the second poisoning wasn't fatal, he can proba-

bly get the charges reduced to reckless endangerment. Mr.
Tanner interviewed Jeff Lugar—"

I sat up. "What?"

Jeff Lugar was the second victim—the tan, buffed boy-
toy who'd been Ricky's date and finished off the poisoned
latte. I'd been desperate for news about his condition. But
after the initial stories reporting the poisoning, the ongoing
details of the case had disappeared from the news cycle. In
a city as big and rich in crazy front page headlines as New
York, even a fatal poisoning at a chic event could become
old news in forty-eight hours. The last report on Lugar's
condition listed him as "critical" and I had assumed he was
in a coma or otherwise unable to give a statement. Obviously, I was wrong.

"Tucker, are you saying your lawyer *talked* to him?" I
asked.

"Yes . . . or someone from Mr. Tanner's office did,
anyway."

"What did he say?"

Tucker shrugged. "Not much. All I know is that from
Lugar's version of the events, Mr. Tanner says he can prove
Jeff was not the intended victim and that his poisoning was
just an unfortunate consequence of the crime . . .".

I sat in silence, mulling over the possibility of getting to
Lugar myself.

"How are you otherwise?" Madame asked in the mean-
time, patting Tucker's hand.

"I think they may move me soon," he said with a
barely suppressed shudder. "Mr. Tanner is trying to get a
psychiatric evaluation for me, which means I would be
moved to a medical facility like Bellevue, but the judge is
resisting . . .".

His voice trailed off and he stared at the wall. Of course I
understood Tucker's concern. Out of solitary confinement,
or "suicide watch," he would be placed with the general
population, mixing with hardened criminals—some already
convicted of heinous crimes. A sheep to snarling wolves.

"It won't come to that," I said firmly. "We'll have you out of here in no time."

"But if we don't manage that trick, I have a few suggestions for surviving this place unscathed," said Madame. "I've learned these tricks from my own experiences."

Both Tucker and I stared at her in amazement. "Are you telling us *you've* been in jail?" asked Tucker.

Madame nodded. "I was imprisoned within this very compound, many years ago," she declared.

"Why?" I asked.

"It's not important," she said with a wave of her hand. "Ancient history . . ."

We both urged Madame to give us details, but she simply refused to elaborate, and her stern expression told us to drop the subject. Of course, we did—one does not "press" Madame.

Eventually, Tucker changed the subject, asking about the coffeehouse, about Esther and Moira. Finally, Madame faced Tucker, took his right hand in hers and looked into his eyes. "I know imprisonment feels like the end of your life, but don't you ever give up hope. Don't look anyone in the eye or they'll take it as a challenge. But don't look away, either, or they will think you are weak."

Tucker nodded with each suggestion.

"Keep to yourself, but do not spurn friendship if it is offered. Deal *carefully* with the guards. If you get too close to them, the inmates will think you're a stool pigeon."

In all the years I'd known Madame, I'd never once heard the words "stool pigeon" (one of my dear old dad's typical terms) come out of her mouth. And as shocked as I was to hear prison advice issued from a woman in floor-length Fen outerwear, I had to admit her suggestions seemed sound.

"Don't be anyone's fool, Tucker," she continued. "But do not assume everyone around you is a criminal or out to harm you simply because they are locked up in here. Most of these inmates are in the same situation you find yourself— blameless, but too impoverished to get bail. They await justice with the hope the system will eventually exonerate them."

Misty eyed, Tucker opened his mouth to speak, but was interrupted by the heavy door swinging open.

"Time's up," said the guard.

We offered Tucker a final hug, and watched unhappily as the guard cuffed him and led him away. The woman who brought us to this windowless room appeared in the door a moment later, then guided us back to the Control Building where we checked out and were given back our cell phones and other personals.

Outside, Madame waved to Mr. Raj, who was parked in the visitor's area. As the Lincoln pulled up to us, Madame sighed deeply. "Oh, Clare, I feel so badly for the boy. I do wish there was something more we could do."

"There is," I replied.

twenty

MADAME and I were both so intimidated by the quiet, ordered oppressiveness of Rikers Island that I don't think we dared breathe normally until we'd crossed the bridge back over the East River and merged with the normal flow of traffic on the Grand Central Parkway.

For once, I felt happy to be stuck in the noisy chaos of pre-rush hour and I gazed out the window, watching an airplane wing its way over Rikers before making a banking approach to one of LaGuardia's runways. I wondered how it would feel to be trapped inside that prison and hear—hour after hour, day in and day out—the whine of airplanes filled with happy, free people going about their lives just over your head.

"Where would you like to go, Mrs. Dubois?" asked Mr. Raj.

Madame offered him a blank stare. "Very good question."

I cursed. "I'm so stupid. I should have asked Tucker where Jeff Lugar is being treated. That's the kind of information that's difficult to pry out of hospital administrators."

Madame leaned forward. "Just make it Manhattan, for

now," she told Mr. Raj, who nodded and continued heading for the Queensboro Bridge.

"Have you a clue where he is, Clare?" Madame asked.

"I believe at least one ambulance came from St. Vincent's," I said.

Madame nodded. "That's a start, my dear." She fumbled in her tiny purse until she located her cell. "Now relax while I make a few inquiries."

Madame dialed her cell, then spoke. "Dr. McTavish, please. It's Mrs. Dubois calling."

The good doctor immediately took the call. No surprise, since Madame had been seeing the man off and on for quite some time now. Well over seventy, Dr. McTavish bore a passing resemblance to Sean Connery. Like the actor who played 007, the esteemed oncologist from St. Vincent's cut an imposing figure even at his advanced age. Unlike Mr. Connery, however, Dr. McTavish had retained most of his iron gray hair.

Madame murmured something sweet to the doctor and the years seemed to melt away from her face as she listened to his response. A few minutes later, she was closing the cell phone and declaring, "It pays to have connections within the healthcare community."

I would have barked, "Spill," but because this was Madame, I politely asked, "What did you discover?"

Madame's eyes brightened—clearly all this detective stuff was up her proverbially dark alley. "Mr. Jeffrey Lugar was brought to St. Vincent's for triage the night of the incident. After he was diagnosed with cyanide poisoning and his condition had been stabilized, he was transferred to the poison treatment center at Bellevue Hospital for long-term care."

Madame leaned over the front seat, touched Mr. Raj's arm. "We'd like to go to Bellevue Hospital. That's on—"

"First Avenue at Twenty-seventh Street. I am quite familiar with the institution, Mrs. Dubois," he replied with a smile.

"Thank you, Mr. Raj."

Madame faced me. "I do hope we can help poor Tucker. He must feel so alone, abandoned, and isolated."

"He knows we're trying to help, that he's not *completely* alone," I replied.

Madame nodded. "Loneliness is a terrible thing. Perhaps *the* most terrible thing. I could face poverty, illness, even death with courage. But not loneliness and isolation . . . I need people in my life, Clare."

"Is that why you received Lottie Harmon so graciously when she returned to New York?"

"That's one reason, of course. But in the past I'd always enjoyed Lottie's company. Unfortunately, the years have changed her."

"Changed her? How?"

"She's just not the same carefree person anymore. Now she's always on edge, you know?"

"What do you mean, on edge? Can you be more specific?"

"Well, let me see . . ." Madame pursed her lips in thought. "Her laugh, for instance. It's so strained. It actually makes me uncomfortable, to tell you the truth. It never used to. And the sidelong glances filled with concern. She's very fussy now . . . a worry wart. Yet she was once so lighthearted, so free and easy. She's just not comfortable in her own skin anymore—it was a trait I'd always admired about her, but now it's vanished."

"I know what you mean. She's too self-conscious. And her manner seems affected—not insincere, so much as strained. Like her laugh—too loud, too strident. Like she's covering up for something."

Madame nodded. "The poise she had. The self-assurance. It's gone . . . But I suppose life can do that to a person."

"What in life, do you think?"

Madame frowned. "A tragedy, perhaps . . . or a succession of romantic or other disappointments . . ." Madame's voice faded. She seemed lost in thought. "I wish I could tell you more," she finally concluded.

It was my turn to frown. "We've run out of clues, I

think. Even this visit to Jeff Lugar—it's an act of desperation. I couldn't tell you what I hope to accomplish."

"Well, don't fret, my dear. It's the decent thing to do," she pointed out. "That man was poisoned in our coffeehouse. The least we could do is pay him a visit. If we don't learn anything from Mr. Lugar, we'll try other avenues."

"Well, whatever happens, I want you to give the good Dr. McTavish *my* thanks."

"He was happy to help. He wasn't aware Jeff Lugar had even been at St. Vincent's or he would have snooped on our behalf much sooner . . . He as much as said so."

I decided to risk Madame's disapproving stare and pry. "Now that we've mentioned him, how are things between the good doctor and yourself?"

It was, of course, a big mistake to bring up romance because Madame turned the question back to me so fast I actually felt a little dizzy—or maybe it was car sickness.

"We were speaking, I believe, about how Lottie Harmon has changed," Madame said stiffly. "And since we are on the subject of *change*, what do you think of Matteo's efforts to remake himself?"

"His newfound entrepreneurial spirit, you mean?"

"I mean the way he looks at you, Clare. Don't you see how differently he treats you?"

"No, actually," I replied, recalling the mysterious lipstick I found on his collar. I sighed, wondering how my relationship with my ex-husband had suddenly become the topic of conversation.

"You must admit that Matteo has taken a new interest in the business."

I nodded, conceding to myself that he'd also taken a new interest in me, at least until something better—something named Breanne—showed up again.

Madame fixed her determined eyes on me. "And I believe he's also shown a new deference and concern for his . . . family."

I sighed. "I admit that Matteo has dropped hints that he'd like to . . . see more of Joy."

"And *you*, my dear."

"He may want that, but it's not something I think is wise for either of us," I replied diplomatically, hoping I'd led Madame to a soft landing.

"But you still love him," Madame shot back—an assertion, not a question. I met Madame's expectant gaze.

"Oh, Madame . . . you know love was never the problem."

Twenty-one

~~~~~~

If I ever write a manual on how to be an amateur detective, I will add a chapter on one of the most important assets any investigator can have—an impeccably dressed elderly woman who arouses absolutely no suspicion and can talk her way into or out of any situation. A woman whose presence is so imperious, so gracious, almost no one will question her motives or rudely ask about her business.

Even in these days of heightened security—bordering on paranoia here in New York City after the 9/11 attacks—Madame was easily able to charm herself past the nurse at Bellevue Hospital's front desk and up to the tenth floor, where we were told Mr. Jeffery Lugar was resting comfortably in a semiprivate room.

Bellevue Hospital occupies a twenty-five-story, multi-million dollar patient-care facility in one of the most exclusive neighborhoods in Manhattan. Founded in the 1600s, the facility includes both adult and pediatric emergency facilities, along with the psychiatric emergency services with which most people associate the place. The entire facility became a part of the New York University School of Medicine in 1968. Currently its attending physician staff numbers twelve hundred and its house staff more than five hundred residents and interns.

Despite its impressive credentials and history, however, once you step out of the elevator and into one of the wards, Bellevue is much like any other hospital—white walls, white-clad nurses and staff, a medicinal smell that barely masks the scent of sickness, decay, and death.

Okay, maybe I'm being a bit too morbid, but aside from the time I spent in the hospital delivering my daughter, Joy, my memories of visiting such facilities are not fond. One of my employees died in such a place, barely a month after I took over management of the coffeehouse again. That was not a good memory, and as I walked the sterile halls, I vowed that I would never again visit a prison and a hospital in the same day.

At the nurses' station, Madame inquired after Jeff Lugar. A middle-aged registered nurse checked the roster. "You'll find Mr. Luger in room ten-fourteen. I believe he already has several visitors, but I'm sure he will be delighted to have a visit from his immediate family."

"Nothing says loving like a visit from Grandma," I whispered.

"Shush, Clare," warned Madame.

But the nurse's assumption proved my assertion—nobody suspects a well-dressed elderly woman of shady behavior. Nobody.

"You'll find Mr. Lugar's room all the way down at the end of the hall, the last room on the left," said the nurse in a chipper voice.

As we proceeded down the corridor, a young man emerged from room 1014 just before we reached it. Before he noticed either of us, I clutched Madame's arm and stopped her.

"Clare? What's the matter?"

"That man," I whispered. "I've seen him before. Twice before."

The person who came out of Jeff Lugar's room was the

young man with the white-blond crewcut—the one Esther Best dubbed the "Billy Idol clone." Mr. Eighties had been hovering around the coffee bar right before the poisoning— at least according to Esther—and then he had been at Tad Benedict's investment seminar. Today the mystery man wore a black silk suit and a narrow scarlet tie; the sleeves of his jacket were rolled up his forearms 1980s style—to reveal a complex map of purple and blue tattoos. A blue and yellow badge dangled from his lapel. I'd seen plastic cards just like them—worn by the Fall Fashion Week staff at Bryant Park when I'd visited Lottie at the large central tent nicknamed the Plaza.

I watched, waiting for the man to turn and see us—and perhaps recognize Madame, too, from our evening aboard the *Fortune*. (Though I'd been in my Jackie O disguise, Madame was now dressed as elegantly as she had been on that night, and a woman of her presence was not easily forgotten.)

A voice called from the room, low and weak. I couldn't make out the words, but I heard Mr. Eighties's reply.

"I'm going to pop downstairs for a soda," he said. "Be right back."

He turned his back to us and headed down the corridor to a second bank of elevators, without noticing us.

"Curiousier and curiousier," I muttered.

Madame lifted her eyebrow, but said nothing. When Mr. Eighties was out of sight, we knocked on the door frame. The man who looked up from the crisp white sheets was a pale ghost of the handsome, virile, tanned young man who had appeared on Ricky Flatt's arm at Lottie's pre-rollout party. His pale face was sunken, his eyes dull. An intravenous tube flowed into his arm and a clear plastic oxygen tube was attached to his upper lip by gauze that wrapped around his head. His flesh was sallow and pale, almost translucent, and his skin seemed as crisp and dry as old parchment paper. When he looked up, Jeff Lugar raised an arm to shield his eyes from the bright afternoon sunlight streaming through a large window. His hand quaked from the effort.

"Jeff Lugar?" I began, stepping over the threshold. "I'm Clare Cosi and this is Mrs. Dubois . . ."

He fixed his eyes on us. They were bright, as if with fever. "Do I know you?" he whispered hoarsely.

I shook my head. "I was at Lottie Harmon's party . . . I saw what happened to you and Mr. Flatt. I just thought I'd pay you a visit . . . see how you're feeling."

Jeff Lugar laughed bitterly. "I'm fine, just fine, or so the doctors tell me."

"Indeed? Why, that's excellent news," Madame said with measured enthusiasm.

"Is it?" Jeff replied. He lifted a hand to brush his shock of hair away from his face. Once again, the limb trembled so much I couldn't look away. Jeff Lugar followed my gaze, then lowered his arm quickly.

"Neural damage caused by oxygen depravation," he explained. "Another delightful effect of the cyanide. There's some brain damage as well, though I'm told it's nominal—whatever *that* means."

Jeff Lugar tried to laugh again, but coughed instead. When the hacking intensified, I stepped forward and poured him some water. He drank with rasping gulps.

"Thanks . . . the oxygen makes my mouth dry." He tried to pass me back the plastic cup, splashed water on my wrist and arm.

"I'm sorry. I'm . . . I'm not the man I used to be."

I sat in silence for a moment, while Madame gently queried Jeff Lugar about his home and family, his health and situation. When I spied an opening in the conversation, I jumped in.

"Do you know why someone would want to poison Ricky Flatt?"

"Maybe because Ricky was a little bitch."

I blinked.

"Look," Jeff Lugar rasped. "I can hardly blame that waiter for poisoning Ricky. Flatt was such a turd sometimes, the way he was goading his ex-boyfriend . . ."

"Were you jealous of Ricky's old flame?"

Jeff shook his head. "No way. I couldn't even stand Ricky. I was only there that night because Ricky insisted I come. Said it would boost my modeling career. It would be good for me to be seen—with him . . . or so he claimed."

"So you're sure it was the waiter who's guilty?"

Jeff shrugged. "Who else? That's who the police say did it and I believe them. Who am I to argue with the police?"

"Maybe Ricky wasn't the intended victim," I prodded. "Maybe someone else was supposed to die and you and Ricky just got in the way."

Jeff nodded. "That's what my friend Bryan said happened. He was there, too. Saw the whole thing. I guess it's possible."

"Who's Bryan?"

"Bryan Goldin. You just missed him."

"White-blond buzz cut? Billy Idol look?"

Jeff Lugar nodded. *Mr. Eighties revealed at last*, I thought.

"Will you be getting out soon?" Madame asked.

"I'm being moved to a rehab facility upstate, a six-month stay—that's how long the doctors say it will take for me to fully recover my . . . capacities . . ."

We conversed for a few more minutes, until I noticed Jeff Lugar getting weaker. I touched Madame's arm and we said our good-byes.

"That poor boy," Madame sighed. "He looks simply terrible."

"At least he's above ground."

"Yes, but I fear he has a long road to recovery."

I could see Madame's heart ached for Jeff Lugar. I was sad for the man, too, but my mind was more focused on Bryan Goldin. In a city of ten million people and a fashion industry of thousands he'd turned up three times now. At the rollout party, Bryan Goldin had seemed unattached, yet on the yacht he appeared to be a member of Lebreaux's entourage. Now here he was again, this time as an apparent friend of the unfortunate Jeff Lugar. Suddenly Matteo's off-the-wall theory about Lebreaux working behind the scenes to destroy the Village Blend's reputation sounded more plausible. Could Lebreaux actually be using Bryan like some kind of demented hit man—even if it meant spiking a latte with cyanide and committing a totally random act of murder? Was it possible that Bryan missed killing Lottie, harmed a friend instead, and now felt guilty?

Madame and I rode the elevator down to the lobby. We were about to leave the hospital when I spied Mr. Eighties on his way back up—presumably to Jeff Lugar's room. He slipped past us without a glance, stepped into an empty elevator.

I squeezed Madame's arm. "I'll be right back," I whispered. Then I stepped into the elevator next to Bryan Goldin. We were the only two occupants as the doors closed and the elevator ascended.

The button for the tenth floor was already glowing, but I tapped it anyway. The doors slid shut, I pressed my back into the corner and glanced at the young model. He glanced at me in return—just a quick look, the way people check one another out in elevators. It was clear he hadn't recognized me, or was very good at feigning indifference if he had. Of course, I didn't exactly stand out in a crowd— not the way Goldin did with his buffed appearance, stylish, expensive clothes, dyed hair, and outlaw tattoos.

The elevator gave a jolt, then started to rise. If I was going to pounce, it was now or never. "Excuse me, but you're Bryan Goldin, right?"

He blinked in naked surprise. Then the curtain of cool indifference descended. "Yes," he said.

"I saw you the other night. At Lottie Harmon's party."

He squinted, took a closer look. "Do you work for a designer label? Or maybe a magazine, Ms . . . ?"

"Cosi. Clare Cosi. Actually I saw you at the party, and the other night, too. On the yacht with Mr. Lebreaux."

Goldin shifted uncomfortably, glanced away, then poked the elevator button impatiently.

"Are you a friend of Lebreaux?" I asked, forcing a smile. "I've known Eduardo for years . . .".

"I know Lebreaux," Goldin said, allowing the statement to hang there.

The elevator stopped at seven. The doors slid open. I thought Bryan was going to bolt but he stayed, using the distraction as a chance to turn his back on me. Two conversing nurses stepped into the elevator. One pressed the button for eight, then someone called from the corridor and the two women hurried out of the elevator again. The doors closed and Goldin and I were alone again.

"I bet you're a model," I cooed.

"Sometimes," Goldin muttered.

I wondered about his connection, if any, to Lottie's runway show with Fen tomorrow. "Do you model for Fen?"

Bryan Goldin curled his lips in a near-perfect imitation of Billy Idol. "Of course."

Of course? Odd choice of words, like it was a given or something. Was it simply confidence bordering on arrogance? Or something else? I was about to ask another question when the elevator stopped on eight and the door opened. No one got on, and we waited for a moment. Then, as the doors were about to close, Bryan Goldin slipped between them and hurried down the corridor. I tried to follow but he'd timed his exit perfectly and the doors closed in my face.

On the tenth floor, I walked back to Jeff Lugar's room and peered inside. Save for the quiet hiss of the respirator, the room was silent. Jeff Lugar was alone, sleeping soundly. I wanted to see if Bryan would return, but after fifteen minutes he still hadn't, so I walked back to the elevator.

Twenty-two

⟨⟨⟨⟨⟨⟨⟨⟨⟨⟨⟨⟨⟨⟨⟨⟨⟨⟨⟨⟨⟨

As Mr. Raj drove us back to the West Side of Manhattan, I told Madame what I'd discovered—which wasn't much, in my estimation.

Bryan Goldin knew Lebreaux and he'd modeled for Fen. But all that got me was a legitimate reason for his being on the *Fortune* and at Lottie's party. I also brought Madame up to date with Rena Garcia's murder. "Eduardo Lebreaux might have had a motive for instigating the poisoning at the Blend. But he has no motive I can see for poisoning Rena Garcia, which pretty much rules out Matteo's theory that Lebreaux is behind all this."

"Eduardo is a cad and a criminal," said Madame, "and he may even be capable of murder. But only if it's in his interest, and I must agree with you, Clare, that I don't see the motive for murdering Rena Garcia, that poor girl. If Eduardo were truly behind it, wouldn't he have waited for a more public affair to poison someone with a Village Blend drink?"

"Like tomorrow's runway show," I automatically replied, and then cringed at the thought that the murderer might indeed be striking again at that very event, which meant I had less than twenty-four hours. I massaged my temples, feeling a headache coming on. "I have to solve this, Madame."

"Yes, my dear, but how?"

I leaned back in the car seat and gazed at the passing shops and restaurants, the crowded sidewalks. I tried to remember some of the cases Quinn had discussed with me while he was drinking latte after latte at my coffee bar over the last few months.

Okay, Mike, how would you think through all this?

Think out loud, Clare, I could almost hear him advise me. *Take it step by step. First, tell me what you know. . . .*

"The murderer's first target wasn't random, and it wasn't Ricky or Jeff. It was Lottie. I'm sure of it. And since we know Rena was the second target, what does that tell us? Who would want Lottie and Rena dead?"

"Tad Benedict?" offered Madame.

"Detective Quinn ruled him out and for now I have to agree. But, according to Tad, Fen was blackmailing Rena for control of the label."

Madame's eyes widened. "So *Fen* is the guilty party!" she cried. Then her face fell and she shook her head, looking down at her lovely pecan-colored, fur-trimmed Fen coat. "Oh, what a shame. Such a talented designer."

"Yet . . . it still doesn't quite fit," I said, tapping my chin. "I mean, Fen killing Rena makes sense. He tried to blackmail her. Maybe he found out about her and Tad's plans to cut and run by selling their shares to other investors. He might have become angry and killed her—or had her killed. But why would Fen have tried to kill Lottie herself? She's the sole creative talent behind her label, so killing her means killing the label too."

"It sounds to me like Fen wants to control Lottie Harmon, not kill her," noted Madame. "And there may be more than one motive for that."

"What do you mean, more than one motive?"

Madame smiled enigmatically. "Fen and Lottie were an item years ago."

"An item?"

"Lovers."

"Lovers?" I echoed. "But I've known Lottie for over a year, and I've never even seen her in the company of Fen. There's nothing about them in the gossip columns or paparazzi photos that I can recall either."

"These days, Lottie is only interested in Fen in terms of the business. Nothing else. I was curious about it, of course, and I asked her about him a few times, but she said she has absolutely no interest in her old flame as anything but a business associate and that's the way she wants it."

Sounds like Matteo and me, I thought. *Or at least it did until I screwed up and slept with him.* But I didn't share that particular thought with Madame. Instead, I said, "So you think there might be a sexual dimension to all this? That Fen is trying to possess more than Lottie's label?"

Madame's eyebrow rose. "It certainly explains his going to such extreme lengths to obtain the stock. When passion is the motivation, better judgement tends to go out the window."

"Didn't you say something else about Lottie earlier today? You thought the years had changed her?"

"Yes, that's right. Less comfortable in her own skin. You know, more than once, I asked her why she quit the business, asked her to fill in the blanks about her years living abroad, but she always glossed over the answers, turned the subject to another topic—and always with that strained, high-pitched laugh."

"She did that to me, too. She's very guarded about her past."

I met Madame's eyes and we both nodded, obviously thinking the same thing. Lottie's past was sure to hold some valuable answers. Just then, Mr. Raj pulled up to the coffeehouse. I kissed Madame good-bye and thanked her for her help.

"Do let me know what you discover, my dear," said Madame, her eyes once again bright with obvious curiosity.

"Of course."

As I stepped out of the car, I could see that the "Fugu thrill-seekers" were still out in full force. The East Village crowd—with tattoos and multiple body piercings—loitered on the sidewalk around the Blend's old wrought iron front bench. No doubt they were waiting for one of their numbers to drop dead from a poisoned take-out. As I passed through an odd-smelling cloud, I sensed not everyone was smoking tobacco.

Entering, I saw Esther servicing a line of customers at the counter, Moira and Matt were busily mixing coffee drinks behind the bar. Either things got crazy and my ex had volunteered to pitch in, or Matt was deliberately exercising his barista skills in anticipation of demonstrations for investors in his kiosk scheme.

Esther spied me as I rushed by and was about to call out. I shushed her with my hand, then flashed her ten fingers. "Back in ten minutes" I mouthed to her. Then I raced up the spiral staircase in the dining room.

Inside my small, second-floor office I tossed my purse on the desk, peeled off my coat, and fired up the computer. Since I knew next to nothing about the history of Lottie's label, I decided to use the Internet to see what I could turn up. I began by Googling the name "Lottie Harmon." The search yielded 9,003 entries. I narrowed the search by entering "history of Lottie Harmon label." That brought me a workable 1,456 entries—workable because hundreds of links were essentially the same story, a reprint of a long and uninformative (for my purposes anyway) press release issued by Rena Garcia when the label was resurrected last year. I eliminated all of those entries and narrowed the search to the early 1980s—the first blush of the Lottie Harmon line. I came up with a tidy 717 entries and began calling them up.

After eliminating the useless links, the most common of which was a widely reprinted Associated Press Hollywood glitz and glamour story featuring the passage ". . . Morgan Fairchild and *Lottie Harmon* accessories . . ." I ended up with only 295 entries. Realizing this might take longer than I thought, I began to look through them. I struck gold on the fifth entry, when I followed a link to a 1980s nostalgia Web site.

The homepage for EightiesNeverDied.com featured a montage of pop culture icons posed along the lines of the old album cover for the Beatles' *Sergeant Pepper's Lonely Hearts Club Band*. There were television stars like Larry Hagman as *Dallas* heel J.R. Ewing; Candice Bergen as Murphy Brown; Don Johnson looking suave as Sonny Crockett on *Miami Vice*; Johnny Depp, Richard Grieco, and the rest of the cast from *21 Jump Street*; Michael J. Fox; and Al Bundy.

Music was represented by Devo sporting their signature red plastic domes, Madonna looking anything but virginal, Billy Idol's sneer, Boy George, Duran Duran, George Michael, and Michael Jackson. Featured movie stars came from the signature films of the era—Jennifer Beals in her oversized sweatshirt from *Flashdance*; Tom Cruise in his skivvies from *Risky Business*; Harrison Ford's *Indiana Jones*; Arnold Schwarzenegger flexing pecs as *Conan the Barbarian*; Michael Douglas, hair slicked back as Gordon Gecko from *Wall Street*; and a knife-wielding Glenn Close in *Fatal Attraction*.

In the background, presiding over all, the twinkling eyes of President Ronald Wilson Reagan, The Gipper. Down either side of the page were plenty of links to various aspects of life in the 1980s, all with catchy titles like "Decade of Greed" for the business section (though it seemed to me there'd been as much or more greed and ruthless dishonesty during the dot bomb bubble of the 1990s), "We Are the Music," "The Vices of Television," "Cold War," "Idol Worship," "Go Goth," and more of the same.

I followed the link dubbed "Shoulder-pads and Leg-warmers" and found an eighties fashion page with a list of articles. Most of the features, I learned, had been culled from the fashion magazines of the day, the pages dutifully scanned and posted on the site by its webmaster—probably in violation of numerous copyright laws. There were articles about Michael Jackson's lone glove, the fashion sense in *Dallas* and *Miami Vice*, male makeup. Finally I spied a link called "Spangles" and recalled that Lottie Harmon had invented the famous glittering tie-bar. I hit the link and it took me to a *Trend* magazine article from 1980 titled "Designing Women."

The piece featured a captioned photo taken at New York, New York, one of the trendier Manhattan discotheques of that long-gone era. The scene was a crowded dance floor with three women in the foreground. The central figure appeared to be the scarlet-haired Lottie of over twenty years ago—in her early thirties. Below the photo the caption read "The rewards of working for Lottie . . . sushi, and an evening at a hot new club." I looked at the two other women in the frame. Both appeared to be younger than Lottie. One was a very pretty brunette, the other had a plainer face, blond hair, and was very heavyset.

A second photo showed another scene in the same nightclub, apparently the same night because Lottie and the pretty brunette were wearing the same clothes. Between the two women was a good-looking man in a suit who was about Lottie's age—no identification in the caption.

Lottie stood at the man's right, her armed linked through his. At the man's left was the pretty brunette. She stood gazing at him, her hand on one of his broad shoulders. There was something about the brunette's look that told me she felt more than mere friendship for the handsome man, and I wondered who she was.

I began to read the old article, and in the first few paragraphs was startled to learn that "Lottie Harmon" wasn't a single person. Three people originally had formed the Lottie Harmon label—Lottie Toratelli, Harriet Tasky, and Lottie's younger sister Mona Lisa Toratelli. However, it was Lottie who became the public face of the company. I checked the photos out again, wondering if the pretty brunette at the handsome man's side was Mona Lisa Toratelli or Harriet Tasky.

The article brought up more questions than answers. The biggest? If Lottie Toratelli had returned to New York to resurrect the Lottie Harmon label, then what had happened to Harriet Tasky and Lottie's sister, Mona Lisa? What had happened to the three women's original partnership?

I saved my search results, printed the *Trend* article and the two photographs from the EightiesNeverDied.com Web site, then returned to Google.

This time I typed in "Lottie Toratelli." I received one hit. That same *Trend* article I'd just read. I couldn't believe it. "Just like that, Lottie Toratelli is no more," I murmured.

Clearly, Lottie had taken pains to make sure she was only identified as Lottie Harmon in any future articles or photo captions. I didn't have time to search all the Lottie Harmon references, so I quickly attempted to find out what had happened to her old partners.

First I typed in "Mona Lisa Toratelli." I received seven results. Six didn't tell me anything remarkable, but the seventh held something shocking—Mona Lisa Toratelli's obituary filed by the Reuters news service.

Apparently the young woman had perished in 1988 in a tragic accident. Mona Lisa was described only as a "designer" for Lottie Harmon who had been on a gem-buying expedition in Bangkok, Thailand, when tragedy befell her. Details about her death were sketchy. It seemed Mona Lisa fell from a hotel balcony, but it was easy to read between the lines and see that authorities thought she might have jumped. The obituary also mentioned she was survived by a six-year-old daughter, but there was no reference to the father's name or his whereabouts.

Harriet Tasky was somewhat easier to trace. A Google search led me to a Web site for a vintage clothing business in London called "Tasky's Closet" which was owned and operated by Ms. Tasky. There was no home address or phone number for Harriet Tasky anywhere on the site, however, and the "Contact us" button was addressed to "The Webmaster."

So, I thought, Mona Lisa is dead and Harriet Tasky is

living across the Atlantic on a business venture of her own. I wondered if the original Lottie Harmon partnership had been dissolved as a result of Mona Lisa's death. I also wondered if Lottie and Harriet had parted as friends, or if there had been any acrimony.

Lottie had been living in London, too. If Harriet had some sort of vendetta against her former partner, it seemed to me she would have attempted something before now . . . unless she was jealous of Lottie's resurrecting the label.

I considered e-mailing "The Webmaster" a set of questions for Ms. Tasky, pretending to be a journalist looking for answers. It was pretty much a long shot, but it was worth a try—unfortunately, it would have to wait until later. At the moment, I had to check in on my own business. I glanced at my watch and winced, realizing my "ten minutes" of research had ended up taking over forty-five.

Before I raced down to the Blend's main floor again, I grabbed the pages I'd downloaded from the printer bin. Because of the way it printed out, the last page of the article lay on top of the pile. Only then did I notice the byline on that decades old *Trend* magazine article—Breanne Summour, the current grand dame editor-in-chief of that very magazine. I bit back a curse. Like it or not, I would have to have a talk with Ms. Summour.

I stepped quickly from my office and descended the spiral staircase to the main floor of the coffeehouse. Wan light from the setting sun shone through the tall windows. I spied Gardner behind the counter, Esther moving toward the front door. I headed her off.

"Where's Matt?" I asked. "I need to talk to him."

"He went upstairs after Gardner showed up. Said he had to go out tonight and wanted to get ready."

I gripped Esther's shoulder. "How do you feel about overtime?"

Esther made a pouty face. "Tonight?"

"Time and a half—and a fifty-dollar bonus."

Esther stripped off her coat. "You've got a deal."

"Great!" I raced for the back stairs.

Inside our duplex apartment, I knocked on Matt's bedroom door and received no reply. Then I heard the sound of water running and I moved down the hall to the closed bathroom door.

"Matt? Are you there?"

The door flew open. My ex-husband stood in front of me, his sculpted chest bare, a towel wrapped around his lean hips, shaving cream lathered on his jawline.

"What?"

"I need to speak to Breanne."

His eyes narrowed. "Why?"

I showed him the article.

He scanned it, shrugged, and handed it back. "What's the big deal?"

"Nobody, not even your mother, knew Lottie Harmon was three people. Breanne did. I need to find out what else she knows about these women. Are you going to see Breanne again?"

"I'm seeing her tonight," he admitted, turning back to the mirror and picking up his razor. "I've been invited to the *Trend* magazine Fashion Week bash. . . ."

"I'm going with you."

Matt rolled his eyes and began to shave. The hot water ran as he dragged the razor down his jaw. Drag and rinse. Drag and rinse.

I folded my arms and waited.

Drag and rinse. Drag and rinse.

"Matt!"

"Fine," he finally replied in a tone that told me it wasn't. But he'd been married to me long enough to know arguing would be futile.

"Great," I said.

"One condition," he warned before I dashed off to change.

"What?"

"No dressing like Jackie O."

Twenty-three

⊙⟳⊙⟳⊙⟳⊙⟳⊙⟳⊙⟳⊙⟳⊙⟳⊙⟳⊙⟳⊙⟳⊙⟳⊙

"CLARE, you look beautiful."

At Matt's unexpected compliment, I nearly tripped on my four-inch heels. "Thanks," I replied, thinking he looked pretty good himself, leaning casually against the Blend's coffee bar with his athletic form draped in a slate gray suit, an azure dress shirt worn fashionably open at the collar.

I teetered toward him across the Blend's polished plank floor, trying earnestly to recapture my ability to balance on fashion forward stilts. When I reached the counter, I spread my hands.

"See, not a pillbox hat in sight."

Matt seemed less interested in my lack of Jackie O hat than in my ample J.Lo cleavage, now displayed by the plunging neckline of a chic, aqua Prada wrap dress I'd bought on deep discount at the Chelsea Filene's Basement. I'd worn it once, for Madame's New Year's Eve party last December. Matteo had been in Rio at the time—so, of course, he hadn't seen it, or the striking Y necklace of translucent blue stones that had caught my eye at a local artisan's fair.

"You're going to be the hottest woman at the party," said Matt with a smile.

"That's sweet. But I needed a shoehorn to squeeze into this thing. And let's get real. This party is a Fashion Week event. The women will be so willowy they'll make Twiggy look like a rhinoceros."

"My point exactly, babe," he teased. "Twiggy don't come with that cleavage."

I nearly blushed as Esther, who'd been listening from behind the counter, wrinkled her brow. "Who's Twiggy?"

Matt and I stared at her, then exchanged mournful glances.

"What? What did I say?" she asked defensively.

I waved my hand. "It's an old person thing."

Matt smiled and offered his arm. "Our horsepower and buggy await."

I said goodnight to Esther and Gardner and eagerly took my ex-husband's arm—less out of a desire to feel his prominent bicep than to make certain I didn't fall on my face in front of my staff. With all my crazy running around this week, their respect for me was already waning, and I was still getting used to the heels.

We sauntered through the Blend and out to the waiting limousine, eyes following us, and I knew why: Matt and I made an attractive couple. Instantly, of course, I cursed my own powers of observation. Was I going mental? *This outing with my ex is strictly business. All business. Totally business.*

On the sidewalk, I noticed it had rained briefly while I'd been getting ready, and the wet streets were ablaze with reflected light. At the curb, a limousine driver stood waiting, and I was surprised to see that even our chauffeur was dressed in a formal black uniform, cap included.

Clearly, Matteo had bypassed the typical Queens-based, leisure-suited limo rentals and sprung for the Manhattan executive service. He'd spared no expense in his effort to put forth a sophisticated image to potential investors—though I recalled that the last time I'd seen him looking this polished he'd ended the evening by tumbling over the side of a yacht and into the Hudson River.

"This is nice," I said, my hands running across the supple leather seats. I'd made the comment innocently. By the way Matteo took my hand and squeezed it, however, then smiled suggestively at my cleavage, I realized he'd taken it a whole other way.

"This *is* nice," he replied and leaned toward me. His freshly shaved jawline was sweetened by the subtle scent of an expensive cologne.

I extracted my hand from his and pushed him gently away. "I have enough excitement on my plate tonight."

"As I recall," he said leaning close again, "you never had trouble juggling more than one thing on your plate."

"Matt, please," I said, pushing him back once more. "This isn't a date. I'm only coming tonight to ask Breanne some questions about Lottie."

He sat back, sank into the leather upholstery, and folded his arms. "You know, Clare, this Nancy Drew fantasy you're living. Maybe it's a sign of something."

"Like what?"

"Like maybe you're ready to see more of the world. Do more than just be a mother and a coffeehouse manager."

I laughed. "What do you have in mind? Bungee jumping in Borneo? Surfing in Malaysia? A quickie with you and some beach bunny in Rio?"

"How about coming back with me to Ethiopia, to the plantation, and help us change the way the coffee business is done in that part of the world . . . hopefully for the better."

I almost laughed again, but checked myself when I realized Matteo wasn't kidding. I shook my head. "That isn't going to happen."

"Why not?"

"For one thing, I can't trust you—"

He sat up. "What? That lipstick thing again. I told you, it was Joy—"

"Drop it, Matt. I'm no fool. Not anymore. In that respect I have changed. For the better."

Matt frowned, acting wounded. He glanced out the window.

"Anyway, it's not just the lipstick and you know it," I said in a conciliatory tone. "If you were to let me down again, at least I know I can always run back to New Jersey with my tail between my legs. I did it once and survived— but things would be different in a place like Ethiopia. Where you go, in the wild parts, I'd have to trust you with my life."

"You think I'd let anything happen to you, Clare? Christ, you're the mother of my daughter. The woman I—"

"Let's drop it, Matt," I said quickly. "Now is not the time and this is not the place."

Fortunately uptown traffic was surprisingly light considering Saturday night's pre-theater crush, so before Matt could press his argument any further, we were already rolling up to the front door of the Pierre. Located on Fifth Avenue at Sixty-first Street, this grand hotel sat directly across from Central Park, one of the most expensive addresses on the face of planet Earth. The place was so pricey, in fact, Madame once told me that Dashiell Hammett, who had stayed there in 1932 while working on *The Thin Man*, couldn't pay the massive bill he'd run up, so he'd thrown on a disguise and tiptoed out.

After the limousine halted, Matt emerged, then took my hand and helped me exit. Clearly, there were no hard feelings on his part, or maybe *hard* feelings wasn't the best way to put it. While I was stupidly worried my rebuff had been too harsh, my ex was stealing yet another suggestive glance at my neckline. Obviously, he'd taken my rejection as a challenge. He offered me his arm again and grinned like a conquering victor when I took it. As we approached the glittering entrance, a doorman tipped his hat and we ventured inside, joining the leisurely flow of the high-toned crowd through the gilded, chandelier-draped lobby.

The Pierre, with its French décor and Old World charm, had been a hostelry for very rich since the 1930s when big band sounds were broadcast nationwide via the radio. In the forties, the place served as the home away from home for presidents and prime ministers, princes and kings displaced by war and revolution. Throughout the 1950s, right up to the present, the luxuriously appointed Cotillion Room has been the venue for New York's most exclusive debutante balls.

The Rotunda, where we were now heading, was the hotel's signature room. An extravagant and whimsical space with a domed ceiling, twin curved staircases and a floor-to-ceiling trompe l'oeil mural that covered the circular walls, it was a regular stop among the old money smart set who preferred their high tea and gourmet meals amid five-star surroundings.

Created in 1967, the Rotunda mural really was something to see. The artist, American painter Edward Melcarth, had chosen the three-dimensional trick-of-the-eye style of the Renaissance era but he'd decided to add a twentieth-century twist. The overall intent was to transform the restaurant space into a paradise, giving guests a sense that they were visiting with the gods. Not content with the deities of antiquity, however, Melcarth added to the Pantheon by painting in the cultural giants of his own era. Images of Venus and Neptune were intermingled with more modern figures—including, of all people, a life-sized portrait of Jacqueline Kennedy Onassis.

"You see, Clare, it's good you didn't try to look like you-know-who." Matt said with a laugh as we passed the portrait. "She's already here."

"Ha, ha."

The classic lines of the Rotunda were only marginally spoiled by the hasty hanging of *Trend* magazine banners off the spiral stairs. One of the banners included air-brushed faces of Breanne Summour wearing different expressions, apparently meant to convey her thoughtfulness, her intelligence, her taste.

"Don't look now," sniped a familiar male voice, "but Breanne's taken this whole trompe l'oeil thing to the next level—she's trying to fool us into thinking she has depth."

I glanced into the crowd behind me as casually as I could and saw Lloyd Newhaven in mauve evening clothes and ascot, arm in arm with the strikingly tall, exotic-looking Violet Eyes. The twenty-something Asian woman was wearing royal purple again—a chic, shiny sheath. Her glossy, raven-black hair had been sculpted atop her regal head in high, ribbonlike arches worthy of a Cooper Union architect. I well remembered the last time I'd seen this pair—the night Ricky Flatt was murdered. Then Violet Eyes had turned up on board the *Fortune*.

I squeezed Matt's arm. Hard.

"Ow."

"Shhh, Matt, listen. I need your help—"

"Oh, no, not the conspiratorial whisper."

"Just play along with me, okay?"

"But—"

I turned before Matt could protest further. "Lloyd? Lloyd Newhaven? Look, darling, it's Lloyd." I dragged Matt over, extending my hand.

Lloyd eyeballed me curiously as we daintily shook. For a moment, he looked confused, but then he seemed to remember he'd met me somewhere before. "I met you this week, didn't I?" he asked cautiously.

"Of course! We had a lovely conversation about the stupidity of mandals. Going to Fen's show tomorrow?"

"Wouldn't miss," he said, still looking uncomfortable, but clearly playing along.

I let an awkward moment of silence descend then craned my neck and presented my hand to the tall, exotic Violet Eyes. On the *Fortune* I'd been hiding behind a huge pair of Jackie O tinted glasses, so I doubted very much she'd be able to place me either. Matt was another story, given the trouble he'd gotten into on the yacht's deck—and off it—but I was gambling the girl wouldn't be able to place where or why she recognized him. And, frankly, given this week's massive throng of well-dressed male models, Matt could easily be considered just another pretty face.

"I do believe we've met before," I said, holding firmly to the young woman's hand to keep her focus on me. "But, you know, there are so many new faces this week. Allow me to introduce myself again. I'm C.C."

Violet Eyes looked down at me and shyly nodded. "Pleased to meet you . . . again," she said, her words edged with a slight exotic accent.

I waited but Violet Eyes failed to give her name. *Okay, a little encouragement.* "Do you remember? We do have a mutual friend," I said feigning delight. "Eduardo Lebreaux."

She blinked her big purple ones. "Oh! You're a friend of Eduardo?"

"We go way back, when he used to work for Pierre Dubois. But of course Pierre passed away and now Eduardo is spreading his wings. It's absolutely fabulous, don't you think?"

"Oh, yes! He's a very impressive figure."

"Very impressive!" I echoed.

Matt grunted. I elbowed him.

"But, my dear," I said quickly, "I must confess, I'm not sure how to pronounce your name. May I be so bold to ask you to help me so that the next time I see Eduardo, I can mention I saw you."

"Ratana Somsong," said Violet Eyes slowly. "In Thai, Ratana means crystal."

"Ratana," I repeated. "How beautiful. So, tell me, where exactly did you meet Eduardo?"

"In Bangkok last year, when he first came to meet with my family about our teas. We're very excited to be in business with Eduardo. He is so very kind. He was the one who advised me to hire Lloyd, the absolute best stylist in the world. Lloyd has been so kind to escort me to this week of fabulous shows and parties. What do you think of my outfit and hair—isn't it spectacular? It's all Lloyd!"

"Oh, yes," I said. "It's fabulous, isn't it, darling?" I looked up to see Matt's attention had strayed. I elbowed him a second time. "*Fabulous*, isn't it!"

"Fabulous!" he echoed.

"Excuse me, so sorry, but I see some of my people," said Lloyd, pulling Violet Eyes away. "*Ciao!*"

"*Ciao*, indeed," I muttered.

"What was that all about?"

"Matt, are you not paying attention? Violet Eyes was at the party where Lottie was murdered—*and* she was on the *Fortune*. I wanted to know who she was and why she was with Eduardo."

"Well, now you know. What does it mean?"

"It means Eduardo should definitely stay off the suspect list."

"I don't see why. The bastard's capable of anything."

"But Violet Eyes had a legitimate reason to be on the *Fortune*—Lebreaux is doing business with her family, importing their teas—and she was obviously at the Lottie Harmon party as Lloyd's guest because she's a lucrative client."

"Lebreaux is still scum."

"True. But that doesn't necessarily make him a murderer. You shouldn't let your emotions cloud your judgement—"

I was about to mention that Quinn had been the one to advise me of this, but by this time the milling crowd had moved up to the center of the room—which is where we found Breanne Summour, tall and blond and holding court. Her hair, upswept in an elegant twist, showed off her annoying swanlike neck. Her dress, a costly concoction of haute couture gauze, displayed her shapely legs in front while draping down in back until it trailed dramatically along the floor.

"My god," I muttered, eyeballing the giant shiny rocks dripping from her ears, "those diamonds alone could have covered Dash Hammett's tab."

"What?" asked Matteo.

"Forget it."

Surrounded by fashionistas and sycophants all clamoring for her attention, Breanne appeared to be the chief goddess of the Rotunda's Olympus, appropriately aloof among her coutiers—until her glazed gaze spied my ex.

"Matteo!" the woman cried, breaking from the mob to extend her hand. "I'm delighted you could make it. Then she noticed me. "And I see you brought your—" the eyes narrowed almost imperceptibly—"business partner."

Matteo caressed her hand and they air kissed. "You remember Clare," he said smoothly and tossed me a wink— but his head was turned so far in my direction, I knew Breanne couldn't have seen it.

I nodded at the woman. "Good evening."

"Yes," she said curtly.

Fine, I thought. *I don't like you much, either.* But I knew this was my opening. I was about to ask her some questions about the *Trend* article she'd written over twenty years ago when she moved so quickly to link Matt's arm with her own that she nearly shoved me off my heels.

"I have something special for you," she burbled at Matt while I gave a pretty good imitation of Pisa's leaning tower, and attempted to regain my balance. "In honor of your impending kiosk empire." She signaled to someone waiting in the wings with a snap of her bejeweled fingers.

There was a momentary ripple of anticipation, then I heard gasps of surprise. *Trend* magazine banners parted like curtains as a half dozen waiters appeared, all bearing sterling silver trays lined with flaming wine glasses. Amid the "ohs" and "ahs" I heard my husband's eager-to-please response.

"Café Brulée! Fantastic, Breanne."

"I brought my own chef back from my house in East Hampton and had him whip it up in honor of you."

"I'm flattered, Breanne. Really," Matteo said, glancing sheepishly in my direction.

Breanne touched his arm. "I'll introduce you to Troy later on. He's a protégé of Paul Bradley Mitchell, you know."

I cringed. Paul Bradley Mitchell was the most overrated celebrity chef of the twenty-first century. Joy and I, curious to see what all the hype was about, had recently visited his famous Central Station restaurant. The service was supremely arrogant yet carelessly substandard, which was precisely how the food should have been described in the reviews. Not only *didn't* we ask for a doggy bag, we took the express train right out of that "Station" and into the first Papaya King we saw on our way home, hastily banishing the horrific taste of the man's horrific haute cuisine with a grilled hot dog accompanied by a fruit smoothie—and served to us by a smiling, polite short-order cook, thank you very much!

"Well he's certainly done a superb job," Matteo replied as he accepted his drink. Like a Greek chorus, Breanne's courtiers enthusiastically concurred. The waiters moved among the partygoers, passing out the flaming drinks. And as Breanne led Matt across the room to meet "some people," I felt a presence at my shoulder.

"Interesting."

The voice was soft but strong. I turned to see the speaker was in his forties, with brown, wavy hair. He wasn't unattractive but he wasn't handsome either. His vaguely familiar face was oddly striking with wide-set, almost bulging dark eyes that seemed to be staring at me above a broad nose and pursed-lipped mouth. He stood an inch or two shorter than me, which meant we were probably about the same height in our stocking feet. He held the heated wine glass in one hand, at least ten inches away from his body—and with obvious discomfort. Tongues of flame still licked the rim.

"How do I consume this concoction without being immolated?" he asked, his bulbous eyes still intensely looking into mine.

I laughed politely. "You can blow it out like a birthday candle, or wait until the cognac burns itself out, which means most of it will be cooked away—a tragic waste, in my opinion."

He sighed, raised the glass. "Make a wish." Then he puffed once. When the flames vanished, he sipped the drink and made a medicine face. "What *is* this?" he asked, blinking.

"Café Brulée. Seven parts coffee and one part cognac poured into a heated wine glass rimmed with lemon juice and powdered sugar," I informed him, then blew out the flame on my own drink and carefully sipped. I couldn't hide my reaction, and was grateful Breanne had led Matteo away. The strange man noted my displeasure, however.

"Vile, isn't it?" he remarked.

I sighed, nodded. "The cognac is too good to be cooked away, and the coffee . . . well, it tastes like Colombian, which is fine for a breakfast blend but far too flat and one-dimensional to compete with the cognac. It also tastes like a medium roast. This drink needs a dark roast. And the chef should have chosen a richer, more complex coffee. Something funky and unexpected, like a bean from Indonesia."

The man stared at me in silence for a moment. Then, without smiling, he extended his hand. "I'm David," he said.

"Clare Cosi." I felt as if I should know this man, but I really couldn't place the face or first name. Was he famous? Was it impolite to ask? *Probably.*

We shook. His hands were softer than mine—which had daily kitchen duties at the Blend, with no time for a manicure—but his grip was firm and assured.

"Breanne's newest acquisition," he remarked, gesturing toward Matt. "Tell me, did I overhear correctly? Is he your business partner?"

I nodded. "I'm the manager for the Village Blend coffeehouse. Matteo is the coffee buyer."

"Nothing else between you," he asked with a little smile and a skeptically raised eyebrow. "The way he looks at you . . ."

I smiled weakly. "Matt and I have a history—" I glanced across the room, where he and Breanne were laughing with a small group. "Ancient history."

David laughed. "I see." He took another sip of his drink, then set it down on a gilded, antique table and folded his arms, one hand stroking his chin in thought. "So what do

you think of this Village Blend kiosk idea people are
buzzing about?"

Nice work, Matt. "People are already 'buzzing' about it,
are they?"

He nodded. "It's certainly a viable economic model."

"Is it?"

He laughed again. "You're in business with the man—
and you don't approve?"

Stupid, Clare. "Of course, I approve."

After a moment of silence, he spoke again. "Franchising in some way makes sense, don't you think? I mean, for
a century, your small Village Blend has worked to maintain
high standards and a coffee brewing tradition, yet in just
fifteen short years, a monolithic multinational chain has
swept over the entire marketplace."

"Ah, but I see the mug as half full," I replied, flattered by
his compliment of the Blend. "The way I look at it, coffee
can be gulped like water or savored like wine. That multinational chain has generally uplifted the coffee drinking
experience—made a larger population aware of smaller,
specialty growers in Third World countries. More people
than ever understand what the Europeans have forever."

"Which is?"

"If you're going to pay eight dollars for a good glass of
wine or five dollars for a good beer or hand-rolled cigar,
then it's worth ponying up the dough for a really good cup
of java. Believe it or not, the *Wall Street Journal* did a study
last year and found that wherever there's a chain store, a
mom-and-pop store does a higher volume of business. Sort
of like two gas stations are better than one for attracting
business to any given street corner."

"I see . . . anything that boosts the consumption of specialty coffee helps your store?"

"Yes, of course. Besides, our coffeehouse has a long
and distinguished history and a loyal customer base. The
Blend isn't going anywhere. That big company does its
thing. We do ours."

"But don't you think it's sometimes the little person

who gets ignored, or thrust aside—trampled even—if he or she does not find a way to emerge from the shadows?"

I met David's level gaze, went fishing. "Sounds like you're talking from personal experience . . .".

He looked away, casually scanning the crowd. "I've been to your Village Blend," he replied. "I'm not so sure you'll be able to maintain such high standards with a franchise—even a high-end franchise such as the one your partner is proposing."

A challenge, eh? My spine stiffened. "You might be surprised. Matteo certainly surprised me with his planning and dedication."

"But it's not the direction you would have taken the Blend, is it?"

"No," I admitted. "But as you pointed out, it's a different world now. Next to the corporate giants, we are the little people, so perhaps the Village Blend will have to expand to survive."

David seemed satisfied with my answer. Strangely enough, so did I. In one brief conversation, I'd actually convinced myself Matteo Allegro was on the right track.

"Well it was very nice to meet you, Clare Cosi. I'm sure we'll speak again."

"You are?" I asked, but the mysterious David provided no other explanation. He simply grinned at me as if he were some kind of academic screener and I'd just passed his rigorous exam, then he sauntered off and disappeared into the crowd.

Immediately, I searched the room for Matteo and Breanne. They'd taken a table under the watchful eye of the trompe l'oeil Zeus. Guests were clustered around Breanne like an overdressed fortress, but I strode right through the wall of organza and raw silk.

Breanne saw me coming and her expression darkened. Matteo looked up and nodded when I appeared at his shoulder. Clearly, he was expecting me.

"Excuse me, Ms. Summour, but I'd like to ask you some questions about an article you wrote." I drew the folded print out from my purse and set it on the table in front of the fashion editor. She barely glanced at the paper.

"What's this about?" she asked, annoyed. "Matt mentioned you had some questions for me?"

I lowered my voice to a whisper. "It's about what happened at the Village Blend the other night."

Some of Breanne's hangers-on quite literally craned their necks to hear what I was saying. She noticed the indiscretion and waved them off. I also noticed Lloyd Newhaven and Violet Eyes nearby. They sipped champagne and stared into the crowd, but I was sure they were trying to eavesdrop, too.

"You're speaking of Ricky Flatt," Breanne said. "He never worked for me."

Matteo rose suddenly, and offered me his seat. "I'm going to the bar. Can I bring you two anything?"

I shook my head, but Breanne nodded and handed Matt her unfinished Café Brulée. "Proseco, please. This drink is rather . . . monstrous."

When Matt was gone, Breanne met my stare with her own. "I'm sure I know nothing about Ricky Flatt or why he met his demise. And I don't see how an article I wrote two decades ago has any bearing on his murder."

"Forget about Flatt. I want to know more about Lottie Harmon. You interviewed her for this piece, didn't you?"

"I interviewed Lottie," she replied. "But 'Lottie Harmon' per se is Tony the Tiger, the Eveready Bunny . . . she's a construct, Ms. Cosi, nothing more than the public face of the designer label called Lottie Harmon. The label was formed by two sisters and their lifelong friend. Lottie Toratelli became Lottie Harmon, the public face of the company, and after this article was written she insisted her name be forever after printed as Lottie Harmon. If memory serves, the last name of the label itself is a combination of *Har* from Harriet Tasky and *Mon* from Lottie's sister, whose name escapes me at the moment."

I already knew some of this, of course—except the part about where the "Harmon" name had come from, which was interesting but hardly earth-shattering. I tapped the photograph on top of the article. "Can you identify these people?"

"Well, that's Lottie right there," Breanne said, indicating the laughing woman with the long, bold scarlet hair. Then she sighed and reached into her bag. A moment later she balanced a delicate pair of reading glasses on her patrician nose and examined the photograph more closely.

"The man next to Lottie is Fen. Only he was just plain Stephen Goldin back then. The two were lovers at that time, hot and heavy."

"Goldin," I repeated. "Stephen *Goldin*? Is Fen any relation to Bryan Goldin, the male model?"

Breanne shot me a look that said *duh*. "Bryan is Fen's nephew. That's how the kid got in the business."

Alarms went off in my head, of course. If Bryan Goldin was Fen's nephew, then Fen most definitely had a surrogate at Lottie's party—as well as on board the *Fortune*, where Tad and Rena had been trying to out-fox Fen. And Rena Garcia might have easily accepted a cup of coffee from Bryan if he'd dropped by to see her Thursday night—say, to talk about the runway show on Sunday.

"What about this other woman," I asked, pointing to the very pretty brunette, looking at Fen with big, admiring eyes.

"That's Lottie's sister," said Breanne, tapping her cheek. "God . . . what was her name? She was pretty but such a shy, little nonentity, like the other partner, Harriet. Some famous painting, maybe? Why am I thinking of that bestselling book with a famous painter in the title?"

"You mean *The Da Vinci Code*?"

"That's it! Her name was Mona Lisa." She picked up the printout and stared at the faces in the photograph. "Fen must have dragged her out to the clubs the night this photo was taken. It was Lottie and Fen who did all the networking back then—and believe me Lottie *insisted* it be that way."

Matteo returned with three chilled champagne flutes

bubbling with Proseco and Breanne set the article on the table again. I sipped the alcohol and picked up the printout.

"I see the resemblance now," I murmured, staring at Lottie and Mona Lisa, Fen sandwiched between them. "The noses and chins. Yes, they look like sisters."

"Fen thought so, too," Breanne said with a suggestive tone.

"What do you mean by that?"

"Buzz was he slept with both of the sisters at the same time."

Matteo seemed suddenly interested. "Slept with both women at the same time?"

"No, no," laughed Breanne. "Fen was in love with Lottie, but he had an affair with Mona. Separately." Then she touched Matt's hand. "But I like the way you think, tiger!"

I looked away in disgust, noticed Lloyd Newhaven was urgently gabbing on a purple cell phone. When I glanced back, I found Breanne finally scanning her own article.

"What do you know about the other partner?" I asked. "Harriet Tasky?"

Breanne shrugged. "Not much. She wasn't the big club hopper. Nose to the grindstone type; shy, like Mona, and not very glamorous. Harriet was heavy, too—a big girl, you know." She pointed to the picture of the large blond woman on the dance floor. "That's her, of course, not very photogenic, which is probably why we didn't mention her in the caption. Remember, the eighties was the age of physical fitness. Then again, thin has always been in."

"Marilyn Monroe was a size fourteen," I pointed out. "Or is that piece of fashion history too ancient?"

Breanne made a little moue and squinted. "Whatever."

"Speaking of whatever . . . whatever happened to Mona and Harriet? Do you know?"

I already knew, of course. Mona was dead. And Harriet had opened a vintage clothing business in London. I simply wanted to see how widely known those facts were.

"No idea," said Breanne. "And, frankly, after Lottie Harmon shut down her label in the late eighties, no one cared. There were other designers to spotlight, other fashion forward folk to follow. Maybe those two women are still around, slaving away in Lottie's studio. That's the way she wanted it back then. They created the jewelry, she sold it. Nothing new in the big, bad, big leagues, my dear."

Clearly bored with the topic, Breanne rose, her manicured fingers firmly curling around the finely tailored fabric covering Matteo's chiseled bicep.

To my surprise, Matt actually looked uncomfortable with her possessive touch. He cast an anxious glance in my direction, as if to ask, "Do you really want me to go off with her? Don't you want me for yourself?"

I sat back in my chair and waved my hand. "Go," I silently mouthed. My look said it all: If it wasn't her, it would be some other woman.

"Come, Matt, I have more people for you to meet."

A moment later, they were gone. I rose, folded up the article, stuffed it back into my evening clutch, then headed for the exit. In the Pierre's lobby, I tried to reach Quinn on my cell phone. I got his voicemail, so I left a message, asking him to call me when he got the message—no matter how late or early it was.

I was now more convinced than ever that the designer Fen was in the middle of this mystery, and I wanted to know what Mike had learned during his questioning of the elusive fashion king.

Outside, the early autumn night was cool and crisp. I didn't see the limousine Matteo and I had arrived in, so I asked the doorman to call me a cab. He'd barely raised his hand when one of the line of black limos with darkly tinted windows that had been waiting across the street veered into traffic and screeched to a halt right in front of me.

Matt was obviously going to be staying at the *Trend* party for the duration, and I assumed there'd be plenty of time for me to borrow his limo for a quick trip down to the Blend. Once I got there, I'd send it right back to the Pierre—no harm done. So when the doorman opened the car door, I slipped inside.

The lock clicked as I settled back into the comfortable leather seat, but when I looked up, I realized the man in the driver's seat wasn't the same chauffeur we'd had on the trip up—and there was a second man up front, in the passenger seat.

"I'm sorry," I said. "I'm in the wrong car." I yanked the door handle, but the door was locked and I didn't see any way to unlock it myself. "Can you unlock the door, please?" I asked.

Instead of letting me out, the driver gunned the engine and pulled away from the hotel, into Fifth Avenue's downtown flow.

"Hey!" I cried. "I know you heard me. Let me out!"

I leaned forward to grab his arm, but almost lost my hand when a glass partition quickly rolled up between the front seat and the back. My fist hit the window and I yelled something unintelligible. Then I heard an electronic crackle as a speaker sprang to life somewhere in the back seat compartment.

"Just relax and cooperate, Ms. Cosi," a male voice commanded. "And your ride will be a short one."

Twenty-Four

GOD *almighty, I'm being kidnapped.* My heart was racing, and I began to hyperventilate. *Stay calm, Clare. Think.*

I fumbled in my purse, then brandished my cell phone like a handgun. "Let me out right now or I'll call 911!" I cried, my thumb already hitting the 9.

The driver's eyes flashed angrily in the rearview mirror. He braked the vehicle so violently I had to throw out my arm to avoid being slammed up against the back of the driver's seat. The cell phone flew out of my hand and bounced across the floor.

With a bump and a squeal of tires on pavement, the limo jerked to a halt. The momentum threw me to the carpet. I landed on my knees—convenient, since I wanted to find my cell. But as my fingers closed on my small silver savior, I heard the front passenger door open. A large body slid onto the seat. A strong hand grabbed my wrist and beefy fingers yanked the cell out of my hand.

"Hey, buster! Gimme that," I hollered, pushing hair out of my face. *Note to self. Next time you're being kidnapped, don't threaten to dial 911. Just dial it!*

I lunged for my phone, but the giant wearing jeans and a black leather coat raised his big hands to fend me of easily. His pinky ring looked large enough for me to wear as a bracelet.

"Sit back and enjoy the ride," the man warned in a low octave, hoisting me up on the seat beside him.

He stared at me with Basset Hound dark eyes over a smashed nose. His large round head was topped with short-cropped black hair. His ears stuck out and seemed to be askew. I met his intimidating gaze and raised balled fists.

"Give me my phone and let me out of this car!" I demanded.

As if on cue, the vehicle's abrupt acceleration slammed me back into the leather seat and the limo raced away from the curb and hurled through midtown.

"You want out, lady?" The man reached across me to pop the door open. I gasped as he brutishly brushed my cleavage in the process. The hiss of tires on pavement filled the compartment. We swerved in and out of traffic and only his thick-muscled arm kept the door from flying open, and me pinned to the seat.

"Go on, go then," the man said, laughing.

An electronic crackle sounded, then the voice of the driver, loud over the intercom. "Cut the crap, Tiny."

The door slammed, the automatic lock clicked again and Tiny sat back. Without the weight of his arm crushing me, I could breathe again.

"Pull over!" I screamed.

Suddenly a finger as thick as a banana was under my nose. "Not another word out of you or I'll stuff this phone in your mouth and hold it shut until we get where we're going."

The accent was South Brooklyn—which told me these men were tough customers, and most likely mobbed up. I could almost hear my dear old bookie dad's advice—*Cupcake, sometimes goin' through a brick wall will only get your head broken. You gotta know when to just play along and see what comes.*

My jaw immediately snapped shut, and I spoke no more.

"That's better," said Tiny. Then the man folded his massive arms and stared straight ahead.

I actually admired Tiny's calm, considering the insane manner in which the driver was bobbing in and out of traffic, narrowly avoiding pedestrians and vehicles alike as he raced around corners and through yellow lights.

When I heard sirens and saw flashing red lights, I prayed a traffic cop had observed the man's manic driving and was about to force us over. But the limo driver wasn't the cause of the commotion, and he didn't slow down, not even when a half dozen New York City police cars raced alongside us. I would have waved to the officers, signaled my plight, but I knew the limousine's windows were tinted so darkly no one outside could see in—which is exactly why I hadn't noticed the man in the passenger seat before I'd entered the limo at the Pierre.

As the police cars swerved onto Forty-second Street and sped away, Tiny chuckled. Clearly, the irony had amused him. *A giant named Tiny amused at irony? Imagine that.*

My heart still racing, I sat back and rifled through options. Despite Tiny's order to stay quiet, I considered risking polite conversation—something that might yield a clue as to where I was going and why. But with one more glance at the man's curled lip and glowering expression, I concluded he would not be keen on idle chitchat. And I certainly wasn't keen on eating my own cell phone.

At Thirty-fourth Street, we headed west, turning downtown again at Ninth Avenue. When we hit Fourteenth, the limo slowed with the traffic. A few quick turns and we were near Hudson Street—not far, in fact, from the Village Blend. For an insanely hopeful moment, I thought these two men really did intend to give me a ride home, and I had a fantasy of tripping across the sidewalk and into the cozy, familiar sanctuary of the Blend's interior. Instead we turned down a dark, cobblestone street lined with nineteenth-century industrial buildings fronted by glittering new eateries.

Years ago, when I'd been a young newlywed and first began to manage the Blend, I knew all about the Meatpacking District. By day, its streets were populated by coarse men in bloody aprons, who carried hacksaws, hog carcasses, or haunches of beef on their broad backs. They spoke with outer-boroughs accents and drank beer in the area's dive bars at just about any hour of the day. At night, a different sort of trade ruled those sidewalks, and I was so young and naive it actually took me a little time to figure out why the painted women tottering on high heels were so tall and had such deep voices and sometimes even facial stubble. (Coming from an old Italian neighborhood in Pennsylvania, women and facial hair wasn't all that big a deal, but I figured the Meatpacking deal out eventually.)

Just a few years after that, some of the slaughterhouses (or "abattoirs" as Madame had referred to them) had been replaced by bars and clubs that catered to the harder edged gay community—pardon the pun. Then, in the 1990s, the Meatpacking District was transformed by gentrification. Some excellent butchers could still be found here—like my buddy, Ron Gerson, famed for his prime rib—but for the most part, urban spaces that once held meat processing plants were transformed into chic restaurants and trendy clubs catering to all clientele. With retail gentrification came changes in housing, and many a loft that once quartered factory workers now housed co-ops for the wealthy.

The limousine continued to wend its way through Saturday-night traffic. Sidewalks teemed with laughing partygoers, illuminated by the garish fluorescence of the Hotel Gansevoort. We were moving quite slowly now, and I causally rested my arm on the door handle. As the limo slowed to a crawl, I tried once more to throw the door open, only to find its lock firm as ever. Once again, I heard Tiny's annoying chuckle, a deep rumble.

The limo halted in front of a driveway until there was a break in the pedestrian traffic on the sidewalk, then it veered into a dark, narrow alley lined with garbage cans and dump-sters, a stream of brackish water running down the middle of the cobblestone surface. We stopped in front of a brick wall bearing the flaking remnants of a hand-painted sign, part of a fifty-year-old billboard hawking "Gansevoort Hams, Bacon, and other Quality Pork Products."

The driver stepped out and opened the door from the outside. Tiny's strong hand closed over my upper arm and he pushed me forward. I gripped my evening clutch as my heels hit the stone street. In the alley's dim light, other senses took over. Smell, for one. Rotting garbage, mildew, and urine surrounded me. *Lovely.*

It would be a horrid place to die, and I considered trying to break free of Tiny's grip, kicking off my heels and run-ning back to the crowded sidewalk. But even if I made it out of his grasp, I doubted I would get more than a few feet before he grabbed me again, or worse—

Did he have a gun? I suddenly wondered. If I tried to run, would he shoot me in the back?

While I pondered these charming possibilities, Tiny and his partner, who was short and wiry like my father but barely in his thirties and wearing a penny-dreadful mous-tache, led me to an anonymous steel door unmarked and undistinguished, except by layers and layers of graffiti that covered every inch of its surface. A kind of industrial throbbing sounded from the other side of the portal, as if gigantic engines were constantly turning inside the brick building.

Tiny continued to clutch my arm as he banged the door with one massive hand, his pinky ring clacking loudly against the metal. A bolt was thrown, and the door yawned. From the opening, a ghastly lavender florescent hue illumi-nated the gloom and a pounding wall of techno dance mu-sic washed over me.

A dark shape framed by the light came into view. I could feel the man's eyes studying me, then my abductors.

"Yo, Virgil, it's us," said Tiny.

The silhouette in the doorway nodded, then backed up

to admit us. Tiny pushed me over the threshold, and in the lavender light I saw that the man guarding the door was draped head to toe in a finely tailored ebony suit. Pale green eyes locked with mine.

"Welcome to the Inferno," he said without smiling.

The space I entered seemed massive, yet most of its size was lost in dark shadows. To my right was an island of light where a neon bar served up cocktails to a handful of languid lounge lizards.

"This way," said Tiny, pushing me toward a long inclined ramp that led down to the next level. The floor was concrete, with tall wooden barricades on either side. I realized with a start that I was following the livestock chute. Cattle, pigs, or sheep once ran down this very concrete slope to the slaughter. I hoped I wasn't following in their hoofprints.

At the bottom of the ramp a wooden gate blocked our progress. Tiny looked up and I followed his stare—surprised to see a man in a leather apron and chaps standing on a wooden platform suspended above us. He gripped a large sledgehammer with both hands, the muscles on his hairy arms rippling against its weight.

"Where is he?" Tiny asked the gatekeeper.

"The Fourth Circle," the man with the hammer called back. "And watch what you say. He's in a real pissed-off mood."

A loud clatter sudden enough to make me jump, and the wooden gate rose. Beyond it only a long concrete hallway illuminated by indigo neon tubes lining the floor, the walls, the ceiling. At the end of that corridor I spied black curtains, heard music and voices from the other side. A pornographic mural on the wall announced in elaborate script that we were now among the "Lustful."

Beyond the veil, there was a vast area filled to capacity with boisterous partygoers—young, attractive, and affluent, with a smattering of older men and women, sugar daddies and mommies no doubt. The dance floor was large, but not especially user friendly. All the walls and floor were covered with square white tiles, the ceiling crisscrossed with lead pipes and stark aluminum vents; disco and laser lighting scattered about, bathing the revelers in hues of light and dark crimson.

I noticed drains covered by cast iron grates on the gently sloped floor, once used to dispose of the blood and offal of slaughtered animals. On the walls hung bone saws and carving knives. Blades dangled Damocles-like over the dancers. Smoke wafting through the space told me New York City's rigorous antismoking laws were being only technically enforced—i.e., there was plenty of smoking going on, but none of it smelled like tobacco.

Running along the walls, stainless steel meat-cutting tables doubled for bar space, with a well-stocked raw bar replacing raw meat, and perfectly mixed Bloody Marys substituted for the gore that once pooled here.

It took a few minutes for Tiny and his silent partner to lead me through the throng to the opposite side of the dance floor. We passed a long bar made of glass bricks, illuminated from within by a sanguine red glow. Near the ladies room, I was shown a spiral staircase of heavy cast iron.

"Down you go, lady," shouted Tiny over the throbbing music.

At the bottom of the stairs, I found myself in a dimly lit, brick-lined basement. Tiny stopped in his tracks, then pointed to a door with a sign that read STAFF ONLY, KEEP OUT.

"In you go. He's waiting . . ."

I blinked, not moving. "You're not coming?" I asked.

"What? You suddenly miss me now?"

"I want my cell phone back," I said stubbornly.

Tiny rolled his eyes, reached into his leather jacket and pulled out the phone. He flipped it open and checked the display. Then he closed the phone again, and tossed it at me. I caught it with both hands. A glance told me I would get no signal this far underground, so a call for help was out of the question.

"Now get in there," Tiny barked, slapping my fanny.

Yikes. While I pushed my way through the door, Tiny

and the other man turned and climbed back up the spiral staircase. In front of me was a dimly lit room about the size of a small garage. Three old brick walls were completely covered with gold-framed oil paintings of lounging and posed women, dressed in fashions from periods over the last five hundred or so years. The fourth wall was covered with about a dozen flat-paneled TV screens; four were playing high-fashion runway shows, four were playing financial news including stock tickers scrolling data from the Nikkei and the other international exchanges, and the rest were playing news broadcasts from several different countries. All had the sound off.

Background music flowed from an invisible source— not the techno dance beat continuing to pound upstairs, but a retro mix of big bold brass and sax with violins and electric guitar in the back of it. The music was surreally familiar and I suddenly realized why—it was a track from one of the James Bond movies, which Matt had been pretty much obsessed with back in his twenties.

Whatever the floor had been, it clearly had been replaced by new parquet. A huge leopard skin throw rug covered it and mountains of large silk and embroidered pillows had been heaped on top. Antique chairs rimmed the outer edges of the walls and standing glass shelves held an array of red and white wines, colorful liqueurs, and hard liquor.

Two people were immediately evident, and at my abrupt entrance a man lounging on a pile of pillows and watching one of the stock ticker screens turned his head toward me. I saw the bleached hair and knew at once it was Bryan Goldin. Beside him, a beautiful Japanese woman in a bright yellow kimono, with loose, long black hair, gently stroked his neck with small, delicate hands.

From another pile of pillows, next to a large, elaborately filigreed Moroccan hooka pipe, another figure stirred. His arms were wrapped in the finest Egyptian silk, his long legs were encased in pen jeans, his feet in Bruno Magli leather loafers. Like a spider, the man slowly uncurled himself and rose to face me.

I hadn't seen his image many times in my life, but I recognized him now. Having just seen his younger face, I'd knew he'd once been strikingly handsome, but obviously no Dorian Gray portrait of this guy was aging in some secret vault because the man looked old beyond his years—and it occurred to me that the roadmap of creases he now displayed probably did trace the dissolute excesses of his years.

Appropriately eccentric for the international fashion scene, the man sported small silver loops in each of his ears, and his hair, once dark and wavy, now hung in a long, gray braid down his back. The conventional features of his once common life had obviously been obliterated for the expected affectations of a more famous one. With curious, intense eyes he stared at me but didn't approach.

"You've been asking a lot of questions about me, Ms. Cosi."

"Good evening, Fen. Or should I call you Mr. Goldin?"

An intrigued gray eyebrow arched. "Actually I'm still Stephen Goldin, of Goldin Associates, though few connect my financial endeavors with my line of apparel. While I try to keep a foot in two worlds, I do like to keep them separate."

"You didn't have to kidnap me to have a meeting," I replied. "I've been wanting to talk to you for days."

"You and that tiresome detective, Quinn." Fen waved his hand. "I have little time for such nonsense during Fashion Week."

"There was time enough to grab me off the street, though."

Fen chuckled. "Were you surprised by my associates?"

"Oh, no. In fact, I think I've seen them before—as extras on *The Sopranos*."

"Some things are unavoidable, Ms. Cosi. I design and make my clothing here in America, and you know what that means. Those men . . . my associates . . . they help me avoid strikes and other union problems. They are useful in other areas as well."

"Like kidnapping?"

"Like acquiring this place . . . I purchased it for a song from an entertainment entrepreneur who had an unfortunate gambling addiction, and was prone to borrowing money from the wrong men . . .".

"Loan sharks, you mean. Your associates? How are they at poisoning people?" I shot a sharp glance at Bryan. He gave me a Billy Idol sneer.

Fen sighed. "Now you're being tiresome."

"Oh, am I? Then listen to this. I know you were Lottie Toratelli's lover twenty years ago. I also know that you slept with Lottie's sister during the same period, and that Mona ended up prematurely dead."

Fen looked past me, gestured to his nephew. Bryan Goldin jumped to his feet and fetched a French Provincial chair from the corner. A matching chair came by way of the Japanese woman in the yellow kimono.

"Sit, Ms. Cosi. You have suddenly become interesting again." I sank down, and Fen sat opposite me. He crossed his long legs and leaned toward me. "I had absolutely nothing to do with Mona Toratelli's death. *Nothing*."

Bryan Goldin appeared again and set a delicate carved table between us. The Japanese woman brought us a bottle of plum wine and two crystal glasses. Then she and Bryan Goldin slipped into the shadows of the room, appearing to vanish.

Fen picked up the bottle. While he poured the dark purple liquid into his glass, I examined my own—ran my finger inside it and sniffed. He laughed at me, a mirthless bark. "If I had wanted to poison you, Ms. Cosi, I wouldn't have brought you to my club to do it. And I certainly wouldn't be pouring us both drinks from the same bottle."

I raised an eyebrow as he took the glass from my fingers and poured me a drink. "To your health," he said, handing my glass back to me and raising his own. I watched him take a healthy swallow.

My lips were dry, my mouth parched. Needing something to calm my rattled nerves, I carefully sipped my own drink, detecting no taste of almonds or bitterness. The only two things that registered were the sweetness and the strength of the alcohol.

"Please, tell me more," said Fen, taking another sip from his glass. "What else do you know about me—or think you do?"

I took a second sip of the sweet wine, then another before I spoke.

"I know you tried to force Rena Garcia and Tad Benedict to sell you their shares in Lottie Harmon," I began. "I also know how you entrapped Rena in a fashion design knockoff scheme, blackmailed her, and threatened to expose her unless she sold you her shares. You even waited to make the threat until she and Tad were officially engaged so you could pull him in as well. A two-for-one, so to speak."

Fen's left eye twitched. I took it as a victory and pressed ahead. "I know Tad and Rena tried to outmaneuver you by selling their shares to other investors—in an effort to help Lottie retain control of her company. Poor Rena obviously died because she was trying to protect her boss."

"Rena was a greedy little fool, Ms. Cosi, but I had nothing to do with her death, either. I was as shocked by the news as anyone."

"Nice try. But I don't believe you."

Fen slammed the table with his fist. "Then you are a stupid woman. Her death has thrown her estate into legal limbo. Rena Garcia died without a will. Now I can't touch those stocks—nobody can. Not until the legal mess is worked out."

Fen leaned back. Forcing self-control, he coolly crossed his legs again. "So you see, Ms. Garcia's death in no way benefits me."

I still wasn't convinced, but I let the subject drop. "So

what were you saying about control of the Lottie Harmon label?" I asked, continuing to boost my nerve by gulping down more of the plum wine.

"Not the Lottie Harmon *label*. I don't give a damn about that. I want control of Lottie."

So, I thought, Madame had been right. "You're still in love with her."

Fen sighed and glanced away, his gaze raking the wall of gilded oil paintings, women posed in empire waists and velvet gowns, Elizabethan collars and powdered wigs, hoop skirts and floor-length furs. "She was addictive, back then," he said softly. "Intense. Soft and sensual, but dangerous too. Tempestuous and totally unpredictable. Like a psychotropic drug. I've had countless women since her, but I've never met one whom I could feel even a fraction as strongly about. I want her back in my bed, you see?"

"And you're a man who gets what he wants?"

Fen shrugged.

It was sad, really. Fen's memories of the wildly sensual Lottie just didn't add up to the somewhat restrained woman I knew Lottie to be now. Clearly, the woman had changed over the past twenty years, but Fen hadn't noticed—or didn't want to.

I didn't know much about this Fen/Stephen Goldin character sitting across from me. Maybe the man lived his life in a succession of obsessions and Lottie was just the latest. Or maybe middle-age panic had recently kicked in and regrets were making him yearn desperately for something that simply didn't exist anymore—if it ever did. He certainly wouldn't be the first person to idealize a past relationship to make up for a present emptiness.

I set the glass down on the intricately carved table with a loud clink, and realized this particular plum wine was much more powerful than any I'd ever consumed. "Those feelings," I said, a little woozy, "I suspect they all came back for you when Lottie contacted you again after all these years?"

Fen nodded as he refilled my glass. "Lottie was finished when she walked away all those years ago—from her busi-

ness and me. She'd been washed up for decades. This new
line of hers, the java jewelry thing, it was interesting and
commercially viable—if wholly conventional. But I saw it
could be lucrative. Like something Isaac might produce for
Target. Or David Mintzer for the Bullseye stores—"

My jaw dropped. David Mintzer. Good lord, I thought,
that's who I'd been talking to at the Pierre Hotel, one of the
most successful clothing designers in the industry. Mintzer
owned two restaurant chains; three magazines; and lines of
clothes, handbags, shoes, fragrances, and bath products;
plus exclusive product lines just for the Bullseye chain of
mass merchandisers. *For god's sake, Clare, the man regu-
larly appears on* Oprah, *and you didn't even recognize him!*

I took another swig of the plum wine as Fen continued
to talk. "I knew I could help sell Lottie's collection, of
course, so I helped her, expecting she'd want to become involved with me again—but she's kept me at arm's length
for over a year now, and I've run out of patience."

Then why are you trying to kill her? I wondered. Clearly,
it didn't add up. About then, the room began to spin. "So
what's the big deal, Fenny?" I found myself babbling. "Woo
her. Win her. Marry her even—just like everybody else."

"You don't understand. She wants nothing to do with
me. The past is still alive for her as it is for me. But Lottie
only remembers the hurt I inflicted on her, not the ecstasy
we shared. Now with her line a success, I fear she may
soon not even need our business relationship. And I'm not
taking the chance she'll disappear on me again. I have the
power to take over what means the most to her—so I will.
Then I'll have power over her, too, you see?"

"No, I don't see. If you cared so much for Lottie all those
years ago, then why the hell did you sleep with her sister?"

Instead of answering my question, Fen rose. He seemed
taller now as he loomed over me. I looked up, startled as I
realized the ceiling was a stylized mirror—inside it I saw
the reflections of the oil paintings that covered three of the
room's four walls.

"My god, look at them," I murmured, "all those

women . . ." The room spun faster, and I couldn't seem to control my tongue. "Oh, wait. Now I get it!" I cried, a tad too loudly. "This club of yours is called the Inferno because it's Dante's hell, and we're in the Fourth Circle—the circle of the hoarders. You hoard women, Fen. You're a hoarder!" I was now shaking my finger at the man like a scolding little nun.

He stared at me with pure disgust. "You have grown tiresome again. I would like you to leave."

"Ha! First you kidnap me, then you throw me out. You've got some nerve, Fenny!" I waved my arm to emphasize my point, and knocked over the half-empty wine glass. It fell off the carved table and bounced softly off a silk pillow, staining it beyond redemption.

"No one has kidnapped you, Ms. Cosi. I merely provided a ride—and bodyguard—to keep you safe for your trip downtown. You did willingly get into my car, if you recall. I'm sure the Pierre doorman would testify to that."

"Bull-loney." I rose. Like a listing ship, the entire room seemed to lurch to the side. I stumbled, clutched the edge of the carved table and nearly toppled it, too.

"You say you were kidnapped, Ms. Cosi. But I say you came here to my club inebriated and became quite loud and disorderly. Indeed, you caused a scene, as my staff will attest. Why, a scandalous story like that could even reach the papers."

"You rat!" I hollered. "You drugged me!"

"Just a healthy dose of grain alcohol, nothing to get excited about. We're done now, Ms. Cosi, and I do hope you are, too. All this nosing around in other people's affairs is really not a healthy pursuit. And we did drink to your health, did we not?"

Then Fen was through talking. He no sooner gave me his back than his nephew, Bryan Goldin, emerged from the shadows. Not gently, he ushered me out the door, depositing me at the bottom of the spiral staircase, which might as well have been the base camp at Mount Everest.

"Sweet dreams, Cosi."

After taking a deep breath, I grabbed the wrought iron railings with both hands and began to climb. It took an eternity to move from one step to the next, and I had to stop for oxygen every minute or so and wait for the room to stop spinning. *God, where's a sherpa when you need one?*

Finally, I reached a level I recognized—the dance floor and that long bar made of glass bricks, illuminated from within by a blood red glow. The sight of it, and the thought of all the animals slaughtered in this building, was suddenly making my stomach churn. Just then, I spied the public phone—which was in use—and the ladies room next to it.

Oh, lord, I'm going to be sick. I lunged for the bathroom. No line, thank goodness, so I pushed my way through the door. Inside I found two large stalls, both in use. I heard giggling, then voices echoing from behind one of the partitions. Whoever they were in there, they were taking up a stall without making proper use of it, and that suddenly made me furious. The grain alcohol made me bold, if not certifiably insane, and I began to pound on the stall door.

"Hey, knock it off," a woman cried from the other side. I pounded again, then kicked the thing. It burst open.

Two young women and a young man in a business suit were crammed inside the stall—one of the women was a tall blonde with a daring leather vest and skirt that bared her belly. The other was a pretty brunette with a short velvet dress that revealed lots of leg and plenty of cleavage. Her lipstick was familiar, I suddenly realized, a garish hue I would never wear, but the exact shade I'd found on my husband's collar the day before.

I blinked, not sure, but hoping, it was all just a nightmarish hallucination. The brunette's eyes were as wide as a deer's on a busy highway—not surprising since she'd been caught in the act of holding a tiny spoon full of illegal white power under her nose.

Then her familiar voice cried, "Mom!" and I knew this was no delusion. The brunette holding the cocaine was my daughter, Joy.

Twenty-five

⊛⊛⊛⊛⊛⊛⊛⊛⊛⊛⊛⊛⊛⊛⊛⊛⊛⊛⊛⊛⊛⊛⊛⊛

"Drink this."

"What is it?"

"Water."

Still holding the cool cloth over my eyes and forehead, I blindly accepted the tall glass from Matt. "Where's the coffee?"

"It's coming. For now, your body needs water. Drink it down, Clare. Trust me, I've had enough hangovers to know what helps."

On this subject, I did implicitly trust my globetrotting ex-husband, who seemed to personify the lyric from the old hit song "One Night in Bangkok," which, paraphrased, essentially says, *all countries look the same with your head in a toilet bowl.*

I myself had already worshipped the porcelain god in the Inferno, right after I discovered my barely adult daughter about to shove Bolivian marching powder up one delicate nostril.

The scene after that was a fairly horrific blur—I was about to take Joy by her wrist and drag her out of that club, but I hadn't needed to do anything nearly that dramatic. She was so alarmed at seeing her mother inebriated to the point of passing out, she'd helped me to the door and into a cab. I pulled her in with me, refusing to let her out of my sight, then insisted she stay the night with me in the duplex.

When we got upstairs, we found Matt already home—to my stunned surprise. I would have bet the farm he'd been planning to spend the night in Breanne's bed. But there he was, ready to take care of us both.

He'd given up his own room when he realized Joy was spending the night. After digging out one of his T-shirts to sleep in, he tucked me into the master bedroom's four-poster. I was too shaky to ask where he was going to sleep—and once again assumed he had some other woman's bed in mind anyway.

"Matt, you *have* to talk to Joy," I said, still staring at the inside of my hangover cloth. "Straight talk."

"I will, Clare. First thing in the morning. Let's all just get some rest tonight."

I didn't have it in me to argue. Just then, I heard a delicate tinkling, like a toy piano playing my favorite song from *The Sound of Music.*

"My cell," I moaned. "Matt, I'm sorry, but can you help me out again?"

"Sure." He followed the electronic rendition of "Edelweiss" to the chair where I'd thrown my clutch. Fishing inside, he found my phone and brought it to me.

"Thanks," I said, flipping it open. "Hello?"

"Clare? It's Mike. You left a message to call. I hope it's not too late."

"No. It's fine. Just a minute." I sat up, the cloth falling from my eyes. Matt stared. I met his gaze with a pleading look. "Coffee?" I asked with wide-eyed innocence.

"Be right back," he said. Then he turned and left the room—very slowly. When he was finally out of eavesdropping range, I spoke into the phone again.

"Mike, Fen kidnapped me tonight."

I hadn't wanted Matt to hear that—he was already

pissed at me for the Nancy Drew act. If he found out what it resulted in, I knew he'd hit the ceiling, which is exactly what Quinn was doing.

"What! Clare, what the hell happened? Where are you now? Are you all right? Do you want me to send a patrol car?"

"I'm fine. I'm home. It's okay now. But earlier, he had two thugs pick me up in a limo and take me against my will to this private club in the old Meatpacking District; it's called the Inferno and it's definitely mobbed up."

I could hear Quinn's frustrated sigh. "Yeah, I know about the place. So do the Feds. It's not the only hot spot in the precinct but unless there's obvious criminal activity, it's out of my jurisdiction. Kidnapping, however, is another matter. Do you want to file formal charges? What happened down there, for god's sake?"

"Fen said he heard I was asking a lot of questions and he wanted to talk to me—find out what I knew and pretty much intimidate me into staying out of his business. He slipped some grain alcohol into my wine glass, I assume to loosen my tongue."

"What did you find out?"

"Not much I didn't already guess. He denies having anything to do with Rena's murder."

"He's got a solid alibi."

"Well, check his nephew, Bryan Goldin. I think he's the one who does the dirty work. Of course, Fen's got the entire cast of *The Sopranos* on his payroll, too. But I did uncover something from his past. A woman he'd been sleeping with died under mysterious circumstances in Thailand in 1988. Mona Lisa Toratelli, Lottie Harmon's sister."

"Got it. I'll see what I can find out from Interpol."

"Great."

"Clare? You're sure you're all right?"

"I'll be better when Tucker is out of jail and Rena's killer is arrested."

"Yeah . . . listen, I didn't get anything from Fen, other

than a solid alibi, but your blackmail information was a big help with Starkey and Hut. Tad came clean with it and they're going to help me on the Garcia murder. Even they admit the two poisonings are likely linked and there might be another perp involved."

"Not *another* perp," I insisted. "An altogether *different* perp."

"One step at a time, Detective Cosi."

I smiled, actually picked up the slight teasing in Mike's tone—no easy feat, considering the man usually maintained a poker voice to match his poker face. Half the time, reading Quinn was about as easy as reading a brick wall—a blank one, of course, one without a collection of over-dressed babes covering it.

"Thanks for calling back, Mike."

"Sure, Clare."

I continued to hold the cell to my ear. A long silent moment passed. Neither of us, it seemed, had anything more to say—but neither of us wanted to sign off, either.

"Here you go, sweetheart, fresh coffee!" Matt had returned to the master bedroom with two steaming mugs.

"I have to go now," I softly told Mike.

"Good night, Clare."

"Good night."

I closed the phone and accepted the mug. The warm, nutty fragrance of the dark roast was more than welcome and I drank it down with extreme satisfaction.

"God, I needed that."

"You'll need these too."

Matt dropped two aspirins into my hand and I gulped them down, along with the rest of the water. Then back to the coffee. After a long silence, Matt sat down on the edge of the bed and folded his arms.

"You want to tell me what you told him?"

I squirmed. "Nothing to tell. Really. I just drank too much at the *Trend* party and then ran into a friend who took me to the Inferno, where I saw Joy."

"Liar."

"Oh, Matt. It's close enough to the truth. Just let it go."

"Clare, I'm warning you, don't get in over your head with this detective game. It's too dangerous."

"Please, Matt. Let's not argue." I drained the coffee mug and was about to throw the cold cloth over my eyes again when the phone on the nightstand rang. I lunged for the receiver, miraculously snagging it before Matt.

"Hello?" I said.

"Clare, dear, I didn't wake you, did I?"

"No, Madame."

Matt's eyebrows rose.

"I've been thinking," said Madame in a conspiratorial tone, "about our case, you know?"

Oh, lord, I thought. *Please don't let Matt hear you say that.* With my suspicious ex-husband continuing to stare, I carefully asked, "What's on your mind?"

"Only this . . . do you think it's possible Lottie herself is the culprit?"

"Lottie herself?" I hadn't considered that possibility. "Why would you think that, Madame?"

"Because Lottie may have learned of Tad and Rena's plan to sell their shares. And Rena would have trusted Lottie. She would have easily taken a poisoned latte from her and drunk it down."

"True. But why would Lottie have poisoned herself?"

Matt frowned and glowered, finally hearing a phrase that confirmed I was discussing the case with his mother. I twisted away from his disapproving eyes.

"Well, my dear, I thought that through, too," Madame replied. "It's possible that Lottie found an accomplice to help her set the whole thing up—that she never intended to drink the poison but only to taste it and then accuse Tad and Rena of poisoning her, but, of course, Ricky Flatt and that poor Jeff Lugar drank down the poison instead. Lottie Harmon may have been trying to gain control of her own label by any means necessary."

"It's an interesting possibility, Madame . . . I can't deny it."

"Of course, I could be wrong, but I thought you should hear the theory."

"Yes . . . well . . ." I looked up again to find Matt ready to blow. "I better get some rest now—and so should you. Big day tomorrow!"

"Oh, yes, the runway show. I'll see you there, my dear. Sweet dreams!"

Bryan Goldin had wished me the same, as I recalled, but I doubted very much I'd have them. I hung up the phone and collapsed into the pile of bed pillows, smacking the cold cloth back over my eyes before Matt could grill me.

"Clare."

"Don't, Matt. Don't."

"Fine. Let's go to bed then."

Before I could ask what he meant by "let's," the light was clicking off and my ex-husband was climbing in beside me under the bedcovers.

Oh, god, no, I thought, but was too exhausted to protest. I simply turned on my side, away from the father of my child. A moment later, I felt Matt's muscular arm curling around me and pulling me possessively against him.

I knew it was wrong, that I should resist. But the familiar feel of his strong body tucked around me again was like that cup of java he'd brought me, warm and reassuring, and reminiscent of those days during our marriage when we'd been happy together, young and undamaged, hopeful and optimistic.

With a sigh I relaxed into him and let dreams descend.

Twenty-six

~~~~~~~~~~~~~~~~~~~~~~~~~~~~~~~~

Sunday morning started far too early. I awoke at six with a parched mouth and the fringes of a hangover headache, courtesy of Fen's atomic cocktail.

Matt was still sleeping in my bed and I silently thanked him for making sure the slight discomfort I was experiencing took the place of the blinding pain I would have surely endured without his help.

After showering and dressing like a George Romero zombie, I stumbled downstairs to find Gardner Evans chipper and wide awake despite the fact that he'd closed last night and had just opened this morning. He and two other evening employees would be serving the Blend's regular customers here at the Village store while Esther, Moira, and I catered the Fen runway show in midtown, which was scheduled to go off in less than six hours.

Esther and Moira soon arrived and we all loaded up the van I'd rented days before and parked in the alley behind the Blend: two espresso machines and service for three hundred, including cream, milk, sugar, coffee, disposable cups, stirring sticks, and napkins and paper plates for the baked goods, which would be delivered on site at eight o'clock sharp. We even brought our own water—filtered fresh this morning (good-tasting water being an essential ingredient for a great cup of joe).

To get our hearts jump-started, I prepared a thermos of double-strength Breakfast Blend, a medium roasted mix of Arabicas with the highest caffeine content on our play list, which we all shared before heading out.

"You drive. I don't think I'm up to it," I told Esther, handing her the keys.

Under normal circumstances, I would have resisted turning over the keys—and my life—to a vehicular novice, but at seven on a Sunday morning, traffic in Manhattan was virtually nonexistent and my head pounded too much to care anyway.

I climbed into the van's cab, then called to Moira. "Take off your backpack and you can squeeze into the front seat with Esther and me."

"That's all right, Ms. Cosi, I'll just ride in back."

Moira climbed into the back of the truck and settled in. We could hardly see her among all the stuff packed inside the van.

"God," whispered Esther, roiling her eyes. "Why can't she be sociable? You'd think that pack was glued to her spine."

I shushed Esther and off we went.

By the time we came in sight of the lions in front of the Forty-second Street Library, the morning clouds had cleared and the sun was shining brightly for a late September morning—even though a brisk ocean wind swept across Manhattan from the east, providing a chilly glimpse of the winter to come.

I hadn't been back to Bryant Park since my first visit with Lottie on Fashion Week's opening day. The scene was even more chaotic now—cabs, vans, fashionista trailers, and plenty of people. We pulled up to the barricade on Fortieth Street.

The road was closed to regular traffic during the festivities, but we presented our pass to a uniformed New York City police officer and he waved us in. Esther managed to park our van crookedly between a Metro New York satellite truck and a tour bus emblazoned with the Fen logo.

"Okay," Esther began. "I know Sunday is right in the middle of Fashion Week and the optimum time for a runway premiere, but why did Fen and Lottie schedule the damn thing before noon?"

"Lottie told me they were selling a spring collection, so Fen wanted his models to be brimming with energy. 'Like the first budding of spring,' is how she put it."

"But what about the fashionistas?" Esther complained. "With all their late-night parties, won't they fall asleep?"

"That's why we didn't bring decaf," I replied. "And it seems to me that Fen was on to something."

I pointed to the pack of journalists and buyers already circling the tents, most of whom seemed less than fully alert. Meanwhile the high-stepping models trotting about in gauzy spring fashions in the chilly autumn air seemed energized.

"They move like they're powered by supercharged batteries," I remarked.

"More likely cocaine," quipped Esther.

I frowned, remembering Joy and hoping Matt would come through with his promise to speak with her. I'd spoken to Joy many times over the years about the dangers of illegal drugs. Now I knew she needed to hear the warnings from her larger-than-life father, the former addict—his words would carry a thousand times more weight than mine.

Stepping out of the van, I felt like a junkie myself, and shielded my hangover-sensitive eyes from the harsh stabbing agony of the sun. Suddenly I wished I'd held on to those Jackie Onassis tinted glasses of Madame's.

I noticed Moira McNeely with a hand to her head, too.

"Moira, are you okay?"

She shook her head. "Headache. Massive."

"Join the club." I pulled a pillbox of aspirins out of the

pocket of my jeans and handed it to her. "I've come pre-pared. Take two aspirins and have another cup of coffee."

"No, I can't," she said handing the pillbox back to me with a look of panic. "I told you earlier in the week. I'm allergic."

"Sorry," I said, "I'm still fuzzy."

"I have a cousin who can die from eating peanuts," said Esther. "Can people die from aspirin allergies, too?"

As Esther and Moira continued to talk, I turned to open the van's double doors and spied Bryan Goldin emerging from the Fen bus. Gone were the Billy Idol black leather duds and studded choker. His tattoos were even out of sight. Today, beneath his platinum blond crewcut, the younger Goldin wore a tailored Fen suit, cocoa brown, with a lavender shirt and tie.

As he stepped down from the bus, he paused to adjust his outfit. He glanced around—no doubt looking to see if he'd been noticed—but he didn't spot me. After a moment, he checked his cuffs and headed across the park to the Theater tent. I saw no sign of Fen himself, but figured a man as reclusive—and frankly, reptilian—as Fen was would stay out of sight as long as possible.

For the next hour Moira, Esther, and I moved the espresso machines into the Theater tent and set them up in the spacious main lobby, with the help of a hunky young member of the Fashion Week organizing staff named Chad.

Esther's face lit up and she turned on the charm when he greeted us, and surprisingly, Chad, who looked to be a corn-fed midwestern transplant, did not seem put off by the girl's antifashion braids, oversized sweatshirt, and black-rimmed glasses. In fact, he smiled so warmly at Esther, I suspected she probably resembled one of his old friends back home on the farm.

Moira, however, was all business as she tested the espresso machines, and the three of them worked so effi-ciently together they hardly required my presence.

"Watch for the pastry delivery. It should be here any

minute," I told Esther. "I'm going backstage to have a word with Lottie."

"Have a blast, boss," she replied, clearly distracted by the rippling muscles under Chad's Fashion Week T-shirt.

The public was not yet allowed into the Theater tent, so I crossed an empty lobby and entered the virgin-white runway area. The vast space seemed hollow without spectators, and I heard only the ghostly rush of ventilation fans as I walked past the rows and rows of seats to the front of the room. The white canvas walls were pristine save for carefully mounted banks of stage lights, and the smooth, polished runway was desolate.

The door on stage was bracketed by two mammoth flat screen televisions, each crowned with huge placards bearing the Fen logo. The screens crackled with silent static, and two men in Fashion Week tees were frantically working on the video system, trying to troubleshoot an obvious malfunction.

I wasn't sure where to search for Lottie, but I spotted a small door leading backstage and thought it logical to try there first. At the door, a young, beefy security guard gave my badge only a cursory glance before he let me slip into the milling chaos that was the dressing area.

I knew at once what was distracting the guard—a harem of partially-clad young models traipsed around the room or sat in makeup chairs before wall-sized mirrors. Some wore robes or street clothes, but most were clad in the skimpiest lingerie. One woman—a towering Slavic Amazon—sauntered past the sweating guard wearing high heels and little else, her blond hair down to her waist, her arms casually folded across her breasts.

Among the ranks of nubile women were plenty of familiar faces—supermodels whose names I didn't actually know, but whose faces graced magazine covers every month. Sitting near a makeup table, I spied Ranata Somsong—Violet Eyes—was as striking as ever in a belted mauve minidress. She appeared to be a spectator here, however, observing the backstage preparations with naked delight. Next to her, blow-drying and teasing a model with the biggest hair I'd seen this side of a beehive, was Lloyd Newhaven.

Bryan Goldin was already here. Fen would probably arrive at any moment. Now Lloyd Newhaven and Violet Eyes. The whole gang was here. Were they working together? Separately?

Though I didn't yet have all the pieces of the puzzle, I still felt Fen was the mastermind and the man to watch today. Last night, he'd given me an interesting song-and-dance about how he had nothing to do with the poisonings, but that grain alcohol in my plum wine proved he was capable of tainting a drink to achieve his goals.

I also remembered what Madame had told me on the phone last night. Was Lottie really the one in danger? Or was she herself the one I should be watching?

I passed through the large dressing area twice, but saw no sign of the accessories designer. Then I heard an amplified voice echoing from the theater.

". . . Milan is my favorite show," a woman's voice boomed. "The food, the wine—"

Another loud voice interrupted. "And the men! Don't forget those delicious Italian men . . .".

The comment was followed by a peel of strained, high-pitched laughter I instantly recognized as Lottie Harmon's. I hurried through the door, expecting to find Lottie on the runway, microphone in hand. Instead I saw one of the technicians standing next to a video player. I glanced up at the large screens and saw a rewinding image of three women sitting on a veranda somewhere on a Mediterranean shore.

I ran up to the technician. "Did you just play that tape?"

He nodded.

"What is it?" I asked.

The man shrugged. "A ten-minute retrospective of some kind. It's scheduled to run before the show starts."

"Could you please play it again?"

The man shrugged and hit the play button. The clip I'd heard was from a television interview for the Italian network RAI. A scroll at the bottom of the screen indicated it had been taped during the Milan fashion show of 1984. The interview was conducted in English, with Italian subtitles running at the bottom of the screen.

Lottie Harmon, nee Toratelli, sat in a deck chair, her signature scarlet hair lifting lightly on the Mediterranean breeze; her sundress was bright yellow, her long, tanned legs tucked under her. On a chair beside Lottie, her sister Mona Lisa wore a pale green dress. The resemblance between the two women was all the more striking in a moving image.

Also striking was the difference in their manner—Lottie was loud, extroverted, and flamboyant. Mona Lisa seemed serious, quiet, restrained. Almost invisible behind the glamorous pair, the heavyset Harriet Tasky stood in a black pantsuit, her dirty blond hair stirring a bit in the sea air.

It was Mona Lisa who spoke of Milan being her favorite show, of her love of the food and wine. It was Lottie Harmon who leaned into the camera and added the comment about "those delicious Italian men." But it was *Harriet Tasky* who laughed that distinctive, strained, high-pitched laugh.

The tape ended abruptly in a shower of crackling static. The man at my side cursed and began to play with the wires. Still in a state of confused shock, I turned. Standing right behind me was the woman who had, for the past year, called herself Lottie Harmon. She was staring in horror at the snowy screen.

"You," I rasped. "You're not Lottie Harmon. You're Harriet Tasky!"

Twenty-seven

∽∽∽∽∽∽∽∽∽∽∽∽∽∽∽∽∽∽∽∽∽

Without a word, Harriet took me by the arm and pulled me to a seat in the back row of the empty theater, far from prying eyes and ears.

"I *was* Harriet Tasky," she admitted in a whispered hiss after sitting beside me. "Now I'm Lottie Harmon. What does it matter to you?"

"It matters because my friend is sitting in a jail cell and the only way I know how to get him out is to find out what the hell is going on around here!"

"Shhh, lower your voice," Harriet insisted. Then the woman's shoulders sagged. "This week has been hell. First the poisoning at the party, then Rena's death . . ." She paused to choke back sudden tears, then just began shaking her head and broke down completely.

"I'm sorry about Rena," I said. "I really am. But I need to know what's going on. The truth. Why are you posing as Lottie Harmon?"

"Why do you think?" she said after composing herself and wiping her tears. "Harriet was a nobody in this world. Overweight, shy, unglamorous. Never mind that I created half the pieces that sent the Lottie Harmon label to the top of the fashion world in its heyday. Poor Mona, of course, created the other half."

"And Lottie Toratelli?"

"She was the professional party girl. The very public, very pretty, flamboyant, well-spoken face of Lottie Harmon. I don't deny she was vital. She made the connections, the front and back end deals. She put the label and its designs in the papers—by making the scene, showing off the jewelry and accessories, bringing in just the right clientele—"

"The Eveready Bunny," I murmured.

"Who kept going and going." Harriet said this with such irony I tried to read between the lines.

"Do you mean drugs?"

Lottie shook her head. "Not drugs. Both Lottie and Mona Lisa had some kind of weird, hereditary allergies. But booze, music, and sex with multiple partners—that was what kept Lottie going."

"But not you and Mona?"

Harriet waved her hand. "Oh, Mona went clubbing a lot at first, but then she got pregnant by some one-night stand and decided to have the baby. She settled down and became the more responsible sister. I tried the club scene for awhile, but the way I looked . . . well, let's just say I got tired of buying drinks and drugs for guys who treated me like crap."

I let the words hang for a moment. "I guess it was tough for you and Mona—working hard and never getting the credit you deserved for your design work."

Harriet shrugged. "It didn't matter, really. We were all getting rich. That had been the plan—and the deal—all along. Things were going great, until that bastard Stephen Goldin started playing his games."

"Fen?"

She glanced away, her eyes glazing a bit. "Stephen was really something back then—brilliant, cocksure—a straight young clothing designer in a business saturated with gay men. Lottie was drawn to him immediately; Mona soon after that. Moths to a flame, as it turned out."

"So he encouraged both women's affections?"

"Encouraged? He reveled in it. For years, he played a twisted cat and mouse game with both women—flaunting his relationship with Lottie, while daring Mona to reveal her own affair with him to her wild, possessive sister. Fen was playing a dangerous game, but no one knew how dangerous until it was too late . . .".

Her voice trailed off, but I knew where she was going. "Harriet," I said softly, "I know Mona died in Bangkok."

Lottie nodded, closed her eyes. "I saw most of the crap come down in that sick *menage a tois,* but I managed to miss Armageddon Day, which finally occurred in 1988."

"What happened?"

She sighed, opened her eyes. "Fen took both sisters to Thailand on phony passports. He had one too. They were planning to smuggle gems out of the country and avoid duties and customs. But with his libido, Fen was probably planning to sample Thailand's notorious sex industry, as well. Anyway, Mona took her little daughter on the trip, maybe to use her as a decoy, so the authorities wouldn't suspect them of being smugglers. It was all a stupid, tragic mistake. I didn't find out the truth about Mona's death until years later. Lottie confessed it all to me herself, at the end . . .".

"The only news item I found on Mona's death said she fell off a balcony—"

"She was pushed," Harriet corrected, shaking her head.

"Did Fen do it?"

"Fen and Lottie had been bickering—badly. By this time, they were on the verge of splitting for good. The break finally came in Bangkok, but before Fen stormed off and flew back to New York without them, he threw his affair with Mona in Lottie's face. Lottie had always been impulsive and, at times, short-tempered. The lifestyle she'd been leading—all the alcohol she consumed daily—had made her downright dangerous. She stormed into Mona's hotel room and confronted her. Mona struck out and Lottie struck back. They began to struggle . . . Lottie pushed her own sister over the balcony, and it happened right in front of Mona's young daughter."

"Oh my god."

Harriet paused. "That pretty little girl . . . I think she was only six years old at the time. I didn't know her that well because Mona had hired a full-time nanny at home and brought her by the studio only once or twice. The daughter, what was her name? Maria or Maura, something like that. She must be in her early 20s by now. I just hope she's forgotten what she saw, or made peace with it, anyway."

"What happened after Mona's death?"

"It was hushed up, I can tell you that. The little girl's father was out of the picture so Mona's daughter was sent to live with a relative in the northeast. Boston, I think."

"And Lottie? What happened to her?"

"She got away with murder, that's what happened to her. Mona's death was quickly ruled a suicide. And Lottie returned to New York in time to debut the new season—but she didn't. She dropped out, cancelled orders, shut down the company and went to Europe. Murdering her sister then covering it up, orphaning her niece, and losing Fen, too, it was too much for her. She just quit."

"And Fen?"

"He moved along . . . to other design partners, and presumably other sexual ones. I moved to London to start a new life—I still had plenty of money, so I opened my own vintage clothing business. I lost the weight I'd carried my whole life, and things were going okay. Then I heard about Lottie . . ."

"What about Lottie?"

"Her drinking intensified. One day I got a phone call from a hospital in Paris, asking if I'd be willing to pick up a Lottie Toratelli. She'd given my name as next of kin. I later found out she'd burned through most of her money, and was now a full-blown alcoholic."

"What did you do?"

"I took her back with me to London, put her in rehab, then made her a partner in my business. She didn't have much cash to buy into it, so we agreed that she'd sign over some property to me, including the Village townhouse I've been living in for this past year. We were doing okay, Lottie and I, running the vintage business in London, until a stupid, senseless accident occurred that changed everything. . . ."

Harriet paused. I gave her time to gather her thoughts.

"We had received a consignment of vintage clothing from a British estate in Cornwall—all vintage prewar top of the line fashions, perfectly sealed and preserved. Lottie and I began opening the plastic bags to conduct an inventory. Suddenly Lottie got sick, then she had a seizure. I called an ambulance and took her to a hospital. It was too late to help, and Lottie died the same day."

I blinked in shock. "How?"

"The doctors said it was naphthalene poisoning, from the chemicals in the mothballs. Lottie was always allergic to aspirin. Turns out the adverse reaction to naphthalene is part of the same allergy, only much worse. After Lottie was gone, I saw to everything, including Lottie's deathbed request that she be cremated as quietly as possible, without even her family being notified. I understood how she felt because during her long rehab, she confessed to me that she'd killed her sister."

"So why did you resurrect Lottie Harmon? Did you need money?"

"It wasn't the money I wanted." Harriet sighed. "With the sisters dead, I had the sole claim on the label. I had been doing all that great work for all those years, laboring in obscurity . . . I wanted to know what it was like to be the one applauded, and featured in the magazines, the one invited to the parties . . . the genius, the star . . ."

I recalled David Mintzer's comment about the poor little guys laboring away in the shadows who get ignored, or thrust aside—apparently Harriet Tasky had been one of them, just waiting for her chance to break out, to step into the limelight.

"It wasn't an easy road," Harriet continued. "When I first tried to get things going again, I called Fen, hoping to interest him in a partnership. I wasn't happy about dealing with a snake like him, but I saw it as my only avenue back into the business."

I could imagine what happened, and Harriet confirmed my suspicions. "The prick wouldn't even take my call. After repeated tries, I called him again—but this time I told the receptionist I was Lottie Harmon and was put right through. He took Lottie's call, all right."

"What happened then?"

"I thought I knew Lottie well enough to be able to play her. I had a whole spiel down and it worked pretty well. He thought he was talking to Lottie Toratelli, and I cut off the conversation before he became convinced otherwise. He begged to see me—that is, Lottie—but I put Fen off. When I hung up, I knew what I had to do."

Harriet faced me, her tone defiant. "Maybe it was extreme, to most people, but I saw my next move as a rebirth. I'd already lost the weight, and was trim and toned. A nip and a tuck, a nose job, some work on the chin and cheeks, enhanced breasts, hair dye and a little liposuction—"

"And you were Lottie Harmon . . . a brand new Eveready Bunny."

"I even changed my name—legally. And you know what? It worked," Harriet insisted. "I've had to keep Fen at arm's length—not hard since he frankly repulses me—but things had been going great. So many people have helped me, like Tad and poor Rena . . . ." Lottie began to cry again.

I sat in silence for a moment. It was a lot to take in, a lot to process . . . I was about to tell Harriet about Fen, to see what, if anything, she knew of his scheming against her—when a Fashion Week intern appeared.

"Excuse me, ladies . . . we have to clear the Theater now. We're going to start admitting the guests in the next half hour."

"Goodness!" Harriet rose and wiped away the last of

her tears. "I have a million things to do before the runway show."

I rose too, and she grabbed my hand and squeezed it. "Okay, Clare, now you know. I told you the truth because you guessed and because you asked. I honestly don't know how hearing about the past is going to help you solve your friend's present problem. I hardly knew Ricky Flatt, but I have to ask you to keep my confidence."

"But there's more for us to discuss, Harriet—"

"*Lottie*, please. Call me Lottie. I told you I legally changed my name."

"Yes, of course—"

"Hey, boss! You're nee-ded!" It was Esther Best, hollering from the front row.

"We have to talk more," I told Lottie urgently. "Please, until we do, steer clear of Fen. I think he's trying to harm you."

"Sorry, my dear, but today of all days that's quite impossible." Lottie rushed backstage while I joined Esther.

"Lottie looks upset," Esther observed.

"She's still broken up about Rena Garcia's death."

"God, yes," Esther said with a shudder. "You know, I think Moira and I were just about the last two people to see her alive."

I froze. "What did you say?"

"I said I think Moira and I were the last people to see Rena alive. . . ."

"How do you figure?"

Esther shrugged. "It was Thursday night and you were holed up in your office. Moira and I were waiting for Gardner to take over when Rena stopped by for coffee. I remember because Moira and Rena got talking and they even shared a cab after that—"

"What time?"

Esther blinked at my urgent tone. "Close to nine, I guess."

Moira McNeely. In her early twenties. From Boston. Allergic to aspirin. A student of fashion from Parson's

School of Design. A young, attractive straight girl who be-friended the Blend's gay barista, Tucker, right around the same time that Lottie Harmon started hanging out at the coffeehouse. A quiet person, laboring in the background, the sort of person one hardly notices. She was Mona Lisa Toratelli's daughter. I knew it then. The little girl who'd witnessed her mother's murder at the hands of her aunt—an aunt who'd gotten away with the crime.

"Oh my god," I cried. "Where's Moira now?"

"I left her at the coffee stand. The show's about to start, you know."

I took off in a run, Esther on my heels.

"What's the problem, boss?" she cried. But I didn't have time to answer. Instead I burst into the lobby, pushed my way through the gathering crowd to the coffee stand.

It had been abandoned. The only sign Moira had been there, her backpack—the one she refused to part with on our ride up. It was now unzipped and wide open, lying on the floor.

"I have to find Lottie! She's in danger," I cried.

Esther, panting, caught up to me just then. "What? Back to the theater?" she puffed.

"You wait here, and if you see Matteo, tell him Moira is the one who's been poisoning people."

"What? Clare, wait a minute!" yelled Esther. But I was already gone, pushing my way into the Theater right past the intern, who was now guarding the entrance. "Hey, lady, you can't go in there!"

I ignored him, ran through the Theater to the backstage door. I heard frightened screams, saw models running back and forth in various states of undress.

Moira stood at the center of the chaos, a .38 police spe-cial clutched in one hand. She was pointing the shiny black weapon at Lottie Harmon—and at Fen, who stood at Lot-tie's shoulder.

"Why aren't you dead?" Moira screamed. "You should be dead! I ground up the aspirins myself . . . you're aller-gic, you have to be, it runs in the family. I gave you the aspirin, that night when you came to the Blend to plan your party. But nothing happened . . . so I tried cyanide, at the big party, but that poor man drank the coffee instead . . .".

Moira sobbed and the gun wavered. Then she bit back her tears and straightened the weapon.

"I even tried aspirins again, ground up on those fancy Italian cookies Ms. Cosi brought you the other day . . . but you're still alive. It's like I can't kill the monster . . . so I killed Rena, just to show you what it's like . . . what it's like to lose someone you love . . . and how dare you . . . how dare you treat Rena like a daughter, buying her an apartment, taking her into your business as a partner . . . while all along you conveniently forgot about your own sister's daughter . . .".

Moira clutched her head with one hand, the other still gripped the handgun. A security guard pushed past me and ran out of the room. Since he was unarmed, I assumed (and hoped) he was running for help and not fleeing the scene.

As Lottie/Harriet watched the hysterical girl, realization naturally dawned. "You're Mona Toratelli's daughter . . ." she murmured, stunned.

"Don't speak my mother's name!" Moira shrieked. "You murdered my mother, you bitch. Your own sister . . . I saw you push her over the balcony . . . I see it every night in my dreams . . . how could you kill her like that . . . and then run away? You just left me! You're a *monster* and now it's time for you to die!"

"No, Moira!" I cried.

Moira closed her mouth and her eyes shot in my direction—she looked crazy, maddened by grief and the insane need for revenge.

"You're going after the wrong person," I quickly explained. "The woman you see in front of you isn't your aunt. She's not even related—"

"Shut up! I know who she is," Moira cried. "I told you! I saw her kill my mother. My mother came to me. She told me in my head what I had to do to make the nightmares go away. Lottie has to die."

Standing beside Harriet, Fen didn't appear to be listening to Moria—but intensely watching her instead. The moment he noticed her hand waver again, he lunged for the weapon.

"No!" I cried. Too late. The shot sounded like an exploding canon, and Fen, struck in the chest, folded around Moira's arm. With the last of his strength, he yanked the gun away from her. A moment later, he collapsed, the gun clattering to the floor.

Byran Goldin immediately jumped on top of Moira while Lloyd Newhaven scooped up the gun. Amid the screams of half-dressed models, cowering amid the clothing racks, Harriet dropped to her knees at Fen's side.

Soaked in blood, he stared up at her. All of Fen's swagger, his arrogance was gone, and I saw only sad, desperate affection behind his dying eyes.

"Lottie . . . I . . ."

"Quiet," Harriet whispered, covering his lips with her fingers.

"Forget the pain . . . the bad things . . ." Fen gasped. "Forgive me for those . . . remember only the ecstasy . . . we shared . . .".

Fen's eyes went wide, and then the light left them. Harriet Tasky, now and forever Lottie Harmon, held him in her arms until the paramedics arrived and pronounced him dead.

ℰPILOGUℰ

∽◉∽◉∽◉∽◉∽◉∽◉∽◉∽◉∽◉∽◉∽◉∽◉∽◉∽

I slept fourteen hours that night. No dreams and no night-mares. Just dark, healing rest.

Believe it or not, Fen and Lottie's runway show had gone off without a hitch. In one short hour, Moira Mc-Neely had been taken into custody, Fen's body had been taken to the morgue, and the pre-show activity resumed. Guests arrived, took their seats, and Bryan Goldin himself delivered a tearful, touching eulogy to his uncle at the start of the runway show.

Lottie helped the young man through it all, and by the end of the day, the two appeared to have forged a solid bond. Bryan, it seemed, was the sole heir to the Fen house of fashion, and because of his need for an experienced hand, he asked Lottie to become a full partner.

Fen's death had made headlines all over the world. Con-sequently, the orders for his spring collection—and Lot-tie's java jewelry—were huge.

A week later, Quinn was sitting at my coffee bar again.

"Here you go, Mike."

"Thanks, Clare."

I'd steamed up a latte for him and an espresso for myself. As I added a bit of sugar to my demitasse, I watched Quinn sip his hot drink, make his usual deep sound of satisfaction, and wipe the foam from his upper lip with two fingers.

"Well," I said, "are you ready to spill?"

He lifted the tall glass mug. "It's too good to spill."

I raised an eyebrow.

"Bad joke," he said with slight twitch of his lips. "Okay, what first?"

"Mona Lisa Toratelli."

"Bangkok authorities filed a report in '88. It all checks out. The little girl's statement was taken, but the authorities claimed there were no other witnesses to corroborate that her aunt had been at the hotel so they quickly swept the mess under the rug, concluding the little girl simply made up the story to cope with her mother's suicide. That's how Moira was treated ever since—as if her memories were some delusion. But clearly, Moira Toratelli McNeely had witnessed her mother's murder at the hands of her aunt— and she never forgot."

I shuddered. "The thought that one sister would kill another over a man . . . especially one like Fen . . . it's so sad. And so brutal. It's difficult to comprehend."

"Precisely. Imagine how Moira felt."

I eyeballed Quinn in surprise. "Sentimental? For a murderer's point of view?"

He shook his head. "Empathetic. You better understand your perpetrator if you want to catch him."

"Or her."

"Or her."

I sipped my espresso in silence. Quinn sipped his latte.

"So what will happen to Moira now?" I asked.

"Best guess—she'll plead guilty. Her lawyer will claim criminally insane, and she'll end up in a hospital for twenty-five years of treatment."

"That poor girl . . . and the people she poisoned . . . Rena Garcia and Jeff Lugar and Ricky Flatt . . . and Tad losing his fiancée, poor Tad . . ." I shook my head at the tragic waste, the heartache. "How do you do it, Mike? How do you get over all the bad stuff?"

"You don't."

"Clare?" Matt was calling me from the back stairs.

"I'll be right back," I told Quinn softly, then headed for the Blend's back door. Matt was descending the steps with his baggage. He'd packed with his usual efficiency: one large black pulley suitcase, a black garment bag, and a black leather carry-on. He'd already shipped some of the Special Reserve Ethiopian beans to Tokyo via DHL.

"My car service is here," he said.

I nodded. "Have a good trip."

"Sure I can't change your mind?"

A question like that at a time like this was usually rhetorical. But my ex-husband's eyes looked almost hopeful, proud but edged with enough pleading to make me feel guilty—but only slightly.

"You'll have company," I told him with a small smile.

He sighed. "Clare—"

Three days before, Breanne had left a lengthy message on our answering machine, telling Matt that she had business in Tokyo, too. (Matt was traveling to Japan for a major presentation on his kiosk plan—one arranged by David Mintzer, who, after his conversation with me at the *Trend* party, had decided to heavily invest in Matt's idea.) Ms. Elegant gushed about how she would be happy to join him on the long flight and happier still to take him to some of her favorite sights and restaurants.

Just the day before, Matt had asked me to go with him—and I had been mulling it over when that phone message came. It quickly helped me make up my mind.

"Go," I told him, opening the Blend's back door. "It's what you do."

He stared.

"Good luck, Matt. I mean it."

He sighed again and nodded, then moved to kiss me. I stepped back and extended my hand. Hurt appeared in his eyes again, but I insisted we shake, squeezing his fingers in a sincere gesture of friendship. He didn't respond, his hand limp, and before I knew it he had turned and vanished.

But I wasn't surprised. Disappearing was what some men did best.

"Clare!"

Now Esther was calling me from the Blend's front room, and her voice sounded strained—upset. *What now?!* I ran into the coffee bar, worried at what disaster I was going to find there next. But there was no disaster. Esther had simply been overwhelmed with emotion when she saw who was coming through our front door.

"Hello, Village Blend!" cried Tucker Burton, throwing his hands in the air. "I'm back!"

Mike's eyes were on me. I think I was crying.

"You see, there, Detective Cosi," he said softly. "Maybe you don't get over the bad stuff . . . but there's usually something good to focus on instead. Remember that."

I nodded. Then I quickly moved across the room and hugged my Tucker tight.

RECIPES & TIPS
FROM THE VILLAGE BLEND

The Village Blend's
Caramel-Chocolate Latte

Cover bottom of mug with Clare's homemade caramel-chocolate syrup. Add a shot of espresso. Fill the rest of the mug with steamed milk. Stir the liquid, lifting from the bottom to bring up the syrup. Top with sweetened whipped cream and a chocolate-covered coffee bean.

Clare's Foolproof Homemade
Caramel-Chocolate Syrup

This syrup is out of this world! Try it warm over ice cream or use it for dipping strawberries or biscotti. Delicious! This recipe will yield about 2 cups of syrup, but it can easily be doubled or tripled for a big batch.

1 cup heavy cream
1 cup light Karo syrup
½ cup granulated sugar
½ cup light brown sugar, packed
⅛ teaspoon salt
8 oz milk chocolate or 1 cup of milk chocolate chips
4 tablespoons (½ stick) salted butter

Combine cream, Karo syrup, sugars, and salt in a non-stick or Teflon saucepan. Stir over medium heat until smooth. Bring to a rolling boil and maintain for 8-10 minutes. Continue to stir intermittently—do not let burn. In a separate saucepan, melt butter and chocolate together, stir until smooth. Pour the chocolate mixture into the saucepan with the caramel syrup and stir over heat until smooth. If there are still lumps, remove sauce from non-stick pan and whisk in a bowl until completely smooth. Serve warm. Store in refrigerator. Tip #1: best bet for storing syrup is a sturdy plastic squeeze bottle. Syrup will become thicker as it cools. To reheat syrup, place the squeeze bottle in a warm water bath or reheat in a microwave. Tip #2: use a good quality milk chocolate, such as Ghirardelli. You can also experiment with your own taste preferences, substituting semi-sweet, Mexican, or dark chocolate for the milk chocolate. Have fun!

Café Brulée

Not for the faint of heart. Brew a strong pot of a darkly roasted coffee. Mix seven parts hot coffee with one part cognac in a large, steamed or heated wine glass after its rim has been dipped first into freshly squeezed lemon juice, then rolled in confectioners sugar. Immediately before serving, carefully set the beverage ablaze—and keep a fire extinguisher handy just in case!

Clare's Basic Biscotti

Italians use the term biscotti to refer to any type of cookie. In today's coffeehouse culture, biscotti is used to describe a long, dry, hard twice-baked cookie designed for dunking into wine or coffee. The name biscotti is derived from bis, meaning "encore" in Italian, and cotto, meaning "baked" or "cooked."

There are many basic biscotti recipes. Some use oil instead of butter, some use no butter at all. This particular recipe produces a more tender biscotti, which is generally preferred by the American palate. To create a harder biscotti out of this recipe, reduce the butter by ½ cup (or ½ stick) and increase the flour by ½ cup.

Yields: 2 dozen

1-½ c butter (1-½ sticks)
3 eggs
1 cup granulated sugar
1 tablespoon vanilla extract
3 cups all-purpose flour
2 teaspoons baking powder
½ teaspoon salt
Parchment paper

Preheat oven to 350 degrees Fahrenheit. With an electric mixer, cream butter, add eggs, sugar, and vanilla and mix well. Sift together flour, baking powder, and salt. Gradually add dry ingredients to wet ingredients until soft dough forms. Place dough on lightly floured surface and knead slightly, then divide dough into two even pieces. Roll each piece into a cylinder about 10 inches long and 2 inches wide. Place these 2 logs of dough onto a baking sheet covered with parchment paper—the bottoms of the logs can flatten when you place them on the baking sheet. They don't need to stay round. Make sure the 2 logs are well separated. Bake in the 350-degree oven for 35 minutes. Let the logs cool for about 10 minutes, then carefully slice them on a diagonal angle. (Because this recipe is for a slightly softer biscotti, the dough may be a bit crumbly. The best way to slice is with a very sharp knife, straight down. No sawing.) Each log should yield about 12 cookies sliced approximately ¾ inches wide. Turn the cookies onto their sides, and place on a baking sheet. Put them back in the 350-degree oven for 8 minutes on one side, then turn over and bake another 8 minutes on the other side. Let cool. Store in an airtight container.

The above is a very basic biscotti recipe. Different variations can come from this recipe by adding such things as nuts, dried fruits, and various extracts. Have fun experimenting! Here are some possibilities:

Almond Biscotti: In above recipe, change 1 tablespoon of vanilla to 2 teaspoons vanilla and 2 teaspoons almond extract. And mix 1 cup of chopped, toasted almonds into the dough. (To toast raw almonds, spread on baking sheet and place in 350-degree oven for about 12 minutes.)

Anise Biscotti: In above recipe, change 1 tablespoon of vanilla to 2 teaspoons vanilla and 2 teaspoons anise extract. (Optional) Mix ½ cup of anise seeds into the dough.

Pistachio Biscotti: In above recipe add to the dry ingredients ½ cup of toasted pistachios that have been ground to a powder. After dough forms, add 1 cup of whole, toasted pistachios. (To toast raw pistachios, spread on baking sheet and place in 350-degree oven for about 12 minutes.)

Ricciardelli

Simply marvelous! These sweet, delicate almond cookies have been popular for centuries. During the Renaissance, ricciarelli were served at the most lavish banquets in Italy and France. They are still a popular addition to dessert and cookie trays at festive gatherings. In Tuscany, they are a popular Christmas cookie and have been called "Tuscan Macaroons."

Yield: about 36 cookies

This is a quick and easy version of the traditional recipe— creating a tender, chewy cookie you'll flip over!

1 cup whole, raw almonds
½ cup granulated sugar

½ cup powdered sugar
⅛ cup honey (mild, such as clover)
2 egg whites
2 teaspoons vanilla extract
¾ cup all-purpose flour
Powdered sugar (for dusting)
Parchment paper

Preheat oven to 300 degrees Fahrenheit. First prepare your almonds. Blanche whole, raw almonds by dropping into boiling water for 2 minutes. Drain the almonds and rinse under cold water. Spread on a paper towel. When dry, squeeze each almond between your fingers so that the clean almond pops out of its dark skin. Repeat until all the almonds are skinned, then dry the almonds with a paper towel. Spread these blanched almonds in a single layer in a baking pan. Bake about 20 to 30 minutes—stir a few times throughout the baking process. Let cool. Place these almonds into a food processor. Grind them into a powder. Add the granulated and powdered sugars, then add the honey, egg whites, and vanilla; process these ingredients until they are well mixed. Add flour. If you do not have a food processer, use a blender to grind the nuts, then transfer to a bowl and use a hand mixer to mix in the other ingredients. A soft dough will form. If too soft, add a bit more flour—but do *not* create a stiff dough. Dough should be soft without being runny. Sprinkle a large cutting board generously with powdered sugar. Drop rounded teaspoons of dough into powdered sugar. Roll each piece of dough into a small ball. Drop ball onto baking sheet lined with parchment paper. Flatten into a circle with back of spoon and, if you like, shape into the traditional diamond shape. Dust unbaked cookies with powdered sugar (use a sieve or sifter for even dusting). Bake until cookies are set but not brown, about 10 to 15 minutes. Dust again with powdered sugar as soon as they come out of the oven. When completely cool, store in an airtight container.

The Village Blend's
Guide to Roasting Terms

LIGHT

Cinnamon
Half city

MEDIUM

Full city
American
Regular
Breakfast

DARK

Continental
New Orleans
Vienna

DARKEST

French
Italian
Espresso

Don't Miss the Next
Coffeehouse Mystery

MURDER MOST FROTHY

*For many Greenwich Village residents, summer in the city
means weekends in the Hamptons. With a coffeehouse to run,
Clare Cosi has never spent much time at the fabled collection
of exclusive seaside towns. Then her new friend David Mintzer
makes an offer Clare can't refuse—train the barista staff at his
new Hamptons restaurant and enjoy sun, sand, and surf at his
fabulous mansion. Clare accepts, packs up her daughter, Joy,
her well-connected former mother-in-law, Madame, and the
Village Blend's recipes for frothy iced coffee drinks, and heads
for ocean breezes. After she arrives, however, more than the
coffee gets iced. At the end of David's fabulous July Fourth
bash, a body is found, shot through the head, and Clare
immediately begins to scrutinize possible suspects. What she
uncovers are so many long brewing resentments among the
volatile blend of new money wannabes, old guard blue bloods,
summering Hollywood celebrities, and aggressive, stressed-out
Manhattan weekenders that she quickly realizes the real
question isn't why the first victim was shot, but when the next
one will be.*

Visit Cleo Coyle's Virtual Village Blend at
www.CoffehouseMystery.com
for more coffee tips, trivia, and recipes.